Athens-Clarke County Library
2025 Baxter Street
Athens, GA 30606
(706) 613-3650
Member: Athens Regional Library System

W9-BYN-923

"My name is Templar — Simon Templar."

SIMON TEMPLAR: a/k/a The Saint, the Happy Highwayman, the Brighter Buccaneer, the Robin Hood of Modern Crime.

DESCRIPTION: Age 31. Height 6 ft., 2 in. Weight 175 lbs. Eyes blue. Hair black, brushed straight back. Complexion tanned. Bullet scar through upper left shoulder; 8 in. scar on right forearm.

SPECIAL CHARACTERISTICS: Always immaculately dressed. Luxurious tastes. Lives in most expensive hotels and is connoisseur of food and wine. Carries firearms and is expert knife thrower. Licensed air pilot. Speaks several languages fluently. Known as "The Saint" from habit of leaving drawing of skeleton figure with halo at scenes of crimes.

By Leslie Charteris

DARE DEVIL
THE BANDIT

THE WHITE RIDER
X ESQUIRE

The Saint Series (in order of sequence)

MEET THE TIGER!
ENTER THE SAINT
THE LAST HERO
KNIGHT TEMPLAR (THE
 AVENGING SAINT)
FEATURING THE SAINT
ALIAS THE SAINT
ANGELS OF DOOM (SHE WAS A
 LADY, THE SAINT MEETS HIS
 MATCH)
THE SAINT V. SCOTLAND YARD
GETAWAY
THE SAINT AND MR. TEAL
THE BRIGHTER BUCCANEER
THE MISFORTUNES OF MR. TEAL
THE SAINT INTERVENES
THE SAINT GOES ON
THE SAINT IN NEW YORK
THE SAINT OVERBOARD
ACE OF KNAVES
THIEVES' PICNIC
THE SAINT PLAYS WITH FIRE
FOLLOW THE SAINT
THE HAPPY HIGHWAYMAN
THE SAINT IN MIAMI
THE SAINT GOES WEST
THE SAINT STEPS IN
THE SAINT ON GUARD
THE SAINT SEES IT THROUGH
CALL FOR THE SAINT

SAINT ERRANT
THE SAINT IN EUROPE
THE SAINT ON THE SPANISH
 MAIN
THANKS TO THE SAINT
THE SAINT AROUND THE WORLD
SENOR SAINT
THE SAINT TO THE RESCUE
TRUST THE SAINT
THE SAINT IN THE SUN
VENDETTA FOR THE SAINT
THE SAINT ON T.V.
THE SAINT RETURNS
THE SAINT AND THE FICTION
 MAKERS
THE SAINT ABROAD
THE SAINT'S CHOICE
THE SAINT IN PURSUIT
THE SAINT AND THE PEOPLE
 IMPORTERS
CATCH THE SAINT
THE SAINT AND THE HAPSBURG
 NECKLACE
SEND FOR THE SAINT
THE SAINT IN TROUBLE
THE SAINT AND THE TEMPLAR
 TREASURE
COUNT ON THE SAINT
SALVAGE FOR THE SAINT
THE FANTASTIC SAINT

(Parentheses indicate alternate titles)

The Saint

IN NEW YORK
LESLIE CHARTERIS

A CRIME CLASSIC

INTERNATIONAL POLYGONICS, LTD.
NEW YORK CITY

ATHENS REGIONAL LIBRARY
ATHENS, GEORGIA   439521

THE SAINT IN NEW YORK

Copyright © 1934, 1935 by Leslie Charteris.
Reprinted with permission of Doubleday and
Company, Inc.

Cover and introduction: Copyright © 1988 by
International Polygonics, Ltd.
Library of Congress Card Catalog No. 88-82346
ISBN 0-930330-97-8

Printed and manufactured in the United States
of America.
First IPL printing November 1988.
10 9 8 7 6 5 4 3 2 1

To
MALCOLM JOHNSON
WHO PROPOUNDED THE IDEA,
AND HELPED IN MANY
OTHER WAYS

INTRODUCTION
by
William Ruehlmann

Impudent.

That is the essential adjective for Simon Templar, a.k.a. the Saint, the Happy Highwayman, the Brighter Buccaneer, the Robin Hood of Modern Crime.

Who else, after precipitous Fairbanksian cavorting over sundry balustrades and rooftop surfaces, after snatching back a kidnaped child from the very clutches of her captors at a Long Island stronghold, after vigorously bashing, slicing up and shooting down an assortment of roscoe-bristling bozos, who else would find it requisite to pause at departure, wind open an inch of bullet-proof glass in the getaway limo and sass the opposition?

Who else, indeed.

> "So long, boys," he called back. "Thanks for the ride!" And then the car was swinging out into the road, whirling away into the night with a smooth rush of power, with the horn hooting a derisively syncopated farewell into the wind.

Simon says thumbs down.

Welcome to *The Saint in New York,* a fair sample of vintage Templar at the top of his irrepressible form for long-standing fans and a solid introduction to the Saint saga for newcomers. First published in 1934, it is not nearly the first Saint novel; that was *Meet the Tiger* (1928), in which our hero was still polishing his powerfully skewed halo. But the more mature Simon in full stride here comes accompanied with a useful prologue that effectively sums up a flamboyant past, and this book is the bridge between the Saint's British origins and his American destiny.

After more than half a century, *The Saint in New York* remains a rattling good read. It takes Simon just two days to clean up the mob in post-Prohibition Manhattan, deliver the Big Fellow to the waiting arms of an expectant Inspector Fernack and blow town. Like Shane, he departs almost mythically, carrying a wound; but unlike anybody else in popular fiction, he shows up packing a pistol in a nun's habit.

Impudent?

"He's nuts," Heimie Felder has occasion to observe more than once in the course of these pages, and perhaps there is evidence for certain delusions of grandeur. That he is unabashedly an urban vigilante goes uncontested, a terminally conservative status only somewhat mitigated by the tacit approval of the Law as represented by "square copper" Fernack. "There's times," intones Iron John, "I wish I knew a guy like the Saint was here in New York — doing things like it says in that dossier." To wit, bumping off the Ungodly.

Who, it must be allowed, are, to a man as assembled herein, certainly deserving of extermination, from gut-shooting Jack Irboll to pale-eyed Dutch Kuhlmann of the crocodile tears and teeth.

After all, according to the cerebrations of extortion victim and Greek chorus Zeke Inselheim, the real villains are the rest of us, lounging rodless in our armchairs.

> He knew that without the passive cooperation of a resigned and leaderless public, without the inbred cowardice of a terrorized population, the racketeers and grafting political leaders who protected them could have been wiped off the face of the American landscape at a cost of one hundredth part of the tribute which they exacted annually.

That Messianic strain from the pulps would much later find its final implications in Mickey Spillane's Mike Hammer and the endless screen sequels to *Death Wish;* but the Saint is no Bernard Goetz. His world is simpler and his mission in the costumed rough justice tradition of fop avengers Don Diego Vega/Zorro and Sir Percy Blakeney/The Scarlet Pimpernel. If the imperturbable Simon borders on narcissism in his scapegrace self-assurance, we forgive him the way we once did Gawain for making great claims but undeniably delivering the goods.

William K. Valcross, who enlists the Saint, should know, certainly learns.

> "Other fellows have tried — bigger men than you, son — stronger men than you, cleverer men than you — "
> The Saint smiled back.
> "Admitting for the moment that they ever lived," he remarked amiably, "you never saw anyone luckier than me."

Impudent . . .

And utterly, incontrovertably correct.

Because the supremely confident Saint retains at least one other useful ace in the hole beyond Belle, the throwing knife handily strapped to his left forearm — an ace that absolutely ensures no odds against him will ever be insurmountable, no desperate corner too tight, no culminating course of events ever ultimately calamitous.

That ace, of course, is the interceding hand of his solicitous and admiring creator, Leslie Charteris, who holds the mirror.

2.

Leslie Charles Bowyer Yin, the son of an Englishwoman and a surgeon directly descended from the Shang dynasty, was born May 12, 1907, in Singapore. He attended prep school in England, studied art in Paris and enrolled at King's College in 1925.

The experience, by Yin's own account, was "unhappy."

> At the end of my first year at Cambridge I announced to my parents that I was going to be a writer. My father, a very conventional gentleman who believed all writers were rogues and vagabonds, told me that if I wanted to be a writer I could do it at my own expense. There followed a happy-go-lucky and sometimes ghastly period during which I wrote consistently books and stories which were usually sold but at very slowly increasing prices. In those days I did more things to scrape a living than I can easily remember. I went back to Malaya and worked in rubber plantations, a tin mine, and a wood distillation plant. I prospected for gold in the jungle and tried pearl fishing. I was a seaman on a freighter and I covered the English countryside with a side-show in a traveling fair. I was a bartender in a country inn and I played professional bridge in a London club . . .

The revenge of romance. A voracious reader of sensational fiction and future member of Mensa, the international Yin would have been an inevitable outsider to snobbish Old School insularity, which may account in part for his relentless satire of upper class affectation and enduring impatience with established authority later. He quickly acquired a few affectations of his own, however, including a monocle, an elaborate wardrobe and, in 1928, the legal name of Charteris, after the roguish Col. Francis, gambler, duellist and founder of the Hellfire Club.

Young Charteris was at once precocious and prolific, having written five novels by the age of 22. An early proving ground was Amalgamated Press' weekly pulp publication The Thriller, out of which grew, with editorial help, unsimple Simon.

The Saint in New York was his most adroit work to date when it first appeared in 1934; Charteris was 27. It was his tenth book, the sixth about the Saint, but the first novel-length narrative to directly assault the more lucrative United States market with a full-blown combination of plot, style and pell-mell pace. More than the setting is American; *Thriller's* hardboiled cross-Atlantic counterpart, *Black Mask*, was making its own terse, non-digressive influence felt. There's more than a hint of Hammett in these enameled hoods.

Yeggs, as it were, Benedict.

Though the Robin Hood of Modern Crime had his antecedents, among them the original Sherwood Forest article, E.W. Hornung's raffish Raffles, Louis Joseph Vance's Lone Wolf, the "just men" of Edgar Wallace and H.C. McNeile's dithering daredevil Bulldog Drummond, Simon Templar — bon vivant, dude, gourmet and avenging angel — obviously owed the essence of his extroverted personality to Charteris' greatest fictive creation, himself. The author, despite mild demurrals, invited a confusion of roles. In 1941 he was approached to script a sort of pictorial comic strip in commemoration of the centennial to Poe's "Murders in the Rue Morgue"; "Leslie Charteris consented to collaborate on a detective story for *Life* on one condition: that he play the Saint."

Set in Palm Springs, by then home turf for the author, "The Saint Goes West," a seven-page, 20-panel photo extravaganza, recounts how Simon Templar in the person of his biographer, monocled, mustached and impeccably attired, flushes out a predator at a posh estate, where three "playgirls" take turns trying to impress him. The snapper:

"Saint," sighed Lissa, "you're wonderful."
"Yes," he said.

Insouciant self-celebration; neither the Saint nor his creator ever required a publicist. Charteris became a scriptwriter for Paramount in Hollywood, where the first Saint films were made, initially starring Louis Hayward, then the urbane but blasé George Sanders; in retrospect, the author would have preferred Cary Grant. Charteris became an American citizen in 1946.

He was married four times, one daughter. He produced a Saint radio series, comic strip and detective magazine, which ran from 1953 to 1967. He traveled widely, flew planes, sailed boats, speared fish.

Charteris was characteristically unrepentant upon consigning his creation at last to the inevitable depredations of TV in 1962:

> When, after many years of noble and lofty-minded resistance, I finally broke down and sold the Saint to the Philistines of television, I fear that I must have added one more argument to the armoury of critics who maintain that every man has his price; because I certainly got mine.

Since then, even the books have become the work of several hands.

3.

So what happened to the Saint?

In *The First Saint Omnibus* (1939), Charteris wrote:

> I have been trying to make a picture of a man. Changing, yes. Developing, I hope. Fantastic, improbable — perhaps. Quite worthless, quite irritating, if you feel that way. Or a slightly cockeyed ideal, if you feel differently. It doesn't matter so much, so long as you feel you would recognize him tomorrow.

Change he did. Originally the Saint had an entourage, complete with old retainer, much in the manner of the

Black Gang of Bulldog Drummond. The most enduring of these associates was Patricia Holm, "his lady," and over the years readers wondered if Simon and Pat had tied the knot, like the game and giggly Nick and Nora Charles of "Thin Man" fame. Well, no whisper of domesticity ever contractually seduced the Saint, who was faithful only after his fashion; the imperturbable Pat makes a brief and uninformed appearance at the end of *The Saint in New York,* later to disappear completely from the canon along with Roger Conway, Orace, Peter Quentin and the others.

For a good while bibulous sidekick Hoppy Uniatz played Smiley Burnette to Simon's Autry, but after 1950 the Saint preferred to ride alone. He grew older, increasingly rootless, migrating the globe in an endless succession of smart hotel rooms, dining well but generally solo.

Contrast the arch and impish Saint of "The Million Pound Day" (1931) with the wearier version of "The Russian Prisoner" (1963). The former:

> Mr. Garniman shrugged.
>
> "Need I explain that you have come to the end of your interesting and adventurous life?"
>
> Simon twitched an eyebrow, and slid his mouth mockingly sideways.
>
> "What — not again?" he sighed, and Garniman's smooth forehead crinkled.
>
> "I don't understand."
>
> "But you haven't seen so many of these situations as I have, old horse," said the Saint. "I've lost count of the number of times that this sort of thing has happened to me. I know the tradition demands it but I think they might give us a rest sometimes. What's the programme this time — do you sew me up in the bath and light the geyser, or am I run through the mangle and buried under the billiard table? Or can you think of something really original?"

The latter:

> "Excuse me. You are the Saint. You must help me."
>
> By that time Simon Templar thought he must have heard all the approaches, all the elegant variations. Some were amusing, some were insulting, some were unusual, most were a routine, a few tried selfconsciously to be original and attention-getting. He had, regrettably, become as accustomed to them as any Arthurian knight-errant must eventually have become. After all, how many breeds of dragons were there? And how many different shapes and colorations of damsels in distress?

We all, if we're lucky, get old; but as the years go on, Simon seems to lose something besides his youth, the same something that once allowed him to take on organized crime in New York singlehanded with complete confidence in the outcome — his innocence.

Still, he survived. And influenced, as he was influenced by the popular heroes that preceded him, the ones who came after. Can we not see the precursor of another more contemporary world-traveling warrior with expensive tastes in this deathless little line from *The Saint in New York*?

> "My name is Templar — Simon Templar."

Not that the organization man whose name is Bond — James Bond can ever satisfactorily supplant Simon. The Saint goes on. And Charteris, now living comfortably in a well-deserved European retirement, need never put pen to paper again to ensure his character's currency.

Simon says thumbs up.

Because the old books are never permitted to remain out of print for very long, and the little stick figure Leslie Charles Bowyer Yin first devised as a boy, drawing cartoons for his own four-page magazine at 10, can still be affixed to the end of introductions like this one with the same assurance of printings past:

WATCH FOR THE SIGN OF THE SAINT

HE WILL BE BACK

—William Ruehlmann
Norfolk, Virginia
March 1988

Series consultant William Ruehlmann, Ph.D., is an award-winning feature writer for The Virginian-Pilot *and* The Ledger-Star *and author of* Saint with a Gun: The Unlawful American Private Eye. *He, too, will be back.*

PROLOGUE

The letter was delivered to the Correspondence Bureau in Centre Street. It passed, as a matter of routine, through the Criminal Identification Bureau, the Criminal Alien Investigation Bureau, and the Main Office Division. And in the end it was laid on the desk of Police Commissioner Arthur J. Quistrom himself—it was a remarkable document by any standards, and even the studiously commonplace prose of its author could not make it uninteresting.

METROPOLITAN POLICE,
SPECIAL BRANCH,
SCOTLAND HOUSE, LONDON, S.W. I.

Police Commissioner, New York City.

Dear Sir:
We have to inform you that there are reasons to believe that SIMON TEMPLAR, known as "The Saint," is at present in the United States.

No fingerprints are available; but a photograph, description, and record are enclosed.

As you will see from the record, we have no grounds on which to institute extradition proceedings; but it would be

1

advisable for you, in your own interests, to observe Templar's activities carefully if you are successful in locating him.

> *Faithfully yours,*
>
> *C. E. Teal, Chief Inspector.*

The first enclosure came under the same letterhead:

SIMON TEMPLAR (*"The Saint"*).

DESCRIPTION: *Age 31, Height 6 ft. 2 ins. Weight 175 lbs. Eyes blue. Hair black, brushed straight back. Complexion tanned. Bullet scar through upper left shoulder; 8-in. scar right forearm.*

SPECIAL CHARACTERISTICS: *Always immaculately dressed. Luxurious tastes. Lives in most expensive hotels and is connoisseur of food and wine. Carries firearms and is expert knife thrower. Licensed air pilot. Speaks several languages fluently. Known as "The Saint" from habit of leaving drawing of skeleton figure with halo on scenes of crimes (Specimen reproduced below).*

RECORD:

First came to our attention five years ago as unofficial agent concerned with recovery of quantity of bullion stolen from Confederate Bank of Chicago and transported to this country. Was successful and claimed reward, leaving arrest of thieves to our own agent, Inspector Carn.

For some time afterwards, with assistance of four accomplices, became self-appointed agent for terrorizing criminals against whom we had been unable to secure evidence justifying arrest. Real indentity at this time remained a mystery. Activities chiefly directed against vice. Was instrumental in obtaining arrest and conviction of leaders of powerful drug ring. Believed to have instigated murder of Henri Chastel, white slave trafficker, in Athens, at same period. Admitted killing of Galter, anarchist, in frustrating at-

tempted assassination of Crown Prince Rudolf during state visit to London, following year.

Kidnapped Professor K. B. Vargan while War Office was considering purchase of Vargan's "electron cloud." Vargan was later killed by Norman Kent, member of Templar's gang, Kent himself being killed by Dr. Rayt Marius, foreign secret service agent also trying to secure Vargan's invention. Motive, established by Templar's subsequent letter published in the press, was alleged to be prevention of use in threatened war of what Templar thought to be inhuman method of slaughter. Both Templar and Marius escaped and left England.

Three months later Templar reappeared in England in connection with second plot organized by Marius to promote war, which was unknown to ourselves. Marius finally escaped again and is now believed to be dead; but intrigue was exposed and Templar received free pardon for frustrating attempt to wreck Royal train.

Subsequently continued campaign of fighting crime by criminal methods. Obtained evidence in several cases and secured arrests; also believed, without proof, to have caused deaths of Francis Lemuel, vice trader, Jack Farnberg, gunman, Ladek Kuzela, and others. Suspicion also exists in murder of Stephen Weald, alias Waldstein, and disappearance of Lord Essenden, during period when Templar was working to clear reputation of the late Assistant Commissioner Sir Francis Trelawney, under direct authority of present Chief Commissioner Sir Hamilton Dorn.

Activities continued until he left England again six months ago.

Most of the exploits mentioned above, as well as many others of which for obvious reasons we have no definite knowledge, have also been financially profitable; and Templar's fortune, acquired by these

> *means, has been credibly estimated at £500,000.*
> *Is also well known to police of France and Germany.*

The photograph followed; and at the end of the sheaf were clipped on the brief reports of the departments through which the information had already been passed:

BUREAU OF CRIMINAL IDENTIFICATION:
> *No record. Copies of photograph and description forwarded to Albany and Washington.*

BUREAU OF CRIMINAL ALIEN INVESTIGATION:
> *Inquiries proceeding.*

MAIN OFFICE DIVISION:
> *Inquiries proceeding.*

The commissioner put up a hand and scratched his grey head. He read the letter through a second time, with his bushy eyebrows drawn down in a frown that wrinkled the bridge of his nose. His faded grey-blue eyes had flabby pounches under them, like blisters that have been drained without breaking the skin; and his face was lined with the same weariness. A grim, embittered soul weariness that was his reward for forty years of the futile battle with lawlessness—a lawlessness that walked arm in arm with those who were supposed to uphold the law.

"You think this may have something to do with the letter that was sent to Irboll?" he said, when he had finished the second reading.

Inspector John Fernack pushed back his battered hat and nodded—a curt, phlegmatic jerk of his head. He stabbed at another paper on the commissioner's desk with a square stubby forefinger.

"I'm guessing that way. See the monicker Scotland Yard says this guy goes under? The Saint, it says. Well, look at this drawing. I'm not much on art, and it looks to me like this guy Templar ain't so hot, either; but the idea's there. See that figger. The sort of thing kids draw when they first get hold of a pencil—just a circle for a head, and a straight line for the body and four more for the arms and legs, but you can see it's meant to be sumpn human. An' another circle floating on top of the head. When I was a kid I got took to a cathedral, once," said Fernack, as if he were confessing some dark blot on his professional career, "an' there were a lot of paintings of people with circles round their heads. They were saints, or sumpn; and those circles was supposed to be haloes." The commissioner did not smile.

"What's happening about Irboll?" he asked.

"He comes up in the General Sessions Court to get his case adjourned again this afternoon," said Fernack disgustedly. He spat, with a twisted mouth, missing the cuspidor. "You know how it is. I never had much of a head for figgers, but I make it this'll be the thirty-first or maybe the thirty-second time he's been adjourned. Considering it's only two years now since he plugged Ionetzki, we've still got a chance to seeing him on the hot seat before we die of old age. One hell of a chance!"

Fernack's lips thinned into a hard, down-drawn line. He leaned forward across the desk, so that his big clenched fists crushed against the mahogany; and his eyes bored into Quistrom's with a brightness like the simmer of burning acid.

"There's times when I wish I knew a guy like this Saint was here in New York—doing things like it says in that dossier," he said. "There's times when for two cents I'd resign from the force and do 'em myself. I'd sleep better nights if I knew there was things like that going on in this city.

"Ionetzki was my side kick, when I was a lieutenant in the Fifth Precinct—before they pushed me up here to headquarters. A square copper—and you know what that means. You've been through the works. You know what it's all about. Harness bull—gumshoe—precinct captain—you've been through it all, like the rest of us.

Which makes you about the first commissioner that hasn't had to start learning what kinda uniform a cop wears. Don't get me wrong, Chief. I'm not handin' you any oil. But what I mean, you know how a guy feels— an' what it means to be able to say a guy was a square copper."

Fernack's iron hands opened and closed again on the edge of the desk.

"That's what Ionetzki was," he said. "A square copper. Not very bright; but square. An' he walks square into a hold-up, where another copper might've decided to take a walk round the block and not hear anything. An' that yellow rat Irboll shoots him in the guts."

Quistrom did not answer; neither did he move. His tired eyes rested quietly on the tensed face of the man standing over him—rested there with a queer sympathy for that unexpected outburst. But the weariness in the eyes was graven too deep for anything to sweep it away.

"So we pull Irboll in," Fernack said, "and everybody knows he did it. And we beat him up. Yeah, we sweat him all right. But what the hell good does that do? A length of rubber hose ain't the same as a bullet in the guts. It doesn't make you die slowly, with your inside burning and your mouth chewed to rags so you won't scream out loud with the agony of it. It doesn't leave a good woman without her man, an' good kids without a father. But we sweat him. And then what?

"There's some greasy politician bawling out some judge he's got in his pocket. There's a lawyer around with habeas corpus—bail—alibis—anything. There's trials—with a tame judge on the bench, an' a packed jury, an' somebody in the district attorney's office who's taking his cut from the same place as the rest of 'em. There's transfers and objections and extraditions and adjournments an' retrials and appeals. It drags on till nobody can scarcely remember who Ionetzki was or what happened to him. All they know is they're tired of talking about Irboll.

"So maybe they acquit him. And maybe they send him to jail. Well, that suits him. He sits around and smokes cigars and listens to the radio; and after a few months, when the newspapers have got something else to talk about, the governor of the jail slips him a free pardon, or the parole board gets together an' tells him to run along home and be a good boy or else . . . An' presently some other good guy gets a bullet in the guts from a yellow rat—an' who the hell cares?"

Quistrom's gaze turned downwards to the blotter in front of him. The slope of his broad shoulders was an acquiescence, a grim, tight-lipped acceptance of a set of facts which it was beyond his power to answer for. And Fernack's heavyboned body bent forward, jutting a rocklike jaw that was in strange contrast to the harsh crack in his voice.

"This guy, the Saint, sends Irboll a letter," Fernack said. "He says that whether the rap sticks or not, he's got a justice of his own that'll work where ours doesn't. He says that if Jack Irboll walks outa that court again this afternoon, with the other yellow rats crowding round him and slapping him on the back and looking sideways at us an' laughing out loud for us to hear—it'll be the last time it happens. That's all. A slug in the guts for another slug in the guts. An' maybe he'll do it. If half of what that letter you've got says is true, he will do it. He'll do just what I'd of done—just what I'd like to do. An' the papers'll scream it all over the sky, and make cracks about us being such bum policemen that we have to let some free-lance vigilante do a job for us that we haven't got the brains or the guts to do. An' then my job'll be to hunt that Saint guy down—take him into the back room of a station house and sweat a confession outa him with a baseball bat—put him in court an' work like hell to send him to the chair—the guy who only did what you or me would of done if we weren't such lousy, white-livered four-flushers we think more about holding down a pay check than getting on with the work we're paid to do!"

The commissioner raised his eyes.

"You'd do your duty, Fernack—that's all," he said. "What happens to the case afterwards—that case or any other—isn't your fault."

"Yeah—I'd do my duty," Fernack jeered bitterly. "I'd do it like I've always done it—like we've all been doing it for years. I'd sweep the floor clean again, an' hand the pan right back to the slobs who're waitin' to throw all the dirt back again—and some more with it."

Quistrom picked up the sheaf of papers and stared at them. There was a silence, in which Fernack's last words seemed to hum and strain through the room, building themselves up like echo heaped on reecho, till the air throbbed and thundered with their inaudible power. Fernack pulled out a handkerchief suddenly and wiped his face. He looked out of the window, out at the drab flat facade of the Police Academy and the grey haze that veiled the skyscrapers of upper New York. The pulse of the city beat into the room as he looked out, seeming to add itself to the deadened reverberations of the savage denunciation that had hammered him out of his habitual restraint. The pulse of traffic ticking its way from block to block, the march of twelve million feet, the whirr of wheels and the mighty rhythm of pistons, the titter of lives being made and broken, the struggle and the majesty and the meanness and the splendour and the corruption in which he had his place. . . .

Quistrom cleared his throat. The sound was slight, muted down to a tone that was neither reproof nor concurrence; but it broke the tension as cleanly as a phrased speech. Quistrom spoke a moment afterwards:

"You haven't found Templar yet?"

"No." Fernack's voice was level, rough, prosaic in response as it had been before; only the wintry shift of his eyes recalled the things he had been saying. "Kestry and Bonacci have been lookin' for him. They tried most of the big hotels yesterday."

Quistrom nodded.

"Come and see me the minute you get any information."

Fernack went out, down the long bare stone corridor to his own office. At three-thirty that afternoon they fetched him to the courthouse to see how Jack Irboll died.

The Saint had arrived.

CHAPTER I
HOW SIMON TEMPLAR
CLEANED HIS GUN, AND
WALLIS NATHER PERSPIRED

The nun let herself into the tower suite of the Waldorf Astoria with a key which she produced from under the folds of her black robe—which even to the most kindly and broad-minded eye would have seemed somewhat odd. As she closed the door behind her she began to whistle—which even to the most kindly and broad-minded eye would have seemed still odder. And as she went into the sitting room she caught her toe in a rug, stumbled, and said "God damn!" in a distinctly masculine baritone, and laughed cheerfully an instant afterwards—which would doubtless have moved even the most kindly and broad-minded eye to blink rapidly and open itself wide.

But there was no such inquiring and impressionable eye to perform these acrobatics. There was only a square-chinned white-haired man in rimless spectacles, sitting in an easy chair with a book on his lap, who looked up with a nod and a quiet smile as the nun came in.

He closed his book, marking the place methodically, and stood up—a spare, vigorous figure in grey homespun.

"All right?" he queried.

"Fine," said the nun.

She pushed her veil back from a sleek black head, unbuttoned things and unhitched things, and threw off the long, stuffy draperies with a sigh of relief. She was revealed as a tall, wide-shouldered man in a blue silk shirt and the trousers of a light fresco suit—a man with gay blue eyes in a brown, piratical face, whose smile flashed a row of ivory teeth as he slapped his audience blithely on the back and sprawled into an armchair with a swing of lean athletic limbs.

"You took a big chance, Simon," said the older man, looking down at him; and Simon Templar laughed softly.

"And I had breakfast this morning," he said. He flipped a cigarette into his mouth, lighted it, and extinguished the match with a gesture of his hand that was an integral part of the smile. "My dear Bill, I've given up recording either of those earth-shaking events in my diary. They're things that we take for granted in this life of sin."

The other shook his head.

"You needn't have made it more dangerous."

"By sending that note?" The Saint grinned. "Bill, that was an act of devotion. A tribute to some great old days. If I hadn't sent it, I'd have been cheating my reputation. I'd have been letting myself down."

The Saint let a streak of smoke drift through his lips and gazed through the window at a square of blue sky.

"It goes back to some grand times—of which you've heard," he said quietly. "The Saint was a law of his own in those days, and that little drawing stood for battle and sudden death and all manner of mayhem. Some of us lived for it—worked for it—fought for it. One of us

died for it. . . . There was a time when any man who
received a note like I sent to Irboll, with that signature,
knew that there was nothing more he could do. And
since we're out on this picnic, I'd like things to be the
same—even if it's only for a little while."

He laughed again, a gentle lilt of a laugh that floated
through the room like sunshine with a flicker of steel.

"Hence the bravado," said the Saint. "Of course that
note made it more difficult—but that just gave us a
chance to demonstrate our surpassing brilliance. And it
was so easy. I had the gun under that outfit, and I
caught him as he came out. Just once. . . . Then I let out
a thrilling scream and rushed towards him. I was urging
him to repent and confess his sins while they were
looking for me. There was quite a crowd around, and I
think nearly all of them were arrested."

He slipped an automatic from his pocket and
removed the magazine. His long arm reached out for the
cleaning materials on a side table which he had been
using before he went out. He slipped a rectangle of
flannelette through the loop of a weighted cord and
pulled it through the barrel, humming musically to
himself.

The white-haired man paced over to the window and
stood there with his hands clasped behind his back.

"Kestry and Bonacci were here today," he said.

The Saint's humming continued for a couple of bars.
He moistened his cleaning rag with three measured
drops of oil.

"Too bad I missed them," he murmured. "I've always
wanted to observe a brace of your hard-boiled New
York cops being tactful with an innocent suspect."

"You may get your chance soon enough," said the
other grimly, and Simon chuckled.

As a matter of fact, it was not surprising that
Inspector John Fernack's team had failed to locate the
Saint.

Kestry and Bonacci had had an interesting time. Passing dutifully from one hostelry to another, they had trampled under their large and useful feet a collection of expensive carpets that would have realized enough for the pair of them to retire on in great comfort. They had scanned registers until their eyes ached, discovering some highly informative traces of a remarkable family of John Smiths who appeared to spend their time leaping from one hotel to another with the agility of influenza germs, but finding no record of the transit of a certain Simon Templar. Before their official eyes, aggravating the aforesaid ache, had passed a procession of smooth and immaculate young gentlemen technically described as clerks but obviously ambassadors in disguise, who had condescendingly surveyed the photograph of their quarry and pityingly disclaimed recognition of any character of such low habits amongst their distinguished clientele. Bellboys in caravanserai after caravanserai had gazed knowingly at the large, useful feet on which the tour was conducted, and had whispered wisely to one another behind their hands. There had been an atmosphere of commiserating sapience about the audiences of all their interviews which to a couple of seasoned sleuths professedly disguised as ordinary citizens was peculiarly distressing.

And it was scarcely to be expected that the chauffeur of a certain William K. Valcross, resident of the Waldorf Astoria, would have swum into their questioning ken. They were looking for a tall, dark man of about thirty, described as an addict of the most luxurious hotels; and they had looked for him with commendable doggedness, refusing to be lured into any byways of fantasy. Mr. Valcross being indubitably sixty years old and by no stretch of imagination resembling the photograph with which they had been provided, they passed him over without loss of time—and, with him, his maidservant, his manservant, his ox, his ass, and the stranger within his gates.

"If they do find me," remarked the Saint reflectively, "there will probably be harsh words."

He squinted approvingly down the shining barrel of his gun, secured the safety catch, and patted it affectionately into his pocket. Then he rose and stretched himself and went over to the window where Valcross was standing.

Before them was spread out the ragged panorama of south Manhattan, the wonder island of the West. A narrow hump of rock sheltered from the Atlantic by the broad shoulder of Brooklyn, a mere ripple of stone in the ocean's inroads, on which the indomitable cussedness of Man had elected to build a city—and, not contented with the prodigious feat of overcoming such a dimensional difficulty at all, had made monuments of its defiance. Because the city could not expand laterally, it had expanded upwards; but the upward movement was a leap sculptured in stone, a flight born of necessity that had soared far beyond the standards of necessity, in a magnificent impulse of levitation that obliterated its own source. Molehills had become mountains in an art begotten of pure artifice. In the shadow of those grey and white pinnacles had grown up a modern Baghdad where the ends of the earth came together. A greater Italian city than Rome, a greater Irish city than Dublin, a greater German city than Cologne; a city of dazzling wealth whose towers had once looked like peaks of solid gold to hungry eyes reaching beyond the horizons of the Old World; a place that had sprung up from a lonely frontier to a metropolis, a central city, bowing to no other. A place where civilization and savagery had climbed alternately on each other's shoulders and reached their crest together. . . .

"This has always been my home," said Valcross, with a queer softness.

He turned his eyes from east to west in a glance that

swept in the whole skyline.

"I know there are other cities; and they say that New York doesn't represent anything but itself. But this is where my life has been lived."

Simon said nothing. He was three thousand miles from his own home; but as he stood there at the window he saw what the older man was seeing, and he could feel what the other felt. He had been there long enough to sense the spell that New York could lay on a man who looked at it with a mind not too tired for wonder—the pride and amazement at which cynical sophisticates laughed, which could still move the heart of a man who was not ashamed to sink below the surface and touch the common humanity that is the builder of cities. And because Simon could understand, he knew what was in the other's mind before it was spoken.

"I have to send for you," Valcross said, "because there are other people, more powerful than I am, who don't feel like that. The people to whom it isn't a home, but a battlefield to be looted. That is why you have to come here, from the other side of the world, to help an old man with a job that's too big for him."

He turned suddenly and looked at the Saint again, taking him in from the sweep of his smoothly brushed hair to the stance of his tailored shoes—the rakish lines of the dark, reckless face, the level mockery of the clear blue eyes, the rounded poise of muscular shoulders and the curve of the chest under the thin, jaunty shirt, the steady strength of one brown half-raised hand with the cigarette clipped lightly between the first two fingers, the lean fighter's hips and the reach of long, immaculate legs. No man whom he had ever known could have been so elegantly at ease and at the same time so alert and dangerous—and he had known many men. No other man he had known could ever have measured up in his judgment to the stature of devil-may-care confidence that he had demanded in his own mind and set out to find—and Valcross called himself a judge of men.

His hands fell on the Saint's shoulders; and they had to reach up to do it. He felt the slight, supple stir of the firm sinews and smiled.

"You might do it, son," he said. "You might clean up this rotten mess of crooks and grafters that's organizing itself to become the biggest thing this city of mine has ever had to fight. If you can't do it, I'll let myself be told for the first time that it's impossible. Just be a little bit careful. Don't swagger yourself into a jail or a shower of bullets before you've had a chance to do any good. I've seen those things happen before. Other fellows have tried—bigger men than you, son—stronger men than you, braver men than you, cleverer men than you—"

The Saint smiled back.

"Admitting for the moment that they ever lived," he remarked amiably, "you never saw anyone luckier than me."

But his mind went back to the afternoon in Madrid when Valcross had sat next to him in the Plaza de Toros and had struck up a conversation which had resulted in them spending the evening together. It went back to a moment much later that night, after they had dined together off the indescribable sucking pig at Botin's, when they sat over whiskies and sodas in Valcross's room at the Ritz; when Valcross had admitted that he had spent three weeks chasing him around Europe solely to bring about that casual encounter, and had told him why. He could hear the old man's quiet voice as it had spoken to him that night.

"They found him a couple of weeks later—I don't want to go into details. They aren't nice to think about, even now. . . . Two or three dozen men were pulled in and questioned. But maybe you don't know how things are done over there. These men kept their mouths shut. Some of them were let out. Some of them went up for trial. Maybe you think that means something.

"It doesn't. This business is giving work to all the gangsters and gunmen it needs—all the rats and killers who found themselves falling out of the big money when there was nothing more to be made out of liquor. It's tied up by the same leaders, protected by the same crooked politicians—and it pays more. It's beating the same police system, for the same reason the old order beat it—because it's hooked up with the same political system that appoints police commissioners to do as they're told.

"There wasn't any doubt that these men they had were guilty, Fernack admitted it himself. He told me their records—everything that was known about them. But he couldn't do anything. They were bailed out, adjourned, extradited, postponed—all the legal tricks. In the end they were acquitted. I saw them walk out of the court grinning. If I'd had a gun with me I'd have tried to kill them then.

"But I'm an old man, and I wasn't trained for that sort of thing. I take it that you were. That's why I looked for you. I know some of the things you've done, and now I've met you in the flesh. I think it's the kind of job you might like. It may be the last job you'll ever attempt. But it's a job that only an outlaw can do.

"I've got plenty of money, and I'm expecting to spend it. You can have anything you need to help you that money will buy. The one thing it won't buy is safety. You may find yourself in prison. You're even more likely to find yourself dead. I needn't try to fool you about that.

"But if you can do your justice on these men who kidnapped and killed my son, I'll pay you one million dollars. I want to know whether you think it's worth your while—tonight."

And the Saint could feel the twitch of his own smile again, and hear himself saying: "I'd do it for nothing. When do we go?"

These things came back to him while Valcross's hands still rested on his shoulders; and it was the first time since that night in Madrid that he had given any thought to the magnitude of the task he had undertaken.

Simon Templar had been in New York before; but that was in the more spacious and leisurely days when only 8.04 of the gin was amateur bathtub brew, before the Woolworth Building was ranked as a bungalow, when lawbreakers were prosecuted for breaking the law more frequently than for having falsified their income-tax returns. Times Square and 42nd Street were running a shabby second to the boardwalk at Coney Island; the smart shops had moved off the Avenue one block east to Park; and the ever-swinging doors of the gilded saloons that had formerly decorated every street corner had gone down before that historic wave of righteousness which dyed the Statue of Liberty its present bilious shade of green.

But there was one place, one institution, that the Saint could have found in spite of far more sweeping changes in the geography of the city. Lexington Avenue could still be followed south to 45th Street; and on 45th Street Chris Cellini should still be entertaining his friends unless a tidal wave had removed him catastrophically from the trade he loved. And the Saint had heard no news of any tidal wave of sufficient dimensions for that.

In the circumstances, he had less than no right to be paying calls at all; in a city even at that moment filled with angry and vigilant men who were still searching for him, he should have stayed hidden and been grateful for having any place to hide; but it would have taken more than the combined dudgeon of a dozen underworlds and police forces to keep him away. He had to eat; and in all the world there are no steaks like the steaks that Chris Cellini broils over an open fire with his own hands. The Saint walked with an easy, swinging stride, his hands

tucked in his trouser pockets, and the brim of his hat
tilted at a reckless angle over his eyes. The lean brown
face under the brim of the hat was open for all the world
to see; the blue eyes in it were as gay and careless as if he
had been a favoured member of the Four Hundred
sauntering forth towards an exclusive cocktail party;
only the slight tingling in his superb lithe muscles was
his reward for that light-hearted defiance of the laws of
chance. If he were interfered with on his way—that
would be just too bad. The Saint was prepared to raise
merry hell that night; and he was sublimely indifferent
to the details of where and how the fun broke loose.

But nobody interfered with him on that passage. He
turned in, almost disappointed by the tameness of the
evening, before the basement entrance of a three-story
brownstone house and pressed the bell at the side of the
iron-barred door. After a moment the inner door
opened, and the silhouette of a stocky shirt-sleeved man
came out against the light.

"Hullo, Chris," drawled the Saint.

For a second or two he was not recognized; and then
the man within let out an exclamation:

"*Buon Dio!* And where have you been for so many
years?"

A bolt was drawn, and the portal was swung inwards.
The Saint's hand was taken in an iron grip; another
hand was slapping him on the back; his ears throbbed to
a rich, jovial laughter.

"Where have you been, eh? Why do you stay away so
long? Why didn't you tell me you were coming, so I
could tell the boys to come along?"

"They aren't here tonight?" asked the Saint, spinning
his hat dexterously onto a peg.

Chris shook his head.

"You ought to of telephoned, Simon."

"I'm just as glad they aren't here," said the Saint
looking at him; and Chris was serious suddenly.

"I'm sorry—I forgot. . . . Well, you know you will be all right here." He smiled, and his rich voice brightened again. "You are always my friend, whatever happens."

He led the Saint down the passage towards the kitchen, with a brawny arm around his shoulders. The kitchen was the supplement to the one small dining-room that the place boasted—it was the sanctum sanctorum, a rendezvous that was more like a club than anything else, where those who were privileged to enter found a boisterous hospitality undreamed of in the starched expensive restaurants, where the diners are merely so many intruders, to be fed at a price and bowed stiffly out again. Although there were no familiar faces seated round the big communal table, the Saint felt the reawakening of an old happiness as he stepped into the brightly lighted room, with the smell of tobacco and wine and steaming vegetables and the clatter of plates and pans. It took him back at one leap to the ambrosial nights of drinking and endless argument, when all philosophies had been probed and all the world's problems settled, that he had known in that homely place.

"You'll have some sherry, eh?"

Simon nodded.

"And one of your steaks," he said.

He sat back and sipped the drink that Chris brought him, watching the room through half-closed eyes. The flash of jest and repartee, the crescendo of discussion and the ring of laughter, came to his ears like the echo of an unforgettable song. It was the same as it had always been—the same humorous camaraderie presided over and kept vigorously alive by Chris's own unchanging geniality. Why were there not more places like that in the world, he began to wonder—places where a host was more than a shopkeeper, and men threw off their cares and talked and laughed openly together, without fear or suspicion, expanding cleanly and fruitfully in the glow of wine and fellowship?

But he could only take that in a passing thought; for he had work to do that night. The steak came—thick, tender, succulent, melting in the mouth like butter; and he devoted himself to it with the wholehearted concentration which it deserved. Then, with his appetite assuaged, he leaned back with the remains of his wine and a fresh cigarette to ponder the happenings of the day.

At all events he had made a good beginning. Irboll was very definitely gone; and the Saint inhaled with deep contentment as he recalled the manner of his going. He had no regrets for the foolhardy impulse that had made him attach his own personal signature uncom- promisingly to the deed. Some of the terror that had once gone with those grotesque little drawings still clung to them in the memories of men who had feared them in the old days; and with a little adroit manipulation much of that terror could be built up again. It was good criminal psychology, and Simon was a great believer in the science. Curiously enough, that theatrical touch would mean more to a brazen underworld than anyone but an expert would have realized; for it is a fact that the hard-boiled gangster constitutes a large proportion of the dime novelette's most devoted public.

At any rate, it was a beginning. The matter of Irboll had been disposed of; but Irboll was quite a minor fish in the aquarium. Valcross had been explicit on that point. The small fry were all right in their appointed place: they could be neatly dismembered, drenched in ketchup and tabasco, exquisitely iced, and served up for a cocktail—on the way. But one million dollars of anybody's money was the price of the leaders of the shoal; and apart from the simple sport of rod and line, Simon Templar had a nebulous idea that he might be able to use a million dollars. Thinking it over, he had some difficulty in remembering a time when he could not have used a million dollars.

"If you offered me a glass of brandy," he murmured, as Chris passed the table, "I could drink a glass of brandy."

There was a late edition of the *World-Telegram* abandoned on the chair beside him, and Simon picked it up and cast an eye over the black banner of type spread across the front page. To his mild surprise he found that he was already a celebrity. An enthusiastic feature writer had launched himself on the subject with justifiable zeal; and even the Saint was tempted to blush at the extravagant attributes with which his modest personality had been adorned. He read the story through with a quizzical eye and the faintest suspicion of a smile on his lips.

And then the smile disappeared. It slid away quite quietly, without any fuss. Only the lazy blue gaze that scanned the sheet steadied itself imperceptibly, focusing on a name that had cropped up once too often.

He had been waiting for that—searching, in a detached and comprehensive way, for an inspiration that would lead him to a renewal of the action—and the lavish detail splurged upon the circumstances of his latest sin by that enthusiastic feature writer had obliged. It was, at least, a suggestion.

The smile came back as he stood up, draining the glass that had been set in front of him. People who knew him said that the Saint was most dangerous when he smiled. He turned away and clapped Chris on the shoulder.

"I'm on my way," he announced; and Chris's face fell.

"What, so soon?"

Simon nodded. He dropped a bill on the sideboard.

"You still broil the best steaks in the world, Chris," he said with a smile. "I'll be back for another."

He went down the hall, humming a little tune. On his

way he stopped by the telephone and picked up the directory. His finger ran down a long column of N's and came to rest below the name in the newspaper story that had held so much interest for him. He made a mental note of the address, patted the side pocket of his coat for the reassuring bulge of his automatic, and strolled on into the street.

The clock in the ornate tower of the old Jefferson Market Court was striking nine when his cab deposited him on the corner of Tenth Street and Greenwich. He stood at the curb and watched the taxi disappear round the next corner; and then he settled his hat and walked a few steps west on Tenth Street to pick up the number of the nearest house.

His destination was farther on. Still humming the same gentle breath of a tune, he continued his westward stroll with his hands in his pockets and a cigarette slanting up between his lips, with the same lithe, easy stride as he had gone down Lexington Avenue to his dinner—and with precisely the same philosophy. Only on this journey his feeling of pleasant exhilaration had quickened itself by the exact voltage of the difference between a gesture of bravado and a definite mission. He had no plan of action, but neither had the Saint any reverence for plans. He went forth, as he had done so often in the past, with nothing but a sublime faith that the gods of all good buccaneers would provide. And there was the loaded automatic in his pocket, and the ivory-hilted throwing knife strapped to his left forearm under his sleeve, ready to his hand in case the gods should overdo their generosity. . . .

In a few minutes he had found the number he wanted. The house was of the Dutch colonial type, with its roofs planted firmly in the late Victorian age. Its broad flat facade of red brick trimmed in white was unassuming enough; but it had a smug solidity reminiscent of the ancient Dutch burghers who had first shown their business acumen in the New World by purchasing the island from the Indians for twenty-four dollars and a jug of corn whiskey—Simon had sometimes wondered how the local apostles of Temperance had ever brought themselves to inhabit a city that was tainted from its earliest conception with the Devil's Brew. It was an interesting metaphysical speculation which had nothing whatsoever to do with the point of his presence there, and he abandoned it reluctantly in favour of the appealing potentialities of a narrow alley which he spotted on one side of the building.

His leisurely stroll past the house had given him plenty of time to assimilate a few other important details. Lights showed from the heavily curtained windows on the second floor, and the gloom at the far end of the alley was broken by a haze of diffused light. Knowing something about the particular style of architecture in question, Simon felt reasonably sure that the last-mentioned light came from the library of the house. The illuminations indicated that someone was at home; and from the black sedan parked at the curb, with a low number on its license plate and the official city seal affixed above it, the Saint was entitled to deduce that the home lover was the gentleman with whom he was seeking earnest converse.

He turned back from the corner and retraced his tracks; and although to a casual eye his gait would have seemed just as lazy and nonchalant as before, there was a more elastic spring to his tread, a fettered swiftness to his movements, a razor-edged awareness in the blue eyes that scanned the sidewalks, which had not been there when he first set out.

The legend painted in neat white letters at the opening of the alley proclaimed it the Trade Entrance; but Simon felt democratic. He turned into it without hesitation. The passage was barely three feet wide, bounded at one side by the wall of the building and at the other by a high board fence. As the Saint advanced, the light from the rear became brighter. He pressed himself close to the darker shadows along the wall of the house and went on.

A blacker oblong of shadow in the wall ahead of him indicated a doorway. He passed it in one long stride and pulled up short at the end of the alley against an ornamental picket fence. For a moment he paused there, silent and motionless as a statue. His muscles were relaxed and calm; but every nerve was alert, linked up in an uncanny half-animal coordination of his senses which seemed to bend every faculty of his being to the aid of the one he was using. To his listening ears came the purling of water; and as a faint breeze stirred the foliage ahead of him it wafted to his arched nostrils the faint, delicate odour of lilacs.

A garden beyond, deduced the Saint. The dim light which he had seen from the street came from directly above him now, shining out of a tier of windows at the rear of the house. He watched the irregular rectangles of light printed on the grass beyond and saw them move, shifting their pattern with every breath of thin air. "Draperies at open windows," he added to his deductions and smiled invisibly in the darkness.

He swung a long, immaculately trousered leg over the picket fence, and a second later planted its mate beside it. His eyes had long since accustomed themselves to the gloom like a cat's, and the light from the windows above was more than sufficient to give him his bearings. In one swift survey he took in the enclosed garden plot, made out the fountain and arbour at the far end, and saw that the high board fence, after encircling the yard, terminated flush against the far side of the house. The geography couldn't have suited him better if it had been laid out to his own specifications.

He listened again, for one brief second, glanced at the casement above him, and padded across the garden to the far fence wall. The top was innocent of broken glass or other similar discouragements for the amateur house-breaker. Flexing the muscles of his thighs, Simon leaped upwards, and with a masterly blend of the techniques of a second-story man and a tight-rope walker gained the top of the fence.

From this precarious perch he surveyed the situation again and found no fault with it. Its simplicity was almost puerile. The open windows through which the light shone were long French casements reaching down to within a foot of the fence level; and from where he stood it was an easy step across to the nearest sill. Simon took the step with blithe agility and an unclouded conscience.

It is possible that even in these disillusioned days there may survive a sprinkling of guileless souls whose visions of the private life of a Tammany judge have not been tainted by the cynicism of their time—a few virginal, unsullied minds that would have pictured the dispenser of their justice at this hour poring dutifully over one of the legal tomes that lined the walls of his library, or possibly, in lighter mood, gambolling affectionately on the floor with his small curly-headed son.

Simon Templar, it must be confessed, was not one of these. The pristine luminance of his childhood faith had suffered too many shocks since the last day when he believed that the problems of overpopulation could be solved by a scientific extermination of storks. But it must also be admitted that he had never in his most optimistic hours expected to wedge himself straight into an orchestra stall for a scene of domestic recreation like the one which confronted him.

Barely two yards away from him, Judge Wallis Nather, in the by no means meagre flesh, was engaged in thumbing over a voluptuous roll of golden-backed bills whose dimension made even Simon Templar stare.

The tally evidently proving satisfactory, His Honour

placed the pile of bills on the glass-topped desk before him and patted it lovingly into a thick, orderly oblong. Then he retrieved a sheet of paper from beneath a jade paperweight and glanced over the few lines written on it. With an exhalation of breath that could almost be described as a snort, he crumpled the slip of paper into a ball and dropped it into the wastebasket beside him; and then he picked up the pile of bills again and ruffled the edges with his thumb, watching them as if their crisp rustle transmuted itself in his ears into the strains of some supernal symphony.

Taken by and large, it was a performance to which Simon Templar raised his hat. It had the tremendous simplicity of true greatness. In a deceitful, hypocritical world, where all the active population was scrambling frantically for all the dough it could get its hands on, and at the same time smugly proclaiming that money could not buy happiness, it burned like a bright candle of sincerity. Not for Wallis Nather were any of those pettifogging affectations. He had his dough; and if he believed that it could not buy happiness, he faced his melancholy destiny with dauntless courage.

Simon was almost apologetic about butting in. Nothing but stern necessity could have forced him to intrude the anticlimax of his presence into such a moment. But since he had to intrude, he saw no reason why the conventions should not be observed.

"Good-evening, Judge," he murmured politely.

He would always maintain that he did everything in his power to soften the blow—that he could not have introduced himself with any softer sympathy. And he could only sigh when he perceived that all his good intentions had misfired.

Nather did three things simultaneously. He dropped the sheaf of bills, spun round in his swivel chair as if its axle had suddenly got tangled up in a high-speed power belt, and made a tentative pass for a side drawer of the desk. It was the last of these movements which never came to completion. He found himself staring into the levelled menace of a blue steel automatic, gaping into a pair of the most mocking blue eyes that he had ever seen. They were eyes that made something cringe at the back of his brain, eyes with a debonair gaze like the flick of a rapier thrust—eyes that held a greater terror for the Honourable Judge than the steady shape of the automatic.

He sat there, leaning slightly forward in his chair, with his heavy body stiffening and his fleshy nostrils dilating, for a space of ten terrific seconds. The only sound was the thud of his own heart and the suddenly abnormally loud tick of the clock that stood on his desk. And then, with an effort which brought the sweat out in beads on his forehead, he tried to shake off the supernatural fear that was winding its icy grip around his chest.

He started to heave himself forward, but he got no further than that brief convulsive start. With a faint, flippant smile, the Saint whirled the automatic once around his forefinger by the trigger guard and came on into the room. After that one derisive gesture the butt of the gun settled into his hand again, as smoothly and surely as if there were a socket there for it.

"Don't disturb yourself, comrade," purred the Saint. "I know the book of rules says that a host should always rise when receiving a guest, but just for once we'll forget the formalities. Sit down, Your Honour—and keep on making yourself at home."

The judge shifted his frozen gaze from the automatic to the Saint's face. The cadences of that gentle, mocking voice drummed eerily on through his memory. It was a voice that matched the eyes and the debonair stance of the intruder—a voice that for some strange reason re-wakened the clammy terror that he had known when he first looked up and met that cavalier blue gaze. The last of the colour drained out of his sallow cheeks, and twin pulses beat violently in his throat.

"What is the meaning of this infernal farce?" he demanded, and did not recognize the raw jaggedness of his own voice.

"If you sit down I'll tell you all about it," murmured the Saint. "If you don't—well, I noticed a slap-up funeral parlour right around the corner, with some jolly-looking coffins at bargain prices. And this is supposed to be a lucky month to die in."

The eyes of the two men clashed in an almost physical encounter, like the blades of two duellists engaging; but the Saint's smile did not change. And presently Judge Nather sank back heavily in his chair, with his face a pastry white and the dew of perspiration on his upper lip.

"Thanks a lot," said the Saint.

He relaxed imperceptibly, loosening the crook of his finger fractionally from the trigger. With unaltered elegance he moved himself sideways to the door and turned the key in the lock with a flick of his wrist. Then he strolled unhurriedly back across the deep-piled rug towards His Honour.

He hitched his left hip up onto the corner of the mahogany desk and settled himself there, with one polished shoe swinging negligently back and forth. One challenging blue eye slid over the fallen heap of bills that lay between himself and his host, and his brows tilted speculatively.

He poked at the nest egg with the nozzle of his gun, scattering the bills across the table in a golden cascade.

"Must be quite a cozy little total, Algernon," he remarked. "Almost enough to make me forget my principles."

"So it's robbery, eh?" grated Nather; and the Saint thought he could detect a note of relief in the words.

He shook his head rather sadly, turning wide innocent eyes on his victim.

"My dear Judge—you wrong me, I merely mentioned that I was struggling against temptation. This really started to be just a sociable interview. I want to know where you were born and why, and what penitentiary you graduated from, and what you think about disarmament, and whether your face was always so repulsive or if somebody trod on it. I wasn't thinking of stealing anything."

His gaze reverted to the sheaf of bills, meditatively, as though the thought was nevertheless penetrating slowly into his mind, against his will; and the judge moistened his dry lips.

"What is all this nonsense?" he croaked.

"Just a little friendly call." Simon poked at the bills again, wistfully. It was clear that the idea which Nather had dragged in was gaining ground. "You and your packet of berries—me and my little effort at house-breaking. On second thoughts," said the Saint, reaching a decision with apparent reluctance, "I am afraid I shall have to borrow these. Just sitting and looking at them like this is getting me all worked up."

Nather stiffened up in his chair, his flabby hands curling up into lumpish fists; but the gun in the Saint's hand never wavered from the even keel that held it centred on the helpless judge like a finger of fate. Nather's small eyes flickered like burning agates as the Saint gathered up the stack of notes with a sweeping gesture and dropped them into his pocket; but he did not try to challenge the threat of the .38 Colt that hovered a scanty yard from his midriff. His impotent wrath exploded in a staccato clip of words that rasped gropingly through the stillness.

"Damn you—I'll see that you don't get away with this!"

"I believe you would," agreed Simon amiably. "I admit that it isn't particularly tactful of me to do things like this to you, especially in this man's city. It's a pity you don't feel sociable. We might have had a lovely evening together, and then if I ever got caught and brought up in your court you'd burst into tears and direct the jury to acquit me—just like you'd have done with Jack Irboll eventually, if he hadn't had such a tragic accident. But I suppose one can't have everything. . . . Never mind. Tell me how much I've borrowed and I'll give you a receipt."

The pallor was gone from Nather's cheeks, giving place to a savage flush. A globule of perspiration trickled down his cheek and hung quivering at the side of his jaw.

"There were twenty thousand dollars there," he stated hoarsely.

The Saint raised his eyebrows.

"Not so bad," he drawled quietly, "for blood money."

Nather's head snapped up, and a fleeting panic widened the irises of his eyes; but he said nothing. And the Saint smiled again.

"Pardon me. In the excitement of the moment, and all that sort of thing, I forgot to introduce myself. I'm afraid I've had you at a disadvantage. My name is Templar—Simon Templar"—he caught the flash of stark hypnotic fear that blanched the big man's lips, and grinned even more gently. "You may have heard of me. I am the Saint."

A tremor went over the man's throat, as he swallowed mechanically out of a parched mouth. He spoke between twitching lips.

"You're the man who sent Irboll that note."

"And killed him," said the Saint quietly. The lilt of banter was lingering only in the deepest undertones of his voice—the surface of it was as smooth and cold as a shaft of polished ice. "Don't forget that, Nather. You let him out—and I killed him."

The judge stirred in his chair, a movement that was no

more than the uncontrollable reaction of nerves strained beyond the limits of their strength. His mouth shaped an almost inaudible sentence.

"What do you want?"

"Well, I thought we might have a little chat." Simon's foot swung again, in that easy, untroubled pendulum. "I thought you might know things. You seem to have been quite a pal of Jack's. According to the paper I was reading tonight, you were the man who signed his permit to carry the gun that killed Ionetzki. You were the guy who signed the writ of habeas corpus to get Irboll out when they first pulled him in. You were the guy who adjourned him the last time he was brought up. And three years ago, it seems, you were the guy who acquitted our same friend Irboll along with four others who were tried for the murder of a kid named Billie Valcross. One way and another, Algernon, it looks like you must be quite a useful sort of friend for a bloke to have."

CHAPTER II

HOW SIMON TEMPLAR EAVESDROPPED TO SOME ADVANTAGE, AND INSPECTOR FERNACK WENT FOR A RIDE

Nather did not try to answer. His body was sunk deep into his chair, and his eyes glared venomously up at the Saint out of a face that was contorted into a mask of hate and fury; but Simon had passed under glares like that before.

"Just before I came in," Simon remarked conversationally, "you were reading a scrap of paper that seemed to have some connection with those twenty grand I borrowed."

"I don't know what you're talking about," said the judge.

"No?" Simon's voice was honeyed, but none of the chill had gone out of his blue eyes. "Let me remind you. You screwed it up and plugged it into the wastebasket. It's there still—and I'd like to see it."

Nather's eyelids flickered.

"Why don't you get it?"

33

"Because I'd hate to give you the chance to catch me bending—my tail's tender today. Fetch out that paper!"

His voice crisped up like the flick of a whiplash, and Wallis Nather jerked under the sting of it. But he made no move to obey.

A throbbing stillness settled over the room. The air was surcharged with the electric tension of it. The smile had faded from the Saint's lips when his voice tightened on that one curt command; and it had not come back. There was no variation in the graceful ease with which he held his precarious perch on the edge of the desk, but the gentle rocking of his free foot had died away like the pendulum of a clock that had run down. And a thin pin-prickling temblor frisked up the Saint's spine as he realized that Nather did not mean to obey.

Instead, he realized that the judge was marshalling the last fragments of his strength and courage to make one desperate lunge for the automatic that held him crucified in his chair. It was fantastic, incredible; but there could be no mistake. The intuitive certainty had flashed through his mind at the same instant as it was born in the brain of the man before him. And Simon knew, with the same certainty, that just as surely as that desperate lunge was made, his own finger would constrict on the trigger, ending the argument beyond all human revision, without hesitation and without remorse.

"You wouldn't dare to shoot," said Nather throatily.

He said it more as if he were trying to convince himself; and the Saint's eyes held him on needle points of blue ice.

"The word isn't in my dictionary—and you ought to know it! This isn't a country where men carry guns for ornament, and I'm just getting acclimatized. . . ."

But even while Simon spoke, his brain was racing ahead to explore the reasons for the insane resolution that was whitening the knuckles of the judge's twitching hands.

He felt convinced that such a man as Wallis Nather would not go up against that gaping automatic on account of a mere twenty thousand dollars. That was a sum of money which any man might legitimately be grieved to lose, but it was not large enough to tempt anyone but a starving desperado to the gamble that Nather was steeling himself to make.

There could be only one other motive—the words scrawled on that scrap of paper in the wastebasket. Something that was written on that crumpled slip of milled rag held dynamite enough to raise the ghostly hand of Nemesis itself. Something was recorded there that had the power to drive Nather forward inch by inch in his chair into the face of almost certain death. . . .

With fascinated eyes Simon watched the slight, nerve-tingling movements of the judge's body as Nather edged himself up for that suicidal assault on the gun. For the first time in his long and checkered career he felt himself a blind instrument in the working out of an inexorable fate. There was nothing more that he could do. The one metallic warning that he had delivered had passed unheeded. Only two things remained. In another few seconds Nather would lunge; and in that instant the automatic would bark its riposte of death. . . .

Simon was vaguely conscious of the quickening of his pulse. His mind reeled away to those trivial details that sometimes slip through the voids of an intolerable suspense—there must be servants somewhere in the place—but it would only take him three swift movements, before they could possibly reach the door, to scrawl his sign manual on the blotter, snatch the crumple of paper from the wastebasket, and vanish through the open windows into the darkness. . . .

And then a bell exploded in the oppressive atmosphere of the room like a bomb. A telephone bell.

Its rhythmic double beat sheared through the silence like a guillotine, cleaving the overstrained chord of the spell with the blade of its familiar commonplaceness; and Nather's effort collapsed as if the same cleavage had snapped the support of his spine. He shuddered once and slouched back limply in his chair, passing a trembling hand across his eyes.

Simon smiled again. His shoe resumed its gentle swinging, and he swept a gay, mocking eye over the desk. There were two telephones on it—one of them clearly a house phone. On a small table to the right of the desk stood a third telephone, obviously a Siamese twin of the second, linked to the same outside wire and intended for His Honour's secretary. The Saint reached out a long arm and brought it over onto his knee.

"Answer the call, brother," he suggested persuasively.

A wave of his automatic added its imponderable weight to the suggestion; but the fight had already been drained out of the judge's veins. With a grey drawn face he dragged one of the telephones towards him; and as he lifted the receiver Simon matched the movement on the extension line and slanted his gun over in a relentless arc to cover the other's heart. Definitely it was not Mr. Wallis Nather's evening, but the Saint could not afford to be sentimental.

"Judge Nather speaking."

The duplicate receiver at the Saint's ear clicked to the vibrations of a clear feminine voice.

"This is Fay." The speech was crisp and incisive, but it had a rich pleasantness of music that very few feminine voices can maintain over the telephone—there was a rare quality in the sound that moved the Saint's blood with a queer, delightful expectation for which he could have given no account. It was just one of those voices. "The Big Fellow says you'd better stay home tonight," stated the voice. "He may want you."

Nather's eyes seemed to glaze over; then they switched to the Saint's face. Simon moved his gun under the desk lamp and edged it a little forward, and his gaze was as steady as the steel. Nather swallowed.

"I—I'll be here," he stammered.

"See that you are," came the terse conclusion, in the same voice of bewitching overtones; and then the wire went dead.

Watching Nather, the Saint knew that at least half the audience had understood that cryptic conversation perfectly. The judge was staring vacantly ahead into space with the lifeless receiver still clapped by his ear and his mouth hung half open.

"Very interesting," said the Saint softly.

Nather's mouth closed jerkily. He replaced the receiver slowly on its hook and looked up.

"A client of mine," he said casually; but he was not casual enough.

"That's interesting, too," said the Saint. "I didn't know judges were supposed to have clients. I thought they were unattached and impartial. . . . And she must be very beautiful, with a voice like that. Can it be, Algernon, that you are hiding something from me?"

Nather glowered up at him.

"How much longer are you going on with this preposterous performance?"

"Until it bores me. I'm easily amused," said the Saint, "and up to now I haven't yawned once. So far as I can see, the interview is progressing from good to better. All kinds of things are bobbing up every minute. This Big Fellow of yours, now: let's hear some more about him. I'm inquisitive."

Nather's eyes flinched wildly.

"I'm damned if I'll talk to you any more!"

"You're damned if you won't."

"You can go to hell."

"And the same applies," said the Saint equably.

He stood up and came round the desk, poising himself on straddled feet a pace in front of the judge, lean and dynamically balanced as a panther.

"You're very dense, Algernon," he remarked calmly.
"You don't seem to get the idea at all. Maybe our little
interlude of song and badinage has led you up the wrong
tree. You can make a good guess why I'm here. You
know that I didn't drop in just for the pleasure of admiring your classic profile. You know who I am. I don't
care whàt you pick on, but you can tell me something.
Any of your maidenly secrets ought to be worth listening to. Come through, Nather—or else . . ."

"Or else what?"

The Saint's gun moved forward until it pressed deep
into the judge's flabby navel.

"Or else find out what Ionetzki and Jack Irboll
know!"

Nather's heavy, sullen lips twisted back from yellowed teeth. And Simon jabbed the gun a notch further
into the judge's stomach.

"And don't lie," said the Saint caressingly; "because
I'm friendly to undertakers and that funeral parlour
looked as if it could do with some business."

Nather passed a fevered tongue over hot dry lips. He
had not lived through thirty years of intermittent con-
tacts with the underworld without learning to recognize
that queer bitter fibre in a man that makes him capable
of murder. And the terrific inward struggle of that last
moment before the telephone bell rang had blunted his
vitality. The strength was not in him to screw himself to
that desperate pitch again. He knew, beyond all question, that if he refused to talk, if he attempted to lie, that
bantering tiger of a man who was squeezing the gun ever
deeper into his vitals could destroy him as ruthlessly as
he would have crushed an ant. Nather's larynx heaved
twice, convulsively; and then, before he could speak, a
muffled tread sounded beyond the locked door.

The Saint tautened, listening. From the ponderous,
flat-footed measure of the stride he guessed it to belong
to the butler. Nather looked up with a sudden gleam of

hope; but the steady pressure of the gun muzzle in his yielding flesh did not vary by a milligram. The Saint's light whisper floated to his ears in an airy breath.

"Heroes die young," it murmured pithily.

A knock sounded on the door—a discreet knock that could only have been made by a servant. Nather, with his vengeful eyes frozen on the Saint, lip-read the order rather than heard it. "Ask him what he wants."

"Well?" Nather growled out.

"Inspector Fernack is downstairs, sir. He says it's important."

Nather stared at the Saint. And the Saint smiled. Once again his reckless fighting lips shaped an almost inaudible command.

"Tell him to come up," Nather repeated after him, and could not believe that he was obeying an order.

He sat silent and rigid as the butler's footsteps receded and died away; and at last Simon withdrew the gun barrel which had for so long been boring insidiously into the judge's abdomen.

"Better and better," said the Saint amazingly, flippng a cigarette into his lips. "I was wanting to meet Fernack."

Nather gaped at him incredulously. The situation was grotesque, unbelievable; and yet it had occurred. The automatic had been eased out of his belly—it was even then circling around the Saint's forefinger in one of those carelessly confident gyrations—which it certainly would not have been if any of the Saint's instructions had been disobeyed. The thing was beyond Nather's understanding. The glacial recklessness of it was subtly disquieting, in a colder and more deadly way than the menace of the gun had ever been: it argued a self-assurance that was frightening, and with that fear went the crawling question of whether the Saint's mind had leapt to some strategy of lightning cunning that Nather could not see.

"You'll get your chance," said the judge gruffly, searching for comprehension through a kind of fog.

Simon rasped the head of a match with his left thumbnail, applied the spluttering flame to the tip of his cigarette, and inhaled luxuriously. With a drift of smoke trailing back through his lips, he lounged towards a large tapestried Morris chair that stood between the French windows by which he had entered, and swung the chair around with his foot so that its heavily padded side was presented to the door through which the detective would enter.

He came back, overturned the wastebasket with an adroit twist of his toe, and picked up the crumpled scrap of paper and dropped it into his pocket in one smooth swoop that frustrated the judge's flash of fight even before the idea was conceived. He pulled open the drawer to which Nather's hand had jumped at the first sound of his voice, and transferred the revolver from it to his hip. And then, with the scene set to his satisfaction, he walked back to his chosen chair and settled himself comfortably in it with his right leg draped gracefully over the arm.

He flicked a quarter inch of ash from his cigarette onto the expensive carpet.

"When your man announces Fernack," he directed, "open the door and let him in. And come back yourself. Understand?"

Nather did not understand. His brain was still fumbling dazedly for the catch that he could not find. On the face of it, it seemed like the answer to a prayer. With Fernack on the scene, there must be the chance of a way out for him—a way to retrieve that scrap of paper buried in Templar's pocket and to dispose of the Saint himself. But something told him that the calm smiling man in the chair was not legislating for any such denouement.

Simon read his thoughts.

"The gun won't be in evidence for a while, Nather.

But it'll be handy. And at this range I'm a real sniper. I shouldn't want you to get excited over any notions of ganging up on me with Fernack. Somebody might get hurt."

Nather's gaze rested on him venomously.

"Some day," said the judge slowly, "I hope we shall meet again."

"In Sing Sing," suggested the Saint breezily. "Let's call it a date."

He drew on his cigarette again and listened to the returning footsteps of the butler, accompanied by a heavier, more determined tread. As a matter of fact, he was innocent of all subterfuge. There was nothing more behind his decision than appeared on the face of it. Fernack was there, and the Saint saw no reason why they should not meet. His whole evening had started off in the same spirit of openminded expectation, and it had turned out very profitably. He waited the addition to his growing circle of acquaintances with no less kindly interest.

The butler's knuckles touched the door again.

"Inspector Fernack, sir."

Simon waved the judge on, and Nather crossed the room slowly. Every foot of the distance he was conscious of the concealed automatic that was aiming into his back. He snapped the key over in the lock and opened the door; and Inspector Fernack shouldered his brawny bulk across the threshold.

"Why the locked door, Judge?" Fernack inquired sourly. "Getting nervous?"

Nather closed the door without answering, and Simon decided to oblige.

"I did it," he explained. Fernack, who had not noticed him, whirled round in surprise; and Simon went on: "Would you mind locking it again, Judge—just as I told you?"

Nather hesitated for a second and then obeyed.

Fernack stared blankly at the figure lounging in the armchair and then turned with puzzled eyes to the judge. He pushed back his battered fedora and pulled reflectively at the lobe of his left ear.

"What the hell is this?" he demanded; and Nather shrugged.

"A nut," he said tersely.

Simon ignored the insult, studying the man who had come in. On the whole, Fernack conformed closely enough to the pattern in his mind of what a New York police inspector was likely to be; but the reality went a little beyond that. Simon liked the belligerent honesty of the frosted grey eyes, the strength and courage of the iron jaw. He realized that, whatever else Fernack might be, a good or bad detective, he fell straight and clean-cut into the narrow outline of that rarest thing in a country of corrupted law—a square dick. There were qualities in that mountain of toughened flesh that Simon Templar could have appreciated at any time; and he smiled at the man with an unaffected friendliness which he never expected to see returned.

"What ho, Inspector," he murmured affably. "You disappoint me. I was hoping to be recognized."

Fernack's eyes hardened in perplexity as he studied the Saint's tanned features. He shook his head.

"I seem to know your face, but I'm damned if I can place you."

"Maybe it was a bad photograph," conceded the Saint regretfully. "Those photographs usually are. All the same, seeing it was only this afternoon that you were handing out copies of it to the reporters—"

Illumination hit Fernack like a blow.

His eyes flamed wide, and his jaw closed with a snap as he took three long strides across the room.

"By God—it's the Saint!"

"Himself. I didn't know you were a pal of Algernon's, but since you arrived I thought I might as well stay."

Fernack's shoulders were hunched, his pugnacious chin jutting dangerously. In that instant shock of surprise, he had not paused to wonder why the Saint should be offering himself like an eager victim.

"I want you, young fellow," he grated.

He lunged forward, with his hand diving for his hip.

And then he pulled up short, a yard from the chair. His hand was poised in the air, barely two inches from the butt of his gun, but it made no attempt to travel further. The Saint did not seem to have moved, and his free foot was still swinging gently back and forth; but somehow the blue-black shape of an automatic had come into his right hand, and the round black snout of it was aimed accurately into the detective's breastbone.

"I'm sorry," said the Saint; and he meant it. "I hate being arrested, as you should have gathered from my biography. It's just one of those things that doesn't happen. My dear chap, you didn't really think I stayed on so you could take me home with you as a souvenir!"

Fernack glared at the gun speechlessly for a moment and shifted his gaze back to the Saint. For a moment Simon was afraid—with a chin like that, it was an even chance that the detective might not be stopped; and Simon would have hated to shoot. But Fernack was not foolhardy. He had been bred and reared in a world where foolhardiness went down under an elemental law of the survival of the wisest; and Fernack faced facts. At that range the Saint could not miss, and the honour of the New York police would gain a purely temporary glow from the heroic suicide of an inspector.

Fernack grunted and straightened up with a shrug.

"What the hell is this?" he repeated.

"Just a social evening. Sit down and get the spirit of the party. Maybe you know some smoke-room stories, too."

Fernack pulled out a chair and sat down facing the Saint. After the first stupefaction of surprise was gone he accepted the situation with homely matter-of-factness. Since the initiative had been temporarily taken out of his hands, he could do no harm by listening.

"What are you doing here?" he asked; and there was the beginning of a grim respect in his voice.

Simon swung his gun around towards Nather and waved the judge back to his swivel chair.

"I might ask the same question," he remarked.

Fernack glanced at the judge thoughtfully; and Simon's quick eyes caught the distaste in his gaze, and realized that Nather saw it, too.

"You do your own asking," Fernack said dryly.

Simon surveyed the two men humorously.

"The two arms of the law," he commented reverently. "The guardian of the peace and the dispenser of justice. You could pose for a tableau. The pea-green incorruptibles."

Fernack frowned, and the judge squirmed slightly in his chair. There was a strained silence in the room, broken by the inspector's rough voice:

"Know any more fairy tales?"

"Plenty," said the Saint. "Once upon a time there was a great city, the richest city in the world. Its towers went up through the clouds, and its streets were paved with golden-backed Treasury notes, which were just as good as the old-fashioned fairy-tale paving stones and much easier to carry around. And all the people in it should have been very happy, what with Macy's Basement and Grover Whalen and a cathedral called Minsky's. But under the city there was a greedy octopus whose tentacles reached from the highest to the lowest places— and even outside the city, to the village greens of Canarsie and North Hoosick and a place called Far Rockaway where the Scottish citizens lived. And this octopus prospered and grew fat on a diet of blood and gold and the honour of men."

Fernack's bitter voice broke in on the recitation:

"That's too true to be funny."

"It wasn't meant to be—particularly. Fernack, you know why I'm here. I did a job for you this afternoon—one of those little jobs that Brother Nather is supposed to do and never seems to get around to. Ionetzki was quite a friend of yours, wasn't he?"

"You know a lot." The detective's fists knotted at his sides. "What next?"

"And Nather seems to have been quite a friend of Jack Irboll's. I'm doing your thinking for you. On account of this orgy of devotion, I blew along to see Nather; and I haven't been here half an hour before you blow in yourself. Well, a little while back I asked you why you were here, and I wasn't changing the subject."

Fernack's mouth tightened. His eyes swerved around to the judge; just Nather's blotchy face was as inexpressive as a slab of lard, except for the high-lights of perspiration on his flushed cheekbones. Fernack looked at the Saint again.

"You want a lot of questions answered for you," he stated flatly.

"I'll try another." Simon drew on his cigarette and looked at the detective through a haze of outgoing smoke. "Maybe you can translate something for me. Translate it into words of one syllable—and try to make me understand."

"What?"

"The Big Fellow says you'd better stay home tonight. He may want you!"

Simon flipped the quotation back hopefully enough, without a pause. It leapt across the air like the twang of a broken fiddle string, without giving the audience a half-second's grace in which to brace themselves or rehearse their reactions. But not even in his moments of most malicious optimism had the Saint expected the results which rewarded him.

He might have touched off a charge of blasting

powder at their feet. Nather caught his breath in a gasping hiccough like a man shot in the stomach. Fernack rose an inch from his chair on tautened thighs: his grey eyes bulged, then narrowed to glinting slits.

"Say that again!" he rasped.

"You don't get the idea." The Saint smiled, but his sapphire gaze was as quiet as the levelled gun. "I was just asking you to translate something. Can you tell me what it means?"

"Who wants to know?"

Nather scrambled up from his chair, his fists clenched and his face working. His face was putting in a big day.

"This is intolerable!" he barked hoarsely. "Isn't there anything you can do, Fernack, instead of sitting there listening to this—this maniac?"

Fernack glanced at him.

"Sure," he said briefly. "You take his gun away, and I'll do it."

"I'll report you to the commissioner!" Nather half screamed. "By God, I'll have you thrown out of the force! What do we have laws for when an armed hoodlum can hold me up in my own house under your very nose—"

"And gangsters can shoot cops in broad daylight and get acquitted," added the Saint brightly. "Let's make it an indignation meeting. I don't know what the country's coming to."

Nather choked; and the Saint stood up. There was something in the air which told him that the interview might more profitably be adjourned—and the judge's blustering outburst had nothing to do with it. With that intuitive certainty in his mind, he arched on it in cool disregard of dramatic sequence. That was the way he liked best to work, along his own paths, following a trail without any attempt to dictate the way it should go. But his evening had only just begun.

He strolled to the desk and lifted the lid of a bronze

humidor. Selecting a cigar, he crackled it at his ear and
sniffed it appreciatively.

"You know good tobacco if you don't know anything
else good, Algernon," he murmured.

He discarded the stub of his cigarette and stuck the
Corona-Corona at a jaunty angle between his teeth. As
an afterthought, he tipped over the humidor and helped
himself to a bonus handful of the same crop.

"Well, boys," he said, "you mustn't mind if I leave
you. I never overstay my welcomes, and maybe you have
some secrets to whisper in each other's ears." He backed
strategically to the window and paused there to button
his coat. "By the way," he said, "you needn't bother to
rush up this window and wave me good-bye. These
farewells always make me feel nervous." He spun the
automatic around his finger for the last time and hefted
it in his hand significantly. "I'd hate there to be any
accidents at the last minute," said the Saint; and was
gone.

Fernack stared at the rectangle of empty blackness
and emptied his lungs in a long sigh. After some seconds
he got up. He walked without haste to the open casements and stood there looking silently out into the dark;
then he turned back to the room.

"That's a guy I could like," he said thoughtfully.

Nather squinted at him.

"You'd better get out, too," snarled the judge.
"You'll hear more about this later—"

"You'll hear more about it now," Fernack said coldly; and there was something in his voice which made
Nather listen.

What the detective had to say did not take long.
Fernack on business was not a man to expand himself
wordily at any time, and any euphemistic phrases which
he might have revolved in his mind had been driven out
of it entirely. He stowed his kid gloves high up on the
shelves of his disgust, and propounded his assessment of

the facts with a profane brutality that left Nather white and shaking.

Three minutes after Simon Templar's departure, Inspector Fernack was also barging out of the room, but by a more orthodox route. He thundered down the stairs and shouldered aside the obsequious butler who made to open the door for him, and flung himself in behind the wheel of his prowl car with a short-winded violence that could not be accounted for solely by an ardent desire to remove himself from those purlieus. But his evening was not finished, either; though he did not know this at that moment.

He slammed the door, switched on the ignition, and unlocked the steering column; and then something hard probed its way gently but firmly into his ribs, and the soft voice of the Saint wafted into his right ear.

"Hold on, Inspector. You and I are going for a little joy ride!"

Inspector Fernack's jaw sagged.

Under the stress of his unrelieved emotions, he had not noticed the Saint's arrival or the noiseless opening of the other door. There was no reason on earth why he should have looked for either. According to his upbringing, it was so baldly axiomatic that the Saint would by that time be skating through the traffic three or four miles away that he had not even given the subject a thought. The situation in which he found himself for the second time was so deliriously unexpected that he was temporarily paralyzed. And in that space of time Simon slid in onto the cushions beside him and closed the door.

Fernack's jaw closed, and he looked into the level blue eyes behind the gun.

"What's your idea?"

"We'll go places. I'd like to talk to you, and it's just possible you might like to talk to me. We'll go anywhere you like, bar Centre Street."

The granite lines of the detective's face twitched. There were limits to his capacity for boiling indignation, a point where the soaring curve of his wrath curled over and fell down a precipitous switchback—and the gay audacity of the man at his side had boosted him to that point in two terrific jumps. For a second the detective's temper seemed to teeter breathlessly on the pinnacle like a trolley stalling on a scenic railway; and then it slipped down the gradient on the other side. . . .

"We'll try the park," Fernack said.

A heavy blucher tramped on the starter, and the gears meshed. They turned out of Tenth Street and swung north up Seventh Avenue. Simon leaned comfortably back and used the lighter on the dashboard for his cigar; nothing more was said until they were threading the tangle of traffic at Times Square.

"You know," said the Saint calmly, "I'm getting a bit tired of throwing this gun around. Couldn't we dispense with it and call this conference off the record?"

"Okay by me," rumbled Fernack, without taking his eyes from the road.

Simon dropped the automatic into the side pocket of his coat and relaxed into the whole-hearted enjoyment of his smoke. There was no disturbing doubt in his mind that he could rely absolutely on the truce. They rode on under the blazing lights and turned into Central Park by the wide entrance at Columbus Circle.

A few hundred yards on, Fernack pulled in to the side of the road and killed the engine. He switched on his shortwave radio receiver and lighted his cigar deliberately before he turned. The glow of the tip as he inhaled revealed his rugged face set in a contour of phlegmatic inquiry.

"Well," he said, "what's the game?" Simon shrugged.

"The same as yours, more or less. You work within the law, and I work without it. We're travelling different roads, but they both go the same way. On the whole, my road seems to get places quicker than yours—as witness the late Mr. Irboll."

Fernack stared ahead over his dimmed lights.

"That's why I'm here, Saint. I told the commissioner this morning that I could love any man who rubbed out that rat. But you can't get away with it."

"I've been getting away with it pretty handsomely for a number of years," answered the Saint coolly.

"It's my job to take you in, sweat a confession out of you, and send you up for a session in the hot squat. Tomorrow I may be doing it. You're slick, I'll hand it to you. You're the only man who ever took me for a ride twice in one hour, and made me like it. But to me you're a crook—a killer. The underworld has a big enough edge in this town, without giving it any more. Officially, it's my job to put you away. That's how the cards are stacked."

"Fair enough. You couldn't come any cleaner with me than that. But I've got my own job, Fernack. I came here to do a bit of cleaning up in this town of yours, and you know how it needs it. But it's your business to see that I don't get anywhere. You're hired to see that all the thugs and racketeers in this town put on their goloshes when it rains, and tuck them up in their mufflers and make sure they don't catch cold. The citizens of New York pay you to make sure that the only killing is done by the guys with political connections—"

"So what?"

"So maybe, off the record, you'd answer a couple of questions while there isn't an audience."

Fernack chewed the cigar round to the other corner of his mouth, took it out, and spat expertly over the side of the car. He put the cigar back and watched a traffic light turn from green to red.

"Keep on asking."

"What is this Big Fellow?"

The tip of Fernack's cigar reddened and died down,

and he put one elbow on the wheel.

"I should like to know. Ordinarily, it's just a name that some of these big-time racketeers get called. They called Al Capone 'the Big Fellow.' All these rats have got egos a mile wide. 'The Big Boy'—'the Big Shot'—it's the same thing. It used to make 'em feel more important to have a handle like that tacked onto 'em, and it gave the small rats something to flatter 'em with."

"Used to?"

"Yeah." The detective's cigar moved through an arc at the end of his arm as he flicked ash into the road. "Nowadays things are kind of different. Nowadays when we talk about the Big Fellow we mean the guy nobody knows: the man who's behind Morrie Ualino and Dutch Kuhlmann and Red McGuire and all the rest of 'em—and bigger than any of them ever were. The guy who's made himself the secret king of the biggest underworld empire that ever happened. . . . Where did you hear of him?" Fernack asked.

The Saint smiled.

"I was eavesdropping—it's one of my bad habits."

"At Nather's?"

"Draw your own conclusions."

Fernack turned in his seat, his massive body cramped by the wheel; and the grey eyes under his down-drawn shaggy brows reflected the reddish light of his cigar end.

"Get this," he said harshly. "Everything you say about me and the rest of the force may be true. I'm not arguing. That's the way this town's run, and it's been like that ever since I was pounding a beat. But I'm telling you that some day I'm gonna pin a rap on that mug, judge or no judge—an' make it stick! If that line you shot at me was said to Nather, it means there's something dirty brewing around here tonight; and if there's any way of tying Nather in with it, I'll nail him. And I'll see that he gets the works all the way up the line!"

"Why should it mean that?"

"Because Nather is just another stooge of the Big Fellow's, the same as Irboll was. Listen: If that bunch is going out tonight, there's always the chance something may go blooey. One or two of 'em may get taken in by the cops. That means they'll get beaten up. Don't kid yourself. When we get those guys in the station house we don't pat them with paper streamers. Mostly the only punishment they ever get is what we give them in the back room. An' they don't like it. You can be as tough as you like and never let out a peep, but a strong-arm dick with a yard of rubber hose can still hurt you. So when a bunch is smart, they have a lawyer ready to dash in with writs of habeas corpus before we can even get started on 'em—and those writs have to be signed by a judge. One day a law will be passed to allow racketeers to make out the writs themselves an' save everyone a lot of expense, but at present you still gotta find a judge at home."

"I see," said the Saint gently.

Fernack grunted, and his fingers hardened on the cigar.

"Who gave that order?" he grated.

"I haven't the faintest idea," said the Saint untruthfully. He sympathized with Fernack, but it was too late in his career to overcome an ingrained objection to letting any detective get ahead of him. "The speech came over the phone, and that's all there was."

"What did you go to Nather's for?"

"I asked you the same question, but I don't have to repeat it. I stayed right under the window and listened."

Fernack's cigar fell out of his mouth and struck his knee with a fountain of sparks.

"You what?"

"Just in case you'd decided to follow me," explained the Saint blandly. "This business of haring for the tall timber in front of squads of infuriated policemen is all right for Charlie Chaplin, but it's a bit undignified for me." He grinned reminiscently. "I admired your vocabulary," he said.

The detective groped elaborately for his fallen weed.

"I had to do it," he growled. "That son of a————
pulled just one too many when he acquitted Irboll. I
may be transferred for it, but I couldn't of stayed away
if I'd been told beforehand that I was going to wake up
tomorrow pounding a two-mile beat out on Staten Island."

Simon put his head back and gazed up at the low roof
of the sedan. "What's the line-up?"

Fernack leaned on the wheel and smoked, staring
straight ahead again. Taxis and cars thrummed past
them in conflicting streams, and up in a tree over their
heads a night bird bragged about what he was going to
do to his wife when she came home.

The traffic lights changed twice before he answered.

"Up at the top of this city," he said slowly, "there's a
political organization called Tammany Hall. They're the
boys who fill all the public offices, and before you were
born they'd made electioneering into such an exact science that they just don't even think about it any more.
They turn out their voters like an army parade, their
hired hoodlums guard the polls, and their employees
count the votes. The boss of Tammany Hall is a man
called Robert Orcread, and the nickname he gave himself is Honest Bob. Outside the City Hall there's a fine
bit of a statue called Civic Virtue, and inside there's the
biggest collection of crooks and grafters that ever ran a
city.

"There's a district attorney named Marcus Yeald
who's so crooked you could use him to pull corks with;
and his cases come up before a row of judges like
Nather. Things are different here from what they are in
your country. Over here our judges get elected; and every time a case comes up before them they have to sit
down and figure out what the guy's political pull is, or

maybe somebody higher up just tells 'em so they won't make any mistake, because if a judge sends a guy up the river who's got a big political drag there's going to be somebody else sittin' in his chair when the next election comes round.

"The politicians appoint the police commissioner, and he does what they say and lays off when they say lay off. The first mistake they ever made was when they put Quistrom in. He takes orders from nobody; and somehow he's gotten himself so well liked and respected by the decent element in this city that even the politicians daren't try and chisel him out now—it'd make too much noise. But it all comes to the same thing in the end. If we send a guy up for trial, he's still got to be prosecuted by Marcus Yeald or one of Yeald's assistants, and a judge like Nather sits on the case an' sees that everything is nice and friendly.

"There's a bunch of rats an' killers in this town that stops nowhere, and they play ball with the politicians, and the politicians play ball with them. We've had kidnapping and murder and extortion, and we're goin' to have more. That's the Big Fellow's game, and it's the perfect racket. There's more money in it than there ever was in liquor—and there's less of an answer to it. Look at it yourself. If it was your son, or your wife, or your brother, or your sister, that was bein' held for ransom, and you knew that the rats who were holding 'em were as soft-hearted as a lot of rattlesnakes—wouldn't you pay?"

The Saint nodded silently. Fernack's slow, dispassionate summary added little enough to what he already knew, but it filled in and coloured the picture for him. He had some new names to think about; and that realization brought him back to the question in his mind that he had tactfully postponed.

"Who is Papulos?" he asked; and Fernack grinned wryly.

"You've been getting around. He's pay-off man for Morrie Ualino."

"Pay-off man for Ualino, eh?" Simon might have guessed the answer, but he gave no sign. "And what do you know about Morrie?"

"He's one of the big shots I mentioned just now. One of these black-haired, shiny guys, as good-lookin' as Rudolf Valentino if you happen to like those kind of looks—lives like a swell, acts an' talks like a gent, rides around in an armoured sedan, and has two trigger men always walking in his shadow."

"What's he do for a living?"

"Runs one of the biggest travelling poker games on Broadway. He's slick—and poison. I've taken him to Ossining once, an' Dannemora once, myself, but he never stayed there long enough to wear through a pair of socks." Fernack's cigar spun through the darkness in a glowing parabola and hit the road with a splutter of fire. "Go get him, son, if you want him. I've told you all I can."

"Where do I find him?"

Fernack jerked his head round and stared. The question had been put as casually as if the Saint had been asking for the address of a candy shop; but Simon's face was quite serious.

Fernack turned his eyes back to the road; and after a while he said: "Down on 49th Street, between Seventh and Eighth Avenues, there's a joint called Charley's Place. It might be worth paying a visit—if you can get in. There's a girl called Fay Edwards who might—"

The inspector broke off short. A third voice had cut eerily into the conversation—an impersonal metallic voice that came from the radio under the dashboard:

"*Calling all cars. Calling all cars. Viola Inselheim, age six, kidnapped from home in Sutton Place . . .*"

Fernack snapped upright, and the lights of a passing car showed his face graven in lines of iron.

"Good God!" he said. "It's happened!"

He was switching on the ignition even while the metallic voice droned on.

". . . *Kidnappers escaped in maroon sedan. New York license plate. First three serial numbers 5 F 3 or 5 F 8. Inspector Fernack call dispatcher. Inspector Fernack call dispatcher. Calling all cars . . .*"

The engine surged to life with a staccato roar of power, and Simon abruptly decided to be on his way.

"Hold it!" he called, as the car slipped forward. "That's your party."

Fernack's reply was lost in the song of the motor as it picked up speed. Simon opened the door and climbed out onto the running board. "Thanks for the ride," he said and dropped nimbly to the receding asphalt.

He stood under a tree and listened to the distancing wail of the car's imperative siren, and a slight smile came to his lips. The impulse that had led him back to Fernack had borne fruit beyond his highest hopes.

Beyond Nather was Papulos, beyond Papulos was Morrie Ualino, beyond Ualino was the Big Fellow. And crumpled into the Saint's pocket, beside his gun, was the slip of paper that had accompanied a gift of twenty thousand dollars which Nather had made such an unsuccessful effort to defend. The inscription on the paper —as Simon had read it while he waited for Fernack under the library window—said, quite simply: "Thanks. Papulos."

It seemed logical to take the rungs of the ladder in their natural sequence. And if Simon remembered that this process should also lead him towards the mysterious Fay Edwards, he was only human.

CHAPTER III

HOW SIMON TEMPLAR TOOK A GANDER AT MR. PAPULOS, AND MORRIE UALINO TOOK A SOCK AT THE SAINT

Valcross was waiting for him when he got back to the Waldorf Astoria, reaching the tower suite by the private elevator as before. The old man stood up with a quick smile.

"I'm glad you're back, Simon," he said. "For a little while I was wondering if even you were finding things too difficult."

The Saint laughed, spiralling his hat dexterously across the room to the chifferobe. He busied himself with a glass, a bottle, some cracked ice, and a siphon.

"I was longer than I expected to be," he explained. "You see, I had to take Inspector Fernack for a ride."

His eyes twinkled at Valcross tantalizingly over the rim of his glass. Valcross waited patiently for the exposition that had to come, humouring the Saint with the air of flabbergasted perplexity that was expected of him. Simon carried his drink to an armchair, relaxed into it, lighted a cigarette, and inhaled luxuriously, all in a theatrical silence.

"Thank God the humble Players' can be bought here for twenty cents," he remarked at length. "Your American concoctions are a sin against nicotine, Bill. I always thought the Spaniards smoked the worst cigarettes in the world; but I had to come here to find out that tobacco could be toasted, boiled, fried, impregnated with menthol, ground into a loose powder, enclosed in a tube of blotting paper, and still unloaded on an unsuspecting public."

Valcross smiled.

"If that's all you mean to tell me, I'll go back to my book," he said; and Simon relented.

"I was thinking it over on my way home," he concluded, at the end of his story, "and I'm coming to the conclusion that there must be something in this riding business. In fact, I'm going to be taken for a ride myself."

Valcross shook his head.

"I shouldn't advise it," he said. "The experience is often fatal."

"Not to me," said the Saint. "I shall tell you more about that presently, Bill—the more I think about it, the more it seems like the most promising avenue at this moment. But while you're pouring me out another drink, I wish you'd think of a reason why anyone should be so heartless as to kidnap a child who was already suffering more than her share of the world's woes with a name like Viola Inselheim."

Valcross picked up a telephone directory and scratched his head over it.

"Sutton Place, you said?" He looked through the book, found a place, and deposited the open volume on Simon's knee. Simon glanced over the Inselheims and located a certain Ezekiel of that tribe whose address was in Sutton Place. "I wondered if that would be the man," Valcross said.

The name meant nothing in Simon Templar's hierarchy.

"Who is he?"

"Zeke Inselheim? He's one of the richest brokers in New York City."

Simon closed the book.

"So that's why Nather is staying home tonight!"

He took the glass that Valcross refilled for him, and smoked in silence. The reason for the all-car call, and Fernack's perturbation, became plainer. And the idea of carrying on the night in the same spirit as he had begun it appealed to him with increasing voluptuousness. Presently he finished his drink and stood up.

"Would you like to order me some coffee? I think I'll be going out again soon."

Valcross looked at him steadily.

"You've done a lot today. Couldn't you take a rest?"

"Would you have taken a rest if you were Zeke Inselheim?" Simon asked. "I'd rather like to be taken for that ride tonight."

He was back in the living room in ten minutes, fresh and spruce from a cold shower, with his dark hair smoothly brushed and his gay blue eyes as bright and clear as a summer morning. His shirt was open at the neck as he had slipped it on when he emerged from the bathroom, and the left sleeve was rolled up to the elbow. He was adjusting the straps of a curious kind of sheath that lay snugly along his left forearm: the exquisitely carved ivory hilt of the knife it carried lay close to his wrist, where his sleeve would just cover it when it was rolled down.

Valcross poured the coffee and watched him. There was a dynamic power in that sinewy frame, a sense of magnificent recklessness and vital pride, that was flamboyantly inspiring.

"If I were twenty years younger," Valcross said quietly, "I'd be going with you."

Simon laughed.

"If there were four more of you, it wouldn't make any difference." He turned his arm over, displaying the sheathed knife for a moment before he rolled down his sleeve. "Belle and I will do all that has to be done on this journey."

In ten minutes more he was in a taxi, riding westwards through the ravines of the city. The vast office buildings of Fifth Avenue, abandoned for the night to cleaners and caretakers, reared their geometrical patterns of lighted windows against the dark sky like huge illuminated honeycombs. The cab crossed Broadway and Seventh Avenue, plunging through the drenched luminance of massed theatre and cinema and cabaret signs like a swimmer diving through a wave, and floated out on the other side in the calmer channel of faintly odorous gloom in which a red neon tube spelt out the legend: "Charley's Place."

The house was an indeterminate, rather dingy structure of the kind that flattens out the skyline westwards of Seventh Avenue, where the orgy of futuristic building which gave birth to Chrysler's Needle has yet to spread. It shared with its neighbours the depressing suggestion of belonging to a community of nondescript persons who had once resolved to attain some sort of individuality, and who had achieved their ambition by adopting various distinctive ways of being nondescript. The windows on the ground level were covered by greenish curtains which acquired a phosphorescent kind of luminousness from the lights behind them.

Simon rang the bell, and in a few moments a grille in the heavy oak door opened. It was a situation where nothing could be done without bluff; and the bluff had to be made on a blind chance.

"My name's Simon," said the Saint. "Fay Edwards sent me."

The man inside shook his head.

"Fay ain't come in yet. Want to wait for her?"

"Maybe I can get a drink while I'm waiting," Simon shrugged.

His manner was without concern or eagerness—it struck exactly the right note of harmless nonchalance. If the Saint had been as innocent as he looked he could have done it no better; and the doorkeeper peered up and down the street and unlatched the door.

Simon went through and hooked his hat on a peg. Beyond the tiny hall was a spacious bar which seemed to occupy the remainder of the front part of the building. The tables were fairly well filled with young-old men of the smoothly blue-chinned type, tailored into the tight-fitting kind of coat which displays to such advantage the bulges of muscle on the biceps and the upper back. Their faces, as they glanced up in automatic silence at the Saint's entrance, had a uniform air of frozen impassivity, particularly about the eyes, like fish that have been in cold storage for many years. Scattered among their company was a sprinkling of the amply curved pudding-faced blondes who may be recognized anywhere as belonging to the genus known as "gangsters' molls"—it is a curious fact that few of the men who shoot their way through amazing wealth to sophistication in almost all their appetites ever acquire a sophisticated taste in femininity.

Simon gave the occupants no more than a casual first glance, absorbing the general background in one broad survey. He walked across to the bar and hitched himself onto a high stool. One of the white-coated bartenders set up a glass of ice water and waited.

"Make it a rye highball," said the Saint.

By the time the drink had been prepared the mutter of conversation in the room had resumed its normal pitch. Simon took a sip from his glass and stopped the bartender before he could move away.

"Just a minute," said the Saint. "What's your name?"

The man had an oval, olive-hued, expressionless face,

with beautifully lashed brown eyes and glossily waved black hair that made his age difficult to determine.

"My name is Toni," he stated.

"Congratulations," said the Saint. "My name is Simon. From Detroit."

The man nodded unemotionally, with his soft dark eyes fixed on the Saint's face.

"From Detroit," he repeated, as if memorizing a message.

"They call me Aces Simon," said the Saint evenly. The bartender's unwrinkled face responded as much as a wooden image might have done. "I'm told there are some players in this city who know what big money looks like."

"What do you want?"

"I thought I might get a game somewhere." Simon's blue gaze held the bartender's as steadily as the other was watching him. "I want to play with Morrie Ualino."

The man wiped his cloth slowly across the bar, drying off invisible specks of moisture.

"I don't know anything. I have to ask the boss."

He turned and went through a curtain at the back of the bar; and while he was gone Simon finished his drink. The bluff and the gamble were on. If anything went wrong at this stage it would be highly unfortunate—what might happen later on was another matter. But the Saint's nerves were like ice. After some minutes the man came back.

"Morrie Ualino don't play tonight. Papulos is playing. You want a game?"

Simon did not move a muscle. Through Papulos the trail went to Ualino, and he had never expected to get near Ualino in the first jump. But if Ualino were not playing that night—if he were engaged elsewhere—it was an added chance that the radio message which Fernack had received might supply a reason. The azure steel came and went in the Saint's eyes, but all the bartender saw was a disappointed shrug.

"I didn't come here to cut for pennies. Who is this guy Papulos?"

Toni's soft brown eyes held an imperceptible glint of contemptuous humour.

"If you want to play big, I think he will give you all you want. Afterwards you can meet Ualino. You want to go?"

"Well, it might give me some practice. I haven't anything else to do."

Toni emptied an ashtray and wiped it out. From a distance of a few yards he would have seemed simply to be filling up the time until another customer wanted him, without talking to anyone at all.

"They're at the Graylands Hotel—just up the street on the other side. Suite 1713. Tell them Charley Quain sent you."

"Okay." Simon stood up, spreading a bill on the counter. "And thanks."

"Good luck," said Toni and watched him go with eyes as gentle as a deer's.

The Graylands Hotel lay just off Seventh Avenue. It was one of those caravanserais which are always full and yet always seem to be deserted, with the few guests who were visible hustling furtively between the sanctity of their private rooms and the anonymity of the street. Business executives detained at the office might well have stayed there, but none of them would ever have given it as his address. It had an air of rather forlorn splendour, like a blowzy woman in gold brocade, and in spite of the emptiness of its public rooms there was a suppressed atmosphere of clandestine and irregular life teeming in the uncharted cubicles above.

The gilded elevator, operated by a pimply youth with a precociously salacious air of being privy to all the irregularities that had ever ridden in it, whisked Simon to the seventeenth floor and decanted him into a dimly lighted corridor. He found Suite 1713 and knocked. After a brief pause a key clicked over and the portal opened eight inches. A pair of cold dispassionate eyes surveyed him slowly.

"My name's Simon," said the Saint. He began to feel that he was admitting a lot of undesirable people to an easy familiarity that evening, but the alias seemed as good as any, and certainly preferable to such a fictitious name as, for instance, Wigglesnoot. "Charley Quain sent me around."

The eyes that studied him received the information as enthusiastically as two glass beads.

"Simon, eh? From Denver?"

"Detroit," said the Saint. "They call me Aces."

The guard's head dropped through a passionless half-inch which might have been taken for a nod. He allowed the door to open wider.

"Okay, Aces. We heard you were on your way. If you're lookin' for action I guess you can get it here."

The Saint smiled and sauntered through. He found himself in a rather large foyer, formally furnished. At the far end, two rooms gave off it on either side, and from the closed door on the right came the mutter of an occasional curt voice, the crisp clicking of chips, and the insidious rustle and lisp of cards. It appeared to Simon that he was definitely on his way. Somewhere beyond that door Mr. Papulos was in session, and the Saint figured it was high time he took a gander at this Mr. Papulos.

The guard threw open the second door, and Simon went on in. He saw that the place had originally been intended for a sitting room; but all the normal furniture had been pushed back against the walls, leaving plenty of space for the large round table covered with a green baize cloth which now occupied the centre of the floor. Fringing the circle of men seated around the board were a few hard, lean-faced gentry whose air of hawk-eyed detachment immediately removed any suspicion that they might be there to minister to the sick in case one of the players was taken sick. A single brilliant light fixture blazed overhead, flooding a cone of white luminance over the ring of players. As the Saint came in, every face turned towards him.

"Aces Simon, of Detroit," announced the guard. As a cynical afterthought he added: "He's lookin' for some action, gents."

The lean-faced watchers in the outer shadows relaxed and crossed their legs again; the players acknowledged the introduction with curt nods and returned immediately to their game.

Simon strolled across to the table and pulled out a vacant chair opposite the dealer. One casual glance around the board was enough to show him that the guard had had reason to be cynical—the play was sufficiently high to clean out any small-time gambler in one deal. He lighted a cigarette and studied the faces of the players. They were a variegated crew, ranging from the elite of the underworld to the tawdrier satellites of the upper. On his right was a stout gentleman whose faded eyes held the unmistakable buccaneering gleam of a prominent rotarian from Grand Rapids out on a tear in the big city.

The stout gentleman leaned over confidentially, exhaling a powerful aroma of young Bourbon.

"Lookin' for action, eh?" he wheezed. "Well, this is the place for it. Eh? Eh?"

"Eh?" asked the Saint, momentarily infected by the spirit of the thing.

"I said, this is the place for action, isn't it, eh?" repeated the devotee of rotation with laborious good will; and a thin little smile edged the Saint's mouth.

"Brother," he assented with conviction, "you don't know the half of it."

His eyes were fixed on the dealer, who, from the stacks of chips and neat wads of bills before him, appeared to be also the organizer of the game; and as the seconds went by it became plainer and plainer to the Saint that there was at least one man at that table who would never be asked to pose for the central nymph in a picture to be entitled *Came the Dawn*. The swarthy pockmarked face seemed to have been developed from the bald side of a roughly cubical head. Two small black eyes, affectionately close together, nested high up under the eaves of a pair of prominent frontal bones; and the nose between them had lost any pretensions to classic symmetry which it might once have had in some ancient argument with a beer bottle. A thick neck creased with rolls of fat linked this pellucid window of the soul with a gross bulk of body which apparently completed the wodge of mortal clay known to the world as Papulos. It was not an aesthetic spectacle by any standards; but the Saint had come there to take a gander at Mr. Papulos, and he was taking it. And while he looked, the black beady eyes switched up to meet his gaze.

"Well, Mr. Simon, how much is it to be? The whites are Cs, the reds are finifs, and the blues are G.'s."

The voice was harshly nasal, with a habitual sneer lurking in it. It was the kind of voice which no healthy outlaw could have heard without being moved to pleasant thoughts of murder; but the Saint smiled and blew a smoke ring.

"I'll take twenty grand—and you can keep it in the blues."

There was a sudden quiet in the room. The other players hitched up closer in their chairs; and the lean-faced watchers in the outer shadows eased their right hips instinctively away from obstructing objects. Without the twitch of an eyebrow Papulos counted out two stacks of chips and spilled them in the centre of the table.

"Twenty grand," he said laconically. "Let's see your dough." His eyes levelled opaquely across the table. "Or is it on the cuff?"

"No," answered the Saint coolly. "It's in the pants."

"Let's see it."

The rotarian from Grand Rapids took a gulp at the drink beside him and stared owlishly at the table; and the Saint reached into his trouser pocket. He felt the roll of bills there; felt something else—the crumpled slip of paper that had originally accompanied them. Securing this telltale bit of evidence with his little finger, he pulled the bills from his pocket and counted them out onto the board.

It was an admirable performance, as the Saint's little cameos of legerdemain always were. Under the Greek's watchful eyes he was measuring out twenty thousand dollars, and the scrap of paper had apparently slipped in somewhere among the notes. Halfway through the count it fell out, face upwards. Simon stopped counting; then he made a very clumsy grab for it. The grab was so slow and clumsy that it was easy for Papulos to catch his wrist.

"Wait a minute." The Greek's voice was a sudden rasp of menace in the stillness.

He flicked the scrap of paper towards him with one finger and stared at it for a moment. Then he shifted his gaze to the banknotes. He looked up slowly, with two spots of colour flaming in his swarthy cheeks.

"Where did you get that money?"

He was still holding the Saint's right wrist, and his grip had tightened rather than relaxed. Simon glowered at him guiltily.

"What's the matter with it?" he flung back. "It ought to be good—you passed it out yourself."

"I know," said Papulos coldly. "But not to you."

He made an infinitesimal motion with his head; and Simon knew, without looking round, that two of the hard-faced watchers had closed in behind his chair. Nobody else moved; and the heavy breathing of the rotarian from Grand Rapids who was seeing Life was the loudest sound in the room.

Papulos got to his feet.

"Get up," he said. "I want to speak to you in the other room."

A hand fastened on Simon's shoulder and jerked him up, but he had no idea of protesting at that stage—quite apart from the fact that any protest would have been futile. He turned obediently between the two guards and followed the broad back of Papulos out of the room.

They crossed the hall and entered the bedroom of the suite, and the door was closed and locked behind them. Simon was roughly searched and then backed up against a wall. Papulos confronted him, while the two gorillas ranged themselves on either side. The Greek's beady eyes were narrowed to black pin points.

"Where did you get that twenty grand?"

The Saint glared at him sullenly.

"It's none of your damned business."

With a movement surprisingly fast and accurate for one of his fleshy bulk, Papulos drew back one hand and whipped hard knuckles across the Saint's mouth.

"Where did you get that twenty grand?"

For an instant the Saint's muscles leapt as if a flame had touched them; but he held himself in check. It was all part of the game he was playing, and the score against Papulos could wait for some future date. When he lunged back at the Greek's jaw it was with a wild amateurish swing that never had a hope of reaching its mark; and he came up short with two heavy automatics grinding into his ribs.

Papulos sneered.

"Either you're a fool, punk, or you're nuts! Once more I'm asking you—decent and civil—where did you get that twenty G?"

"I found it," said the Saint, "growing on a gooseberry bush."

"He's nuts," decided one of the guards.

Papulos raised his hand again and then let it go with a twisted grin.

"Okay, wise guy. I'll find out soon enough. And if you got it where I think you did, it's going to be just too bad."

He plumped himself on one of the beds and picked up the telephone. The guards stood by phlegmatically, waiting for the connection to go through. One of them gazed sourly at a cigar that had gone out, and picked up a box of matches. The fizz of a match splashed through the silence; and then the Greek was talking.

"Hullo, Judge. This is Papulos. Listen, I got a monkey down here who just flashed a twenty-grand roll in C notes, and a certain slip of paper. . . ."

The Saint saw him stiffen and grind the receiver harder into his ear. The guard with the relighted cigar blew out a cloud of malodorous smoke and drew patterns on the carpet with a pointed toe. The receiver clacked and spattered into the stillness, and Simon flexed his forearm for the reassuring pressure of the knife sheathed inside his sleeve.

Papulos dropped the instrument back in its bracket with an ominous click and turned slowly back to the Saint. He got to his feet, with his flattened face jutting forward on his shoulders, and stared at Simon, with his eyes bright and glistening.

"Mr. Simon, eh?" he rasped.

The Saint smiled engagingly.

"Simon Templar is the full name," he said, "but I thought you might feel I was going upstage on you if I insisted on it all."

Papulos nodded.

"So you're the Saint!" His voice was venomous, but deeper still there was a vibration of the hate that can only be born of fear. "You're the rat who plugged Irboll this afternoon. You're the guy who's going to clean up New York." He laughed abruptly, but there was no humour in the sound. "Well, punk—you're through!"

He turned on his heel and issued a series of sharp orders to the two guards.

One word out of the arrangements for his disposal was enough for Simon Templar's ears. His strategy had worked exactly as he had psychologized it from the beginning. By permitting himself to be trapped by Papulos he had taken one more step up the ladder. He was being passed on to the man higher up for the final disposition of his fate; and that man was Morrie Ualino. And where Ualino was, the Saint felt sure, there was a good sporting chance that the heiress of all the Inselheims might also be.

"March," ordered the first guard.

"But what about my twenty grand?" protested Simon aggrievedly.

The second guard grinned.

"Where you're going, buddy, they use asbestos money," he said. "Shove off."

Papulos unlocked the door. The twenty thousand dollars was in the side pocket of his coat, just as he had stuffed it away when he rose from the poker table; and Simon Templar never took prophecies of his eventual destination too seriously. He figured that a nation which had Samuel Insull in its midst would not be unduly impoverished by the loss of twenty thousand berries; and as he reached the door he stopped to lay a hand on the Greek's shoulder with a friendliness which he did not feel.

"Remember, little buttercup," said the Saint outrageously, "whatever you do, we shall always be sweethearts—"

Then one of the guards pushed him on; and Simon stowed twenty thousand dollars unobtrusively away in his pocket as they went through the hall.

Simon rode beside the first torpedo, while the other drove the sedan north and east. If anything, the pressure of the gun that bored suggestively into his side had the pleasantly familiar touch of an old friend. It was a gentle reminder of danger, a solid emblem of battle and sudden death; and there were a few dozen men in hell who would attest to the fact that he was a stranger to neither.

They rolled smoothly across the Queensborough Bridge, which spans the East River at 59th Street, and the car picked up speed as they blared their way through the semideserted streets of Astoria. Then the broad open highways of Long Island stretched before them; and the Saint lighted a cigarette and turned his brain into a perfectly functioning machine that charted every yard of the route on a memory like a photographic plate.

The outlying suburbs of New York flashed by in quick succession—Flushing, Garden City, Hempstead. They had travelled some miles beyond Springdale when the car slowed down and turned abruptly into a bumpy unfinished driveway that terminated a hundred yards farther on in front of a sombre and shuttered two-story house, where another car was already parked.

One of the guards nudged him out, and three of them mounted the short flight of steps to the porch in single file. The inevitable face peered through a grille, recognized the leading guard, and said, "Hi, Joe." The bolts were drawn, and they went in.

The hall was lighted by a single heavily frosted orange bulb which did very little more than relieve the blackest shades of darkness. On the right, an open door gave a glimpse of a tiny room containing a small zinc-topped bar; on the left, a larger room was framed between dingy hangings. The larger room had a bare floor with small booths built around the walls, each containing a table covered with a grubby cloth. There was an electric piano in one corner, a dingy growth of artificial vines straggling over the tops of the booths and tacking themselves along the low ceiling, and a half-dozen more of the same feeble orange bulbs shedding their watery glimmer onto the scene. It was a typical gangster's dive, of a pattern more common in New Jersey than on Long Island, and the atmosphere was intended to inspire romance and relaxation, but it was one of the most depressing places in which Simon Templar had ever been.

"Upstairs?" queried the gorilla who had been recognized as Joe; and the man who had opened the door nodded.

"Yeah—waitin' for ya." He inspected the Saint curiously. "Is dis de guy?"

The two guards made simultaneous grunting noises designed to affirm that dis was de guy, and one of them took the Saint's arm and moved him on towards the stairway at the back of the hall. They mounted through a curve of darkness and came up into another dim glow of light on the floor above. The stairs turned them into a narrow corridor that ran the length of the house; Simon was hurried along past one door before which a scrawny-necked individual lounged negligently, blinking at them, as they went by, with heavy-lidded eyes like an alligator's; they passed another door and stopped before the third and last. One of his escorts hammered on it, and it was yanked open. There was a sudden burst of brighter light from within; and the Saint went on into the lion's den with an easy, unhurried stride.

Simon had seen better dens. Except for the brighter illumination, the room in which he found himself was no better than the social quarters on the ground floor. The boards underfoot were uncarpeted, the once dazzlingly patterned wallpaper was yellowed and moulting. There was a couch under the window where two shirt-sleeved hoodlums sat side-saddle over a game of pinochle; they glanced up when the Saint came in, and returned to their play without comment. In the centre of the room was a table on which stood the remains of a meal; and at the table, facing the door, sat Ualino.

Simon identified him easily from Fernack's description. But he saw the man only for one fleeting second; and after that his gaze was held by the girl who also sat at the table.

There was no logical reason why he should have guessed that she was the girl Fay who had spoken to Nather on the telephone—the Fay Edwards of whom Fernack had begun to speak. In a house like that there were likely to be numbers of girls, coming and going; and there was no evidence that Morrie Ualino was an ascetic. But there was something to this girl that might quite naturally have spoken with a voice like the one which Simon had heard. In that stark shabby room her presence was even more incongruous than the immaculate Ualino's. She was slender and fair, with eyes like amber, and her mouth was a soft curve of amazingly innocent temptation. Perhaps she was twenty-three or twenty-four, old enough to have the quiet confidence which adolescence never has; but still she was young in an ageless, enduring way that the years do not change. And once again that queer intuitive throb of expectation went through the Saint, as it had done when he first heard the voice on Nather's telephone; the stirring of a chord in his mind whose note rang too deep for reason. . . .

It was to her, rather than to Ualino, that he spoke.

"Good-evening," said the Saint.

No one in the room answered. Ualino dipped a brush into a tiny bottle and stroked an even film of liquid polish on the nail of his little finger. A diamond the size of a bean flashed from his ring as he inspected his handiwork under the light. He corked the bottle and fluttered his graceful hand back and forth to dry off the polish, and his tawny eyes returned at leisure to the Saint.

"I wanted to have a look at you." Simon smiled at him.

"That makes us both happy. I wanted to have a look at you. I heard you were the Belle of New York, and I wanted to see how you did it." The ingenuousness of the Saintly smile was blinding. "You must give me the address of the man who waves your hair one day, Morrie —but are you sure they got all the mud pack off last time your face had a treatment?"

There was a hideous clammy stillness in the room, a stillness that sprawled out of sheer open-mouthed incredulity. Not within the memory of anyone present had such a thing as that happened. In that airlessly expanding quiet, the slightest touch of fever in the imagination would have made audible the thin whisper of eardrums waving soggily to and fro, like wet palm fronds in a breeze, as they tried dazedly to recapture the unbelievable vibrations that had numbed them. The faces of the two pinochle players revolved slowly, wearing the blank expression of two men who had been unexpectedly slugged with blunt instruments and who were still wondering what had hit them.

"What did you say?" asked Ualino pallidly.

"I was just looking for some beauty hints," said the Saint amiably. "You know, you remind me of Papulos quite a lot, only he hasn't got the trick of those Dietrich eyebrows like you have."

Ualino stroked down a thread of hair at one side of his head.

"Come over here," he said.

There was no actual question of whether the Saint would obey. As if answering an implied command, each of the two gorillas on either side of the Saint seized hold of his wrists. His arms were twisted up behind his back, and he was dragged round the table; and Ualino turned his chair round and looked up at him.

"Did you ever hear of the hot box?" Ualino asked gently.

In spite of himself, the Saint felt an instant's uncanny chill. For he had heard of the hot box, that last and most horrible product of gangland's warped ingenuity. Al Capone himself is credited with the invention of it: it was his answer to the three amazing musketeers who pioneered the kidnapping racket in the days when other racketeers, who had no come-back in the law, were practically the only victims; and Red McLaughlin, who led that historic foray into the heart of Cook County—who extorted hundreds of thousands of dollars in ransom from Capone's lieutenants and came within an ace of kidnapping the Scarface himself—died by that terrible death. A cold finger seemed to touch the Saint's spine for one brief second; and then it was gone, leaving its icy trace only in the blue of his eyes.

"Yeah," said the Saint. "I've heard of it. Are you getting it ready for Viola Inselheim?"

Again that appalling silence fell over the room. For a full ten seconds nobody moved except Ualino, whose manicured hand kept up that steady mechanical smoothing of his hair.

"So you know about that, too," he purred at last.

The Saint nodded. His face was expressionless; but he had heard the last word of confirmation that he wanted. His inspiration had been right—his simple stratagem had achieved everything that he had asked of it. By letting himself be taken to Ualino as a helpless prisoner, already doomed, he had been shown a hideout that he could never otherwise have found, for which Fernack and his officers could search for weeks in vain.

"Sure I know," said the Saint. "Why else do you think I should have let your tame gorillas fetch me along here? There isn't any other attraction about the place— except that chat about complexion creams that you and I were going to have."

"He's nuts," explained one of the guards vaguely, as if seeking comfort for his own reeling sanity.

Simon smiled to himself and looked towards the open window. Through it he could see the edge of the roof hanging low over the oblong of blackness, the curved metal of the gutter catching a gleam of light from the bulb over the table. From the sill, it should be within easy reach; and the rest lay with the capricious gods of adventure. . . . And he found his gaze wandering back with detached curiosity, even in that terrific moment, to the girl who must be Fay Edwards. He could see her over Ualino's shoulder, watching him steadily; but he could read nothing in her amber eyes.

Ualino took the hand down from caressing his hair and stuck the thumb in his vest pocket. He seemed to be playing with a vial of sadistic malignance as a child might play with a ball, for the last time.

"What did you think you'd do when you got here?" he asked; and the Saint's level gaze returned to his face with the chill of antarctic ice still in it.

"I'm here to kill you, Ualino," Simon said quietly.

One of the pinochle players moved his leg, and a card slipped off the sofa and hit the floor with a tiny scuff that was as loud as a drumbeat in the soundless void. A stifling silence blanketed the air that was like no silence which had gone before. It was a stillness that reached out beyond the deadest infinities of disbelief, an unfathomable immobility in which even incredulity was punch-drunk and paralyzed. It rose out of the waning vibrations of the Saint's gentle voice and throbbed back and forth between the walls like a charge of static electricity; and the Saint's blue eyes gazed through it in an inclement mockery of bitter steel. It could not last for more than a second or two—the fierce tension of it was too intolerable—but for that space of time no one could have interrupted. And that quiet, gentle voice went on, with a terrible softness and simplicity, holding them with a sheer ruthless power that they could not begin to understand:

"I am the Saint; and I have my justice. This afternoon Jack Irboll died, as I promised. I am more than the law, Ualino, and I have no corrupt judges. Tonight you die."

Ualino stood up. His tawny eyes stared into the Saint's with a greenish glow.

"You're pretty smart," he said venomously; and then his fist lashed at Simon's face.

The Saint's head rolled coolly sideways, and Ualino's sleeve actually brushed his cheek as the blow went by. A moment later the Saint's right hand touched the hilt of his knife and slid it up in its sheath—with both his arms twisted up behind his back it was hardly more difficult than it would have been if his hand and wrist had come together in front of him. Ualino's eyes blazed with sudden raw fury as he felt his clenched fist zip through into unresisting air. He drew his arm back and smashed again; and then a miracle seemed to happen.

The man on the Saint's right felt a stab of fire lance across the tendons of his wrist, and all the strength went out of his fingers. He stared stupidly at the bush of blood that broke from the severed arteries; and while he stared, something flashed across his vision like a streak of quicksilver, and he heard Ualino cry out.

That was about as much as anybody saw or understood. Somehow, without a struggle, the Saint was free; and a steel blade flashed in his hand. It swept upwards in front of him in a terrible arc; and Ualino clutched at his stomach and sank down, with his knees buckling under him and a ghastly crimson tide bursting between his fingers. . . . Nobody else had time to move. The sheer astounding speed of it numbed even the most instinctive process of thought—they might as easily have met and parried a flash of lightning. . . . And then the knife swept on upwards, and the hilt of it struck the electric light bulb over the table and brought utter darkness with an explosion like a gun.

Simon leapt for the window.

A hand touched his arm, and his knife drew back again for a vicious thrust. And then, with a sudden effort, he checked it in mid-flight. . . .

For the hand did not tighten its grip. Halting in the black dark, with the shouts and blunderings of infuriated men roaring around him, his nostrils caught a faint breath of perfume. Something cold and metallic touched his hand, and instinctively his fingers closed round it and recognized it for the butt of an automatic. And then the light touch on his sleeve was gone; and with the trigger guard between his teeth he sprang to the windowsill and reached upwards and outwards into space.

CHAPTER IV

HOW SIMON TEMPLAR READ NEWSPAPERS, AND MR. PAPULOS HIT THE SKIDS

He lay out on the tiles at a perilous downward angle of forty-five degrees, as he had swung himself straight up from the windowsill, with his feet stretched towards the sky and only the grip of his hands in the gutter holding him from an imminent nosedive to squishy death. Directly below him he could see the torsos and bullet heads of two gorillas illuminated in the light of a match held by a third, as they leaned out from the window and raked the dark ground below with straining, startled eyes. Their voices floated up to him like the music of checked hounds to a fox that has crossed its own scent.

"He must of gone that way."

"Better get down an' see he don't take the car."

"Take the car hell—I got the keys here."

The craning bodies heaved up again and vanished back into the room. He heard the quick thumping of their feet and the crash of the door; and then for a space another silence settled on the Long Island night.

Simon shifted the weight on his aching shoulders and

grinned gently under the stars. In its unassuming way it had been a tense moment, but the advantage of the unexpected was still with him. The minds of most men run on well-charted rails, and perhaps the mind of the professional killer in times of sudden death has fewer sidetracks than any other. To the four raging and bewildered thugs who were even then pounding down the stairs to guard their precious car and comb the surrounding meadows, it was as inconceivable as it had been to Inspector Fernack that any man in the Saint's position, with the untrammelled use of his limbs, should be interested in any other diversion than that of boring a hole through the horizon with the utmost assiduousness and dispatch. But like Inspector Fernack, the four public enemies who fell into this grievous error were enjoying their first encounter with that dazzling recklessness which made Simon Templar an incalculable variant in any equation.

With infinite caution the Saint began to manoeuvre himself sideways along the roof.

It was a gymnastic exercise for which no rules had been devised in any manual of the art. He had circled up to the roof in that position because it was quicker than any other; and, once he was up there, it was practically impossible to reverse it. Nor would he have gained anything if he had by some incredible contortions managed to get his feet down to the gutter and his head up to its proper elevation, for his only means of telling when he had reached his destination was by peering down over the gutter at the windows underneath. And that destination was the room outside which the scrawny-necked individual had been lounging when he arrived.

Once a loose section of metal gave him the most nerve-racking two-yard journey of his life; more than once, when one of the men who were searching for him prowled under the house, he had to remain motionless, with all his weight on the heels of his hands, till the muscles of his arms and shoulders cracked under the strain. It was a task which should have taken the concentration of every fibre of his being, but the truth is that he was thinking about Fay Edwards for seven-eighths of the way.

What was she doing now? What was she doing at any time in that bloodthirsty half-world? Simon realized that even now he had not heard her speak—his assumption that she was the girl of Nather's telephone was purely intuitive. But he had seen her face an instant after his knife had laid Ualino open from groin to breastbone, and there had been neither fear nor horror in it. Just for that instant the amber eyes had seemed to blaze with a savage light which he could not understand; and then he had smashed the electric bulb and was on his way. He might have thought that the whole thing was a moment's hallucination, but there was the metal of the automatic still between his teeth to be explained. His brain tangled with that ultimate amazing mystery while he warped himself along the edge of yawning nothingness; and he was no nearer a solution when the window that he was aiming for came vertically under his eyes.

At least there was nothing intangible or mysterious about that; and he knew that there was no prospect of the general tempo of whoopee and carnival slackening off before he got home to bed. With one searching glance over the ground below to make sure that there was no lurking sentinel waiting to catch him in midair, the Saint slid himself forward head first into space, neatly reversed his hands, and curled over into the precarious dark.

He hung at the full stretch of his arms, facing the window of his objective. It was closed; but a stealthily inquiring pressure of one toe told him that it was fastened only by a single catch in the centre.

There was no further opportunity for caution. The

rest of his evening had to be taken on the run, and he knew it. Taking a deep breath, he swung himself backwards and outwards; and as his body swung in again towards the house on the returning pendulum he raised his legs and drove his feet squarely into the junction of the casements.

The flimsy fastening tore away like tissue paper under the impact, and the casements burst inwards and smacked against the inside wall with a crash of breaking glass. A treble wail of fright came out to him as he swung back again; then he came forward a second time and arched his back with a supple twist as his hands let go the gutter. He went through the window neatly, skidded on a loose rug, and fetched up against the bed.

The room was in darkness, but his eyes were accustomed to the dark. A small white-clad shape with dark curly hair stared back at him, big eyes dilated with terror, whimpering softly. From the floor below came the thud of heavy feet and the sound of hoarse voices, but the Saint might have had all the time in the world. He took the gun from between his teeth and pushed down the safety catch with his right hand; his left hand patted the girl's shoulder.

"Poor kid," he said. "I've come to take you home."

There was a surprising tenderness in his voice, and all at once the child's whimpering died down.

"You want to go home, don't you?" asked the Saint.

She nodded violently; and with a soft comforting laugh he swung her up in the crook of his arm and crossed the room. The door was locked, as he had expected. Simon held her a little tighter.

"We're going to make some big bangs, Viola," he said. "You aren't frightened of big bangs, are you? Big bangs like fireworks? And every time we make a big bang we'll kill one of the wicked men who took you away." She shook her head.

"I like big bangs," she declared; and the Saint laughed

again and put the muzzle of his gun against the lock.

The shot rocked the room like thunder, and a heavy thud sounded in the corridor. Simon flung open the door. It was the scrawny-necked individual on guard outside who had caused the thud: he was sprawled against the opposite wall in a grotesque huddle, and nothing was more certain than that he would never stand guard anywhere again. Apparently he had been peering through the keyhole, looking for an explanation of the disturbance, when the Saint shot out the lock; and what remained of his face was not pleasant to look at. The child in Simon's arms crowed gleefully.

"Make more bangs," she commanded; and the Saint smiled.

"Shall we? I'll see what can be done."

He raced down the passage to the stairs. The men below were on their way up but he gained the half-landing before them with one flying leap. The leading attacker died in his tracks and never knew it, and his lifeless body reared over backwards and went bumping down to the floor below. The others scuttled for cover; and Simon drew a calm bead on the single frosted bulb in the hall and left only the dim glow from the bar and the dance room for light.

A tongue of orange fire spat out of the dark, and the bullet spilled a shower of plaster from the wall a yard over the Saint's head. Simon grinned and swung his legs over the banisters. Curiously enough, the average gangster has standards of marksmanship that would make the old-time bad man weep in his grave: most of his pistol practice is done from a range of not more than three feet, and for any greater distances than that he gets out his sub-machine-gun and sprays a couple of thousand rounds over the surrounding county on the assumption that one of them must hit something. The opposition was dangerous, but it was not certain death. One of the men poked an eye warily round the door of the bar and leapt back hurriedly as the Saint's shot splintered the frame an inch from his nose; and the Saint let go the handrail and dropped down to the floor like a cat.

The front door was open, as the men had left it when they rushed back into the house. Simon made a rapid calculation. There were four men left, so far as he knew; and of their number one was certainly watching the windows at the back, and another was probably guarding the parked cars. That left two to be taken on the way; and the time to take them was at once, while their morale was still shaken by the diverse preposterous calamities that they had seen.

He put the girl down and turned her towards the doorway. She was moaning a little now, but fear would lend wings to her feet.

"Run!" he shouted suddenly. "Run for the door!"

Her shrill voice crying out in terror, the child fled. A man sprang up from his knees behind the hangings in the danceroom entrance; Simon fired once, and he went down with a yell. Another bullet from the Saint's gun went crashing down a row of bottles in the bar; then he was outside, hurdling the porch rail and landing nimbly on his toes. He could see the girl's white dress flying through the darkness in front of him. A man rose up out of the gloom ahead of her and lunged, and she screamed once as his outstretched fingers clawed at her frock. Simon's gun belched flame, and the clutching hand fell limp as a soft-nosed slug tore through the fleshy part of the man's forearm. The gorilla spun round and dropped his gun, bellowing like a bull, and Simon sprinted after the terrified child. An automatic banged twice behind him, but the shots went wide. The girl shrieked as he came up with her, but he caught her into his left arm and held her close.

"All right kiddo," he said gently. "It's all over. Now we're going home."

He ducked in between the parked cars. He already knew that the one in which he had arrived was locked: if Ualino's car was also locked there would still be difficulties. He threw open the door and sighed his relief—the key was in its socket. What was it Fernack had said? "He rides around in an armoured sedan." Morrie Ualino seemed to have been a thoughtful bird all round, and the Saint was smiling appreciatively as he climbed in.

A scattered fusillade drummed on the coachwork as he swung the car through a tight arc in reverse, and the bullet-proof glass starred but did not break. As the car lurched forward again he actually slowed up to wind down an inch of window.

"So long, boys," he called back. "Thanks for the ride!" And then the car was swinging out into the road, whirling away into the night with a smooth rush of power, with the horn hooting a derisively syncopated farewell into the wind.

Simon stopped the car a block from Sutton Place and looked down at the sleepy figure beside him.

"Do you know your way home from here?" he asked her.

She nodded vigorously. Her hysterical sobbing had stopped long ago—in a few days she would scarcely remember.

He took a scrap of paper from his pocket and made a little drawing on it. It was a skeleton figure adorned with a large and rakishly slanted halo.

"Give this to your daddy," he said, "and tell him the Saint brought you home. Do you understand? The Saint brought you back."

She nodded again, and he crumpled the paper into her tiny fist and opened the door. The last he saw of her was her white-frocked shape trotting round the next corner; and then he let in the clutch and drove on. Fifteen minutes later he was back at the Waldorf Astoria, and Morrie Ualino's armour-plated sedan was abandoned six blocks away.

Valcross in pyjamas and dressing gown, was dozing in the living room. He roused to find the Saint smiling down at him a little tiredly, but in complete contentment.

"Viola Inselheim is home," said the Saint. "I went for a lovely ride."

He was wiping the blade of his knife on a silk handkerchief; and Valcross looked at him curiously.

"Did you meet Ualino?" he asked; and Simon Templar nodded.

"Tradition would have it that Morrie sleeps with his fathers," he said, very gently; "but one can't be sure that he knows who they were."

He opened the bureau and took out a plain white card. On it were written six names. One of them—Jack Irboll's—was already scratched out. With his fountain pen he drew a single straight line through the next two; and then, at the bottom of the list, he wrote another. It was *The Big Fellow*. He hesitated for a moment and then wrote an eighth, lower down, and drew a neat panel round it: *Fay Edwards*.

"Who is she?" inquired Valcross, looking over his shoulder; and the Saint lighted a cigarette and pushed back his hair.

"That's what I'd like to know. All I can tell you is that her gun saved me a great deal of trouble, and was a whole lot of grief to some of the ungodly. . . . This is a pretty passable beginning, Bill—you ought to enjoy the headlines tomorrow morning."

His prophecy of the reactions of the press to his exploits would have been no great strain on anyone's clairvoyant genius. In the morning he had more opportunities to read about himself than any respectably self-effacing citizen would have desired.

Modesty was not one of Simon Templar's virtues. He sat at breakfast with a selection of the New York dailies strewn around him, and the general tenor of their leading pages was very satisfactory. It is true that the *Times* and the *Herald Tribune,* following a traditional policy of treating New York's annual average of six hundred homicides as regrettable *faux pas* which have no proper place in a sober chronicle of the passing days, relegated the Saint to a secondary position; but any aloofness on their part was more than compensated by the enthusiasm of the *Mirror* and the *News.* SAINT RESCUES VIOLA, they howled, in black letters two and a half inches high. UALINO SLAIN. RACKET ROMEO'S LAST RIDE. UALINO, VOELSANG, DIE. SAINT SLAYS TWO, WOUNDS THREE. LONG ISLAND MASSACRE. SAINT BATTLES KIDNAPPERS. There were photographs of the rescued Viola Inselheim with her stout papa, photographs of the house where she had been held, gory photographs of the dead. There was a photograph of the Saint himself; and Simon was pleased to see that it was a good one.

At the end of his meal, he pushed the heap of vociferous newsprint aside and poured himself out a second cup of coffee. If there had ever been any lurking doubts of his authenticity—if any of the perspiring brains at police headquarters down on Centre Street, or any of the sizzling intellects of the underworld, had cherished any shy reluctant dreams that the Saint was merely the product of a sensational journalist's overheated imagination—those doubts and dreams must have suffered a last devastating smack on the schnozzola with the publication of that morning's tabloids. For no sensational journalist's imagination, overheated to anything below melting point, could ever have created such a story out of unsubstantial air. Simon lighted a cigarette and stared at the ceiling through a haze of smoke with very clear and gay blue eyes, feeling the deep thrill of other and older days in his veins. It was very good that such things could still come to pass in a tamed and supine world, better still that he himself should be their self-appointed spokesman. He saw the kindly grey head of William Valcross nodding at him across the room.

"Just now you have the advantage," Valcross was saying. "You're mysterious and deadly. How long will it last?"

"Long enough to cost you a million dollars," said the Saint lightly.

He went over to the bureau and took out the card on which the main points of his undertaking were written down, and carried it across to the open windows. It was one of those spring mornings on which New York is the most brilliant city in the world, when the air comes off the Atlantic with a heady tang like frosted wine, and the white pinnacles of its towers stand up in a sky from which every particle of impurity seems to have been washed by magic; one of those mornings when all the vitality and impetuous aspiration that is New York insinuates itself as the only manner of life. He filled his lungs with the cool, clean alpine air and looked down at the specks of traffic crawling between the mechanical stops on Park Avenue; the distant mutter of it came up to him as if from another world into which he could plunge himself at will, like a god going down to earth; and on that morning he understood the cruelty and magnificence of the city, and how a man could sit there in his self-made Olympus and be drunk with faith in his own power. . . . And then the Saint laughed softly at the beauty of the morning and at himself, for instead of being a god enthroned he was a brigand looking down from his eyrie and planning new forays on the plain; and perhaps that was even better.

"Who's next on the list?" he asked, and looked at the card in his hand.

Straight away west on 49th Street, beyond Seventh

Avenue, the same urgent question was being discussed
in the back room of Charley's Place. It was too early in
the day for the regular customers, and the bar in the
front part of the building had a dingy and forsaken
aspect in the dim rays of daylight that struggled through
the heavy green curtains at the windows. White-coated,
smooth-faced and inscrutable as ever, Toni Ollinetti
dusted the glass-topped tables and paid no attention to
the murmur of voices from the back room. He looked
neither fresh nor tired, as he looked at any hour out of
the twenty-four: no one could have told whether he had
just awoken or whether he had not slept for a week.

The scene in the back room was livelier. The lights
were switched on, flooding the session with the peculiarly cold yellow colour that electricity has in the daytime.
There was a bottle of whisky and an array of glasses on
the table to stimulate decision, and the air was full of
tobacco smoke of varying antiquities.

"De guy is nuts," Heimie Felder had proclaimed,
more than once.

His right arm was in a sling, as an advertisement of
the Saint's particular brand of nuttiness. He enjoyed the
distinction of being one of the few men who had done
battle with the Saint and survived to tell of it, and it was
a pity that his vocabulary was scarcely adequate to deal
with the subject. He had given much painful thought to
the startling events of the previous night, but he had
been unable to make any notable advance on his first
judgment.

"You ought to of seen him," said Heimie. "When we
took him in de udder room, over in de hotel, he was just
surly an' kep' his mout' shut like he was an ordinary
welsher. We asks him, "Whereja get dat dough?' an'
Pappy gives him a poke in de kisser, an' he hauls off an'
tried to take a sock at Pappy dat was so slow Pappy
could of gone off an' played anudder hand an' come
back an' it still wouldn't of reached him. So Pappy rings

up Judge Nather, an' Nather says: 'Yeah, de guy holds me up an' takes de dough off of me a couple hours ago.' So we take him along to Morrie Ualino, out there on Long Island where dey got de kid; an' it seems de Saint knows about dat, too. But nobody ain't worryin' about what he knows any more, becos we're all figurin' dat when he goes out of there he won't be comin' back unless his funeral procession goes past de house. De guy is nuts. He stands there an' starts ribbin' Morrie about him bein' a dude, an' you know how mad dat useta make Morrie. You can see Morrie is gettin' madder 'n' madder every minute, but dis guy just grins an' goes on kidding. I tell ya, he's nuts. An' then he's got hold of a knife from somewhere, an' he cuts my wrist open till I has to let go; an' then, zappo, he's got his knife in Morrie's guts an' broke de electric light bulb, an' while we're chasin' him he ducks over de roof somehow an' gets de kid. He's gotten a Betsy from somewhere, an' he shoots up de jernt an' gets away in Morrie's car. De guy is nuts," explained Heimie, clinching the matter.

Dutch Kuhlmann poured himself out a half-tumbler of whisky and downed it without blinking. He was a huge fleshy man with flaxen hair and pale blue eyes; and he looked exactly like an amiable waiter from a Bavarian beer garden. No one, glancing at him in ignorance, would have suspected that before the unhonoured demise of the Eighteenth Amendment he was the man who supplied half the thirsty East with beer, reigning in stolid sovereignty over the greatest czardom of illicit hops in American history. No one would have suspected that the brain which guided the hulking flabby frame had carved out and consolidated and maintained that sovereignty with the ruthlessness of an Attila. His record at police headquarters was clean: to the opposition, accidents had simply happened, with nothing to connect them with Dutch Kuhlmann beyond their undoubtedly fortunate coincidence with the route of his ambitions: but those who moved in the queer dark stratum which touches the highest and the lowest points in Manhattan's geology told their stories, and his trucks ran unchallenged from Brooklyn to New Orleans.

"Dot is a great shame, about Morrie," said Kuhlmann. "Morrie vass a goot boy."

He took out a large linen handkerchief, dried a tear from the corner of each eye, and blew his nose loudly. The passing of Morrie Ualino left Dutch Kuhlmann the unquestioned captain of the coalition whose destinies were guided by the Big Fellow, but there was no doubt of the genuineness of his grief. After he had given the orders which sent his own cousin and strongest rival in the beer racket on the long one-way ride, it was said that Kuhlmann had wept all night.

There was a brief respectful silence in honour of the defunct Morrie—several members of the Ualino mob were present, for without the initiative or personality to take his place they drifted automatically into the cohorts of the nearest leader. And then Kuhlmann pulled his sprawling bulk together.

"Vot I vant to know," he said with remorseless logic, "is, vot is the Saint gettin' out of this?"

"He got twenty grand from Nather," said Papulos. "Probably he's collected a reward from Inselheim for bringing the kid back. He's getting plenty!"

Kuhlmann's pale eyes turned slowly onto the speaker, and under their placid scrutiny Papulos felt something inside himself turning cold. For, if you liked to look at it in a certain way, Morrie Ualino had died only because Papulos had passed the Saint along to him—with that terrible knife which had somehow escaped their search. And the men around him, Papulos knew, were given to looking at such things in a certain way. The subtleties of motive and accident were too great a strain on their limited mentalities: they regarded only ultimate results and the baldly stated means by which those results had even-

tuated. Papulos knew that he walked on the thinnest of
ice; and he splashed whisky into his glass and met
Kuhlmann's gaze with a confidence which he did not
feel.

"Yeah, dot is true," Kuhlmann said at length. "He
gets plenty money—plenty enough to split t'ree-four
ways." There was a superfluous elaboration of the
theme in that last phrase which Papulos did not like.
"But dot ain't all of it. You hear vot Heimie says. Ven
they got him in the house he says to Morrie: 'I came here
to kill you.' An' he talks about justice. Vot is dot for?"

"De guy is nuts" explained Heimie peevishly, as if the
continued inability of his audience to accept and be content with that obvious solution were beginning to bother
him.

Kuhlmann glanced at him and shrugged his great
shoulders.

"Der guy is not nuts vot can shoot Irboll right in the
courthouse und get avay," he exploded mightily. "Der
guy is not nuts vot can find out in one hour dot Morrie
has kidnapped Viola Inselheim, und vot can get some
fool to take him straight to the house vhere Morrie has
der kid. Der guy is not nuts vot can pull out a knife in
dot room und kill Morrie, und vot can pull out a gun
from nowhere und shoot Eddie Voelsang and shoot his
vay past four-five men out of the house mit the kid!"

There was a chorus of sycophantic agreement; and
Heimie Felder muttered sulkily under his breath. "I
heard him talkin'," he protested to his injured soul. "De
guy is—"

"Nuts!" snarled an unsympathetic listener; and
Kuhlmann's big fist crashed on the table, making the
glasses dance.

"This is no time for your squabbling!" he roared suddenly. "It is you dot is nuts—all of you! In von day der
Saint has killed Irboll and Morrie and Eddie Voelsang
und taken twenty t'ousand dollars of our money. Und

you sit there, all of you fools, and argue of vether he is nuts, vhen you should be asking who is it dot he kills next?"

A fresh silence settled on the room as the truth of his words sank home; a silence that prickled with the distorted terrors of the Unknown. And in that silence a knock sounded on the door.

"Come in!" shouted Kuhlmann and reached again for the bottle.

The door opened, and the face of the guard whose post was behind the grille of the street door appeared. His features were white and pasty, and the hand which held a scrap of pasteboard at his side trembled.

"Vot it is?" Kuhlmann demanded irritably.

The man held out the card.

"Just now the bell rang," he babbled. "I opened the grille, an' all I can see is a hand, holdin' this. I had to take it, an' while I'm starin' at it the hand disappears. When I saw what it was I got the door open quick, but all I can see outside is the usual sort of people walkin' past. I thought you better see what he gave me, Dutch."

There was a whine of pleading in the doorkeeper's voice; but Kuhlmann did not answer at once.

He was staring, with pale blue eyes gone flat and frozen, at the card he had snatched from the man's shaking hand. On it was a childishly sketched figure surmounted by a symbolical halo; and underneath it was written, as if in direct answer to the question he had been asking: *Dutch Kuhlmann is next.*

Presently he returned his gaze to the doorkeeper's face; and only the keenest study would have discovered any change in its bleak placidity. He threw the card down on the table for the others to crowd over, and hitched a cigar from the row which protruded from his upper vest pocket. He bit the end from the cigar and spat it out, without changing the direction of his eyes.

"Come here, Joe," he said almost affectionately; and the man took an uneasy step forward. "You vas a goot boy, Joe."

The doorkeeper licked his lips and grinned sheepishly; and Kuhlmann lighted a match.

"It vas you dot let der Saint in here last night, vasn't it?"

"Well, Dutch, it was like this. This guy rings the bell an' asks for Fay, an' I tells him Fay ain't arrived yet but he can wait for her if he wants to—"

"Und so you lets him in to vait inside, isn't it?"

"Well, Dutch, it was like this. The guy says maybe he can get a drink while he's waiting, an' he looks okay to me, anyone can see he ain't a dick, an' somehow I ain't thinkin' about the Saint—"

"So vot are you thinking about, Joe?" asked Kuhlmann genially.

The doorkeeper shifted his feet.

"Well, Dutch, I'm thinkin' maybe this guy is some sucker that Fay is stringin' along. Say, all I do is stand at that door an' let people in an' out, an' I don't know everything that goes on. So I figures, well, there's plenty of the boys inside, an' this guy couldn't do nothing even if he does get tough, an' if he is a sucker that they're stringin' along it won't be so good for me if I shut the door an' send him away—"

"Und so you lets him in, eh?"

"Yeah, I lets him in. You see—"

"Und so you lets him in, even after you been told all der time dot nobody don't get let in here vot you don't know, unless he comes mit one or two of the boys. Isn't dot so?"

"Well, Dutch—"

Kuhlmann puffed at his cigar till the tip was a circle of solid red.

"How much does he give you, Joe?" he asked jovially, as if he were sharing a ripe joke with a bosom friend.

The man gulped and swallowed. His mouth was half open, and a sudden horrible understanding dilated the pupils of his eyes as he stared at the beaming mountain of fat in the chair.

"That's a lie!" he screamed suddenly. "You can't frame me like that! He didn't give me anything—I never saw him before—"

"Come here, Joe," said Kuhlmann soothingly.

He reached out and grasped the man's wrist, drawing him towards his chair rather like an elderly uncle with a reluctant schoolboy. His right hand moved suddenly; and the doorkeeper jerked in his grasp with a choking yell as the red-hot tip of Kuhlmann's cigar ground into his cheek.

Nobody else moved. Kuhlmann released the man and laughed richly, brushing a few flakes of ash from his knee. He inspected his cigar, struck a match, and re-lighted it.

"You're a goot boy, Joe," he said heartily. "Go and vait outside till I send for you."

The man backed slowly to the door, one hand pressed to his scorched cheek. There was a wide dumb horror in his eyes, but he said nothing. None of the others looked at him—they might have been a thousand miles away, ignoring his very existence on the same planet as themselves. The door closed after him; and Kuhlmann glanced round the other faces at the table.

"I'm afraid we are going to lose Joe," he said; and a sudden lump of pure grief caught in his throat as he realized, apparently for the first time, what that implied.

Papulos fingered his glass nervously. His fingers trembled, and a little of the amber fluid spilled over the rim of the glass and ran down over his thumb. He stared straight ahead of Kuhlmann, realizing at that moment what a narrow margin separated him from the same attention as the doorkeeper had received.

"Wait a minute, Dutch," he said abruptly. Every oth-

er eye in the room veered suddenly towards him, and
under their cold scrutiny he had to make an effort to
steady his voice. He plunged on in a spurt of unaccoun-
table panic. "They's no use rubbin' out a guy for a mistake. If he tried to cross us it'd be a different thing, but
we don't know that it wasn't just like he said. What the
hell, anyone's liable to slip up—"

Papulos knew he had made a mistake. Kuhlmann's
faded blue gaze turned towards him almost intro-
spectively.

"What's it matter whether he crossed us or made a
mistake?" demanded another member of the conference,
somewhere on Papulos's left. "The result's the same. He
screwed up the deal. We can't afford to let a guy get
away with that. We can't take a chance on him."

Papulos did not look round. Neither did Kuhlmann;
but Kuhlmann nodded slowly, thoughtfully, staring at
Papulos all the time. Thoughts that Papulos had frantically tried to turn aside were germinating, growing up,
in that slow, methodical Teutonic brain; Papulos could
watch them creeping up to the surface of speech, inex-
orably as a rising flood, and felt a sick emptiness in his
stomach. His own words had shifted the focus to himself; but he knew that even without that rash intervention he could not have been passed over.

He picked up his glass, trying to control his hand. A
blob of whisky fell from it and formed a shining pool on
the table—to his fear-poisoned mind the spilt liquid was
suddenly crimson, like a drop of blood from a bullet-
torn chest.

"Dot is right," Kuhlmann was saying deliberately.
"You're a goot boy too, Pappy. Vhy did you send der
Saint straight avay to see Morrie?"

Papulos caught his breath sharply. With a swift movement he tossed the drink down his throat and heard the
other's soft-spoken words hammering into his brain like
bullets.

"Vhy did you send der Saint straight avay to see Morrie, as if he had been searched, und let him take a knife and a gun mit him?"

"You're crazy!" Papulos blurted harshly. "Of course I sent him to Morrie—I knew Morrie wanted to see him. He didn't have a knife an' a gun when he left me. Heimie'll tell you that. Heimie searched him—"

Felder started up.

"Why you—"

"Sit down!" Papulos snarled. For one wild moment he saw hope opening out before him, and his voice rose: "I'm sayin' nothing about you. I'm sayin' Dutch is crazy. He'll want to put you on the spot next. An' how d'you know he'll stop there? He'll be calling every guy who's ever been near the Saint a double-crosser—he'll be trying to put the finger on the rest of you before he's through—"

His voice broke off on one high, rasping note; and he sat with his mouth half open, saying nothing more.

He looked into the muzzle of Dutch Kuhlmann's gun, levelled at him across the table; and the warmth of the whisky he had drunk evaporated on the cold weight in his stomach.

"You talk too much, Pappy," said Kuhlmann amiably. "It's a goot job you don't mean everything you say."

The other essayed a smile.

"Don't get me wrong, Dutch," he pleaded weakly. "What I mean is, if we got to knock somebody off, why not knock off the Saint?"

"Dat's right," chimed in Heimie Felder. "We'll knock off de Saint. Why didn't any of youse mugs t'ink of dat before? I'll knock him off myself, poissonal."

Dutch Kuhlmann smiled, without moving his gun.

"Dot is right," he said "Ve'll knock off der Saint, und not have nobody making any more mistakes. You're a goot boy, Pappy. Go outside and vait for us, Pappy—we have a little business to talk about."

The thumping died down in the Greek's chest, and suddenly he was quite still and strengthless. He sighed wearily, knowing all too well the futility of further argument. Too often he had heard Kuhlmann pronouncing sentence of death in those very words, smiling blandly and genially as he spoke: "You're a goot boy. Go outside and vait for us. . . ."

He stood up, with a feeble attempt to muster the stoical jauntiness that was expected of him.

"Okay, Dutch," he said. "Be seein' ya."

There was an utter silence while he left the room; and as he closed the door behind him his brief display of poise drained out of him. Simon Templar would scarcely have recognized him as the same sleek, self-possessed bully that he had encountered twelve hours ago.

The doorkeeper sat in a far corner, turning the pages of a tabloid. He looked up with a start as Papulos came through but the Greek ignored him. Under sentence of death himself, probably to die on the same one-way ride, a crude pride held him aloof. He walked up to the bar and rapped on the counter, and Toni came up with his smooth expressionless face.

"Brandy," said Papulos.

Toni served him without a word, without even an inquisitive glance. Outside of that back room from which Papulos had just emerged, no one knew what had taken place; the world went on without a change. No one could have told what Toni thought or guessed. His olive-skinned features seemed to possess no register of emotion. The finger might be on him, too: he had served the Saint, and directed him to the Graylands Hotel, at the beginning of all the trouble—he might have received his own sentence in the back room, three hours ago. But he said nothing and turned away as Papulos drank.

There was a swelling emptiness below the Greek's breastbone which two shots of cognac did nothing to fill. Even while he drank, he was a dead man, knowing perfectly well that there was no Appellate Division in the underworld to find a reversible error which might give him a chance for life. He knew that in a few useless hours death would claim him as certainly as if it had been inscribed in the book of Fate ten thousand years ago. He knew that there was no one who would join him in a challenge to Kuhlmann's authority—no one who could help him, no one who could rescue him from the vengeance of the gang. . . .

And then suddenly the flash of a wild idea illumined some dark recess of his memory.

In his mind he saw the face of a man. A bronzed reckless face with cavalier blue eyes that seemed to hold a light of mocking laughter. The lean hard-muscled figure of a man whose poise held no fear for the vengeance of all the legions of the underworld. A man who was called the Saint. . . .

And in that instant Papulos realized that there was one man who might do what all the police of New York could not do—who might stand between him and the crackling death that waited for him.

He pushed his glass forward wordlessly, watched it refilled, and drained it again. For the first time that morning his stomach felt the warmth of the raw spirit. The doorkeeper knew nothing; Toni Ollinetti knew nothing—could not possibly know anything. If Kuhlmann came out and found him gone the mob would trail him down like bloodhounds and inevitably find him even though he fled to the uttermost ends of the continent; but then it might be too late.

Papulos flung a bill on the counter and turned away without waiting for change. His movements were those of an automaton, divorced from any effort of will or deliberation, impelled by nothing but an instinctive surging rebellion against the blind march of death. He waved an abrupt, careless hand. "Be seein' ya," he said;

and Toni nodded and smiled, without expression. The doomed doorkeeper looked up as he went by, with a glaze of despair in his dulled eyes: Papulos could feel what was in the man's mind, the dumb resentful envy of a condemned man seeing his fellow walking out into the sweet freedom of life: but the Greek walked by without a glance at him.

The bright morning air struck into his senses with its intolerable reminder of the brief beauty of life, quickening his steps as he came out to the street. His movements had the desperate power of a drowning man. If an army had appeared to bar his way, he would have drawn his gun and gone down fighting to break through them.

His car stood at the curb. He climbed in and stamped on the self-starter. Before the engine had settled down to smooth running he was flogging it to drag him down the street, away from the doom that waited in Charley's Place. He had no plan in his mind. He had no idea how he would find the Saint, where all the police organizations of the city had failed. He only knew that the Saint was his one hope of reprieve, and that the inaction of waiting for execution like a bullock in a slaughter line would have snapped his reason. If he had to die, he would rather die on the run, struggling towards life, than wait for extinction like a trapped rat. But he looked in the driving mirror as he turned into Seventh Avenue, and saw no one following him.

But he saw something else.

It was a hand that came up out of the back of the car —a lean brown hand that grasped the back of his seat close to his shoulder and dragged up a man from the floor. His heart leapt into his throat, and the car swerved dizzily under his twitching hands. Then he saw the face of the man, and a racing trip hammer started up under his ribs.

The man squeezed himself adroitly over into the va-

cant front seat and calmly proceeded to search the
dashboard for a lighter to kindle his cigarette.

"What ho, Pappy," said the Saint.

CHAPTER V

HOW MR. PAPULOS WAS TAKEN OFF, AND HEIMIE FELDER MET WITH FURTHER MISFORTUNES

Papulos steadied the car clumsily and flashed it under the indignant eyes of a traffic cop who was deliberating the richest terms in which he could describe a coupla mugs who seemed to think they had a P.D. plate in front of 'em, and who deliberated a second too long. The trip hammer inside his ribs slowed up to a heavy, rhythmical pounding.

"I'm glad to see you," he said, in a voice that croaked oddly in his throat. "I was goin' out lookin' for you."

With the glowing lighter at the end of his cigarette, Simon half turned to glance at him.

"Were you, Pappy?" he murmured pleasantly. "What a coincidence! It seems as if we must be soul mates, drifting through life with our hearts singing in tune. Tell me some more bedtime stories, brother—I like them."

Papulos swallowed. The Saint's almost miraculous appearance had caught him before he had even had time to consider a possible line of approach; and for the first time since he had plunged out of Charley's Place on that mad quest he became aware of the hopeless obstacles that didn't even begin to crop up until he had found his quarry. Now, unasked and uninvited, his quarry had obligingly found him; and he was experiencing some of the almost hysterical paralysis that would seize an ardent huntsman if a fox walked up to him and rolled over on its back, expectantly wagging its tail. The difference in this case was that the quarry was much larger and more cunning and more dangerous than any fox; it had a wickedly mocking gleam in its steel-blue eyes; and under the bantering surveillance of that clear and glittering gaze Mr. Papulos recalled, in a most unwelcomely apt twist of reminiscence, that on the last occasion when he had seen the quarry face to face, and there were a considerable number of armed and husky hoodlums within call, he, Mr. Papulos, had been misguided enough to poke the said quarry in the kisser. The prospects of establishing a rapid and brotherly *entente* seemed a shade less bright than they had appeared in his first exuberant enthusiasm for the idea.

"Yeah—I was lookin' for you," he repeated jerkily. "I thought you and me might have a talk."

"One gathers that you were in no small hurry to exercise your jaw," Simon remarked. "You nearly left the back part of the bus behind when you started off. What's after you?"

Something inside the Greek rasped through to the surface under the pressure of that gentle bantering voice. His breath grated in his throat.

"If you want to know what's after me," he blurted, "it's a bullet. A whole raft of bullets."

"Do they travel on rafts?" asked the Saint interestedly. "I didn't know you were joining the navy."

Papulos gulped.

"I'm not kidding," he got out desperately. "The

finger's on me—on account of you. I sent you to Morrie, with that knife on you, an' they're saying I double-crossed 'em. You gotta listen to me, Saint—I'm on the spot!"

The Saint's eyebrows lifted.

"So you figure that if you go out and bring my head back in an Oshkosh they may forgive you—is that it?" he drawled. "Well, well, well, Pappy, I'm not saying it wasn't a grand idea; but I've got a morbid sort of ambition to be buried all in one piece—"

"I tell you I'm not kidding!" Papulos pleaded wildly. "I gotta talk to you. I'll talk turkey. Maybe we can make a bargain—"

"How much credit do you reckon to get on that sock you gave me last night?" inquired the Saint.

Papulos swallowed again and found difficulty in doing it. His eyes, mechanically picking a route through the traffic, were reddened and frantic.

"For God's sake," he gasped, "I'm talkin' turkey. I'm tryin' to make a deal—"

"Not for sanctuary?"

"Yeah—if that's the word for it."

The Saint's eyes narrowed. His smile suddenly acquired a tremendous skepticism.

"That sounds like an awful lot of fun," he murmured. "How do we play this game?"

"Any way you like. I'm on the level, Saint! I wouldn't double-cross you. I'm shootin' square with you, Saint. The mob's after me. They're putting me on the spot—an' you're the only guy in the world who might get me off of it. . . . Yeah, I took that sock at you last night—but that was different. You can take a sock back at me any time—you can take twenty! I wouldn't stop you. But what the hell, you wouldn't see a guy rubbed out just because he took a sock at you—"

Simon pondered gently; but beneath his benign exterior it was apparent that he regarded the Greek with undiminished suspicion and distaste.

"I don't know, Pappy," he said reflectively. "Blokes have been rubbed out for less—much less."

"I was just nervous, Saint. It didn't mean a thing. I guess you might of done the same yourself. Lookit, I could help you a lot if you forgot last night an' helped me—"

"In exchange for what?" asked the Saint, and his voice was even less reassuring than before.

Papulos licked his lips.

"I could tell you things. Say, I ain't the only guy in the racket. I know you were waitin' to take me for this ride when I came out, but—"

For the first time since he had been there the Saint laughed. There was no comfort for Papulos in that laugh, no more than there had been in his soft voice or his pleasant smile; but he laughed.

"You flatter yourself, Pappy," he said. "You aren't nearly so important as that. We step on things like you on our way, wherever they happen to wriggle out—we don't make special appointments for 'em. I thought this car belonged to Dutch. But since you happen to be here, Pappy, I'm afraid you'll have to do. As you kindly reminded me, we have one or two slight arguments to settle—"

"You want Dutch, don't you? You want Dutch more'n you want me—ain't that right? Well, I could help you to get Dutch. I can tell you everything he does, an' when he does it, an' where he goes, an' how he's protected. I could help you to get the whole mob, if you want 'em. Listen, Saint, you gotta let me talk!"

Simon smiled pleasantly. His face was tolerant and kindly, but Papulos did not see that. Papulos saw only the cold blue steel in his eyes—and a vision of death that had come to Irboll and Voelsang and Ualino. Papulos heard the hard ring behind the gentle tones of his voice and knew that he had yet to convince the Saint of his terrible sincerity.

The Saint gazed at him through a wreathing screen of smoke; and his left hand did not stir from his coat pocket, where it had rested ever since he had been in sight.

A checkered and perilous career had done much to harden that tender trustfulness in which Simon Templar's blue eyes had first looked out upon the light of day. Regretfully, he admitted that the gross disillusionments of life had left their mark. It is given to human faith to survive just so much and no more; and a man who in his time has been scarred to the core by the bitter truth about fairies and Santa Claus cannot be blamed if a certain doubt, a certain cynicism, begins in later life to taint the virgin freshness of his innocence. Simon had met Papulos before and had taken his measure. He did not believe that Papulos was a man who could be driven by the fear of death to betray the unwritten code of his kind.

What he forgot was the fact that most men live in frightful fear of death—frightful fear of that black oblivion which will snatch their lusts and their enjoyments from them in a single tortured instant. He forgot that though a man like Papulos would fight in the battles of gangland like a maniac, though he would stand up brutally unafraid under the hails of hot death that come whistling through the open streets, he might become nothing but a cringing coward in the threat of cold-blooded unanswerable obliteration. Even the stark panic that showed in the Greek's eyes did not convince him.

"I wouldn't lie to you," Papulos was babbling hoarsely. "This is on the level. I got nothin' to gain. You don't have to promise me nothin'. You gotta believe me."

"Why?" asked the Saint callously.

Papulos swung the car round Columbus Circle and

headed blindly to the east. His face was haggard with utter despair.

"You think this is a stall—you don't believe I'm on the level?"

"Yes," said the Saint," and no."

"What d'ya mean?"

"Yes, brother," said the Saint explicitly, "I do think it's a stall. No, brother, I don't believe you're on the level. . . . By the way, Pappy, which cemetery are you heading for? It'd save a lot of expense if we did the job right on the premises. You can take your own choice, of course, but I've always thought the Gates of Heaven Cemetery, Valhalla, N. Y., was the best address of its kind I ever heard."

Papulos looked into the implacable blue eyes and felt closer to death than he had ever been.

"You gotta listen," he said, almost in a whisper. "I'm shootin' the works. I'll talk first, an' you can decide whether I'm tellin' the truth afterwards. Just gimme a break, Saint. I'm shootin' square with you."

Simon shrugged.

"There's lots of time between here and Valhalla," he pointed out affably. "Shoot away."

Papulos caught at the breath that would not seem to fill the void in his lungs. The sweat was running down his sides like a trickle of icicles, and his mouth had stiffened so that he had to labour over the formation of each individual word.

"This is straight," he said. "Puttin' the snatch on that kid was an accident. That ain't the racket any more—it's too risky, an' there ain't any need for it. Protection's the racket, see? You say to a guy like Inselheim: 'You pay us so much dough, or it'll be too bad about your kid, see?' Well, Inselheim stuck in his toes over the last payment. He said he wouldn't pay any more; so we put the arm on the kid. You didn't do him no good, takin' her back."

"You don't tell me," said the Saint lightly; but his

voice was grim and watchful.

Papulos babbled on. He had spent long enough getting a hearing; now that he had it, the words came in a flood like a breaking dam. In a matter of mere minutes, it might be too late.

"You didn't do no good. Inselheim got his daughter back, but he's still gotta pay. We won't be snatching her again. Next time, she gets the works. We phoned him first thing this morning: 'Pay us that dough, or you won't have no daughter for the Saint to rescue.' Even a guy like you can't bring a kid back when she's dead."

"Very interesting," observed the Saint, "not to say bloodthirsty. But I can't somehow see that even a story like that, Pappy, is going to keep you out of the Gates of Heaven. You'll have to talk much faster than this if we're going to fall on each other's shoulders and let bygones be bygones."

The Greek's hands clenched on the wheel.

"I'll tell you anything you want to know!" he gabbled wildly. "Ask me anything you like—I'll tell you. Just gimme a break—"

"You could only tell me one thing that might be worth a trade for your unsavoury life, you horrible specimen," said the Saint coldly. "And that is—who is the Big Fellow?"

Papulos turned, white-faced, staring.

"You can't ask me to tell you that—"

"Really?"

"It ain't possible! I'd tell you if I could—but I can't. There ain't nobody in the mob could tell you that, except the Big Fellow himself, Ualino didn't know. Kuhlmann don't know. There's only one way we talk to him, an' that's by telephone. An' only one guy has the number."

Simon drew the last puff from his cigarette and pitched it through the window.

"Then it seems just too bad if you aren't the guy, Pappy," he said sympathetically; and Papulos shrank away into the farthest corner of the seat at the ruthless quietness of his voice.

"But I can tell you who it is, Saint! I'm coming clean. Wait a minute—you gotta let me talk—"

His voice rose suddenly into a shrill scream—a scream whose sheer crazed terror made the Saint's head whip round with narrowed eyes stung to a knife-edged alertness.

In one split second he saw what Papulos had seen.

A car had drawn abreast of them on the outside—a big, powerful sedan that had crept up without either of them noticing it, that had manoeuvred into position with deadly skill. There were three men in it. The windows were open, and through them protruded the gleaming black barrels of submachine-guns. Simon grasped the scene in one vivid flash and flung himself down into the body of the car. In another instant the staccato stammer of the guns was rattling in his ears, and the steel was drumming round him like a storm of death.

The window on his right shattered in the blast and spilled fragments of glass over him; but he was unhurt. He was aware that the car was swerving dizzily; and a moment later there was a terrific crashing impact that flung him into a bruised heap under the dashboard, with his head singing as if a dozen vicious mosquitoes were imprisoned inside his skull. And after that there was silence.

Some seconds passed before other sounds reached him as if they came out of a fog. He heard the rumble of invisible traffic and the screeching of brakes, the shrilling of a police whistle and the scream of a woman close by. It took another second or two for his battered brain to grasp the fundamental reason for that strange impression of stillness: the ear-splitting crackle of the machine guns had stopped. It was as if a tropical squall had struck a small boat, smashed it in one savage instant, and whirled on.

The Saint struggled up. The car was listing over to starboard, and he saw that the front of it was inextricably entangled with a lamppost at the edge of the sidewalk. A crowd was already beginning to gather; and the woman who had screamed before screamed again when she saw him move. The car which had attacked them had vanished as suddenly as it had appeared.

He looked for Papulos. After that one abruptly strangled shriek the man had not made a sound. In another moment Simon understood why. The impact had hurled the Greek halfway through the windscreen: he lay sprawled over the scuttle with one arm limply spread out, but it was quite clear that he had been dead long before that happened. And the Saint gazed at him for an instant in silence.

"I was wrong, my lad," he said softly. "Maybe they were after you."

There was scarcely room for any further apologies to the deceased. In the far distance Simon could see a blue-clad figure lumbering towards him, blowing its whistle as it ran; and the crowd was swelling. They were on 57th Street, near the corner of Fifth Avenue, and there was plenty of material around to develop an audience far larger than the Saint would have desired. A rapid departure from those regions struck him as being one of the most immediate requirements of the day.

He got the nearest door open and stepped out. The crowd hesitated: most of them had been reading newspapers long enough to gather that standing in the way of escaping gunmen is a pastime that is severely frowned upon by the majority of insurance companies: and the Saint dropped a hand to his coat pocket in the hope of reminding them of the fact. The gesture had its desired effect. The crowd melted away before him; and he raced

round the corner and sprinted southwards down Fifth
Avenue without a soul attempting to hinder him.

A cruising taxi went by, and he leapt onto the running
board and opened the door before the driver could ac-
celerate. In another second the partition behind the
driver was open, and the unmistakable cold circle of a
gun-muzzle pressed gently into the back of the man's
neck.

"Keep right on your way, Sebastian," advised the
Saint, coolly reading the chauffeur's name off the license
card inside, "and nothing will happen to you."

The driver kept right on his way. He had been driving
taxis in New York for a considerable number of years
and had developed a fatalistic philosophy.

"Where to, buddy?" he inquired stolidly.

"Grand Central," ordered Simon. "And don't worry
about the lights."

They cut away to the left on 50th Street under the very
nose of a speeding limousine; and the chauffeur half
turned his head.

"You're de Saint, aintcha, pal?" he said.

"How did you know?" Simon answered carefully.

"I t'ought I reckenized ya," said the driver, with some
satisfaction. "I seen pictures of ya in de papers."

Simon steadied his gun.

"So what?" he prompted caressingly.

"So nut'n. I'm pleased ta meetcha, dat's all. Say, dat
job ya pulled on Long Island last night was a honey!"

The Saint smiled.

"We ought to have met before, Sebastian," he
murmured.

The chauffeur nodded.

"Sure, I read aboutcha. I like dat job. I been waitin'
to see Morrie Ualino get his ever since I had to pay him
protection t'ree years ago, when he was runnin' de taxi
racket. Say, dat was some smash ya had back dere.
Some guys tryin' to knock ya off?"

"Trying."

The driver shook his head.

"I can't figger what dis city is comin' to," he confessed. "Ya ain't hoit, though?"

"Not the way I was meant to be," said the Saint.

He was watching the traffic behind them now. The driver had excelled himself. After the first few hectic blocks he had reverted to less conspicuous driving, without surrendering any of the skill with which he dodged round unexpected corners and doubled on his own tracks. Any pursuit which might have got started soon enough to be useful seemed to have been shaken off: there was not even the distant siren of a police car to be heard. The man at the wheel seemed to have an instinctive flair for getaways, and he did his job without once permitting it to interfere with the smooth flow of his loquacity.

As they covered the last stretch of Lexington Avenue, he said: "Ja rather go in here, or Forty-second Street?"

"This'll do," said the Saint. "And thanks."

"Ya welcome," said the driver amiably. "Say, I wouldn't mind doin' a job for a guy like you. Any time you could use a guy like me, call up Columbus 9-4789. I eat there most days around two o'clock."

Simon opened the door as the cab stopped, and pushed a twenty-dollar bill into the driver's collar.

"Maybe I will, some day," he said and plunged into the station with the driver's "So long, pal," floating after him.

Taking no chances, he dodged through the subways for a while, stopped in a washroom to repair some of the slight damage which the accident had done to his appearance, and finally let himself out onto Park Avenue for the shortest exposed walk to the Waldorf. Once again he demonstrated how much a daring outlaw can get away with in a big city. In the country he would have been a stranger, to be observed and discussed and inquired into; but a big city is full of strangers, and nearly all of them are busy. None of the men and women who hurried by, either in cars or on their own feet, were at all interested in him; they scurried intently on towards their own affairs, and the absent-minded old gentleman who actually cannoned into him and passed on with a muttered apology never knew that he had touched the man for whom all the police and the underworld were searching.

Valcross came in about lunchtime. Simon was lounging on the davenport reading an afternoon paper; he looked up at the older man and smiled.

"You didn't expect to see me back so early—isn't that what you were going to say?"

"More or less," Valcross admitted. "What's wrong?"

Simon swung his legs off the sofa and came to a sitting position.

"Nothing," he said, lighting a cigarette, "and at the same time, everything. A certain Mr. Papulos, whom you wot of, has been taken off; but he wasn't really on our list. Mr. Kuhlmann, I'm afraid, is still at large." He told his story tersely but completely. "Altogether, a very unfortunate misunderstanding," he concluded. "Not that it seems to make a great deal of difference, from what Pappy was saying just before the ukulele music broke us up. Pappy was all set to shoot the works, but the works we want were not in him. However, in close cooperation with the bloke who carries a scythe and has such an appalling taste in nightshirts, we may be able to rectify our omissions."

Valcross, at the decanter, raised his eyebrows faintly.

"You're taking a lot of chances, Simon. Don't let this —er—bloke who carries the scythe swing it the wrong way."

"If he does," said the Saint gravely, "I shall duck. Then, in sober and reasonable argument, I shall endeavour to prove to the bloke the error of his ways.

Whereupon he will burst into tears and beg my forgiveness, and we shall take up the trail again together."

"What trail?"

Simon frowned.

"Why bring that up," he protested. "I'm blowed if I know. But it occurs to me, Bill, that we shall have to be a bit careful about the taking off of some of these other birds on our list—if they all went out like Pappy there wouldn't be anyone left who could lead us to the Big Fellow, and he's a guy I should very much like to meet. But if Papulos was talking turkey there may be a line to something in the further prospective tribulations of Zeke Inselheim; and that's why I came home."

Valcross brought a filled glass over to him.

"Does that supply the need?" he asked humorously.

The Saint smiled.

"It certainly supplies one of them, Bill. The other is rather bigger. I think you told me once that the expenses of this jaunt were on you."

The other looked at him for a moment, and then took out a checkbook and a fountain pen.

"How much do you want?"

"Not money. I want a car. A nice, dark, ordinary-looking car with a bit of speed in hand. A roadster will do, and a fairly new second-hand one at that. But I'll let you go out and buy it, for the reason you mentioned yourself—things may be happening pretty fast around the Chateau Inselheim, and I'd rather like to be there."

He had no very definite plan in mind; but the penultimate revelation of the late Mr. Papulos was impressed deeply on his memory. He thought it over through the afternoon, till the day faded and New York donned her electric jewels and came to life.

The only decision he came to was that if anything was going to happen during the next twenty-four hours it would be likely to happen at night; and it was well after dark when he set out in the long underslung roadster that Valcross had provided. After the day had gone, and the worker had returned to his fireside, Broadway came into its own; the underworld and its allies, to whom the sunset was the dawn, and who had a very lukewarm appreciation of firesides, came forth from their hiding places to play and plot new ventures; and if Mr. Ezekiel Inselheim and his seed were still the target, they would be likely to waste no time.

It was, as a matter of fact, one of those soft and balmy nights on which a fireside has a purely symbolical appeal. Overhead, a full moon tossed her beams extravagantly over an unappreciative city. A cool breeze swept across the Hudson, whipping the heat from the granite of the mighty metropolis. Over in Brooklyn, a certain Mr. Theodore Bungstatter was so moved by the magic of the night that he proposed marriage to his cook, and swooned when he was accepted; and the Saint sent his car roaring through the twinkling canyons of New York with a sublime faith that this evening could not be less productive of entertainment than any which had gone before.

As a matter of fact, the expedition was not embarked on quite so blindly as it might have appeared. The information supplied by the late Mr. Papulos had started a train of thought, and the more Simon followed it the more he became convinced that it ought dutifully to lead somewhere. Any such racket as Papulos had described depended for its effectiveness almost entirely upon fear —an almost superstitious fear of the omnipotence and infallibility of the menacing party. By the failure of the previous night's kidnapping that atmosphere had suffered a distinct setback, and only a prompt and decisive counter-attack would restore the damage. On an expert and comprehensive estimate, the odds seemed about two hundred to one that the tribulations of Mr. Inselheim were only just beginning; but it must be confessed that Simon Templar was not expecting quite such a rapid vindication of his arithmetic as he received.

As he turned into Sutton Place he saw an expensive limousine standing outside the building where Mr. Inselheim's apartment was. He marked it down mechanically, along with the burly lounger who was energetically idling in the vicinity. Simon flicked his gear lever into neutral and coasted slowly along, contemplating the geography of the locale and weighing up strategic sites for his own encampment; and he had scarcely settled on a spot when a dark plump figure emerged from the building and paused for a moment beside the burly lounger on the sidewalk.

The roadster stopped abruptly, and the Saint's keen eyes strained through the night. He saw that the dark plump figure carried a bulky brown-paper package under its arm; and as the brief conversation with the lounger concluded, the figure turned towards the limousine and the rays of a street lamp fell full across the pronounced and unforgettable features of Mr. Ezekiel Inselheim.

Simon raised his eyebrows and regarded himself solemnly in the driving mirror.

"Oho," he remarked to his reflection. "Likewise aha. As Mr. Templar arrives, Mr. Inselheim departs. We seem to have arrived in the nick of time."

At any rate, the reason for the burly lounger's presence was disposed of, and it was not what the Saint had thought at first. He realized immediately that after the stirring events of the last twenty-four hours the police, with their inspired efficiency in locking the stable door after the horse was stolen, would have naturally posted a guard at the Inselheim residence; and the large-booted idler was acquitted of any sinister intentions.

The guilelessness of Mr. Inselheim was less clearly established, and Simon was frowning thoughtfully as he slipped the roadster back into gear and watched Inselheim entering the limousine. For a few moments, while the limousine's engine was warming up, he debated whether it might not have been a more astute tactical move to remain on the spot where Mr. Inselheim's offspring might provide a centre of more urgent disturbances. And then, as the limousine pulled out from the curb, he flicked an imaginary coin in his mind, and it came down on the memory of a peculiar brown-paper package. With a slight shrug he pulled out a cigarette case and juggled it deftly with one hand as he stepped on the gas.

"The hell with it," said the Saint to his attractive reflection. "Ezkekiel is following his nose, and there may be worse landmarks."

The limousine's taillight was receding northwards, and Simon closed up until he was less than twenty yards behind, trailing after it through the traffic as steadily as if the two cars had been linked by invisible ropes.

After a while the dense buildings of the city thinned out to the quieter, evenly spaced dwellings of the suburbs. There the moon seemed to shine even more brightly; the stars were chips of ice from which a cool radiance came down to freshen the summer evening; and the Saint sighed gently. In him was a certain strain of the same temperament which blessed our Mr. Theodore Bungstatter of Brooklyn: a night like that filled him with a sense of peace and tranquility that was utterly alien to his ordinary self. He decided that in a really well-organized world there would have been much better things for him to do on such an evening than to go trailing after a bloke who boasted the name of Inselheim and looked like it. It would have been a very different matter if the mysterious and beautiful Fay Edwards, who had twice passed with such surprising effect across the horizons of that New York venture, had been driving the limousine ahead. . . .

He thrust a second cigarette between his lips and

struck a match. The light revealed his face for one flashing instant, striking a rather cold blue light from thoughtfully reckless eyes—a glimpse of character that might have interested Dutch Kuhlmann not a little if that sentimentally ruthless Teuton had been there to see it. The Saint had his romantic regrets, but they subtracted nothing from the concentration with which he was following the job in hand.

His hand waved the match to extinction, and in his next movement he reached forward and switched out all the lights in the car. In the closer traffic of the city there was no reason why he should not legitimately be following on the same route as the limousine, but out on the less populated thoroughfares his leech-like devotion might cause a nervous man some inquisitive agitation which Simon Templar had no wish to arouse. His left arm swung languidly over the side as the roadster ripped round a turn in the road at an even sixty and roared on to the northwest.

The road was a level strip of concrete laid out like a silver tape under the sinking moon. He steered on in the wake of the limousine's headlight, soothing his ears with the even purr of tires swishing over the macadam, his nerves relaxed and resting. Above the hum of the engines rose a faint and not unmelodious sound. Simon Templar was serenading the stars. . . .

The song ended abruptly.

Something flashed in the corner of his eye—something jerky and illuminating like an electric torch. It flashed three times, with the precision of a lighthouse; and then the darkness settled down again.

Simon's hands steadied on the wheel, and he shut off the engine and declutched with two swift simultaneous movements. His foot shifted to the brake and brought the roadster to a standstill as quickly as it could be done without giving his tires a chance to scream a protest.

In the last mile or two, out on the open road, he had

fallen behind a bit, and now he was glad that he had done so. The red taillight of the limousine leapt into redder brilliance as Inselheim jammed on the brakes, pulling it over to the side of the road as it slowed down. Then, right at its side, the flashlight beamed again.

From a safe distance, Simon saw a dark object leave the window at the side of the limousine, trace an arc through the air, and vanish into the bushes at the side of the highway. Then the limousine took off like a startled hare and shot away into the night as if it had seen a ghost; but by that time the Saint was out of his car, racing up the road without a sound.

The package which Inselheim had thrown out remained by the roadside where it had fallen, and Simon recognized it at once as the parcel which the millionaire had carried under his arm when he left his apartment. That alone made it interesting enough, and the manner of its delivery established it as something which had to be investigated without delay—although Simon could make a shrewd grim guess at what it contained. But his habitual caution slowed up his steps before he reached it, and he merged himself into the blackness beneath a tree with no more sound than an errant shadow. And for a short time there was silence, broken only by the soft rustle of leaves in the night wind.

The package lay in a patch of moonlight, solitary and forlorn as a beer bottle on a Boy Scout picnic ground. The Saint's eyes were fixed on it unwinkingly, and his right hand slipped the gun out of his pocket and noiselessly thumbed the safety catch out of gear. A gloved hand moved out of the darkness, reaching for the parcel, and Simon spoke quietly.

"I don't think I'd touch that, Ferdinand," he said.

There was a gasp from the darkness. By rights there should have been no answer but a shot, or the sounds of a speedy and determined retreat; but the circumstances were somewhat exceptional.

The leaves stirred, and a cap appeared above the greenery. The cap was followed by a face, the face by a pair of shoulders, the shoulders by a chest and an abdomen. The appearance of this human form rising gradually out of the blackness as if raised on some concealed elevator had an amazingly spooky effect which was marred only by the physiognomy of the spectre and the pattern of its clothes. Simon could not quite accept an astral body with such a flamboyant choice of worsteds, but he gazed at the apparition admiringly enough.

"Well, well, well!" he remarked. "If it isn't my old college chum, wearing his old school tie. Can you do any more tricks like that, Heimie?—it's fun to be fooled, but it's more fun to know!"

Heimie Felder goggled at him dumbly. The developments of the past twenty-four hours had been no small strain on his limited intellect, and the stress and surprise of them had robbed him of much of his natural elasticity and *joie-de-vivre*. Standing waist-high in the moonlight, his face reflected a greenish pallor which was not entirely due to the lunar rays.

"Migawd," he said, expressing his emotions in the mildest possible terms.

The Saint smiled.

"In a year or two you'll be quite used to seeing me around, won't you?" he remarked chattily. "That is, if you live as long as a year or two. The mob you belong to seems to have such suspicious and hasty habits, from what Pappy was telling me. . . . Excuse me if I collect this."

He stooped swiftly and picked up the brown-paper parcel from its patch of moonlight. Heimie Felder made no attempt to stop him—the power of protest seemed to have deserted him at last, never to return. But his lips shaped a dazed comment of one word which groped for the last immutable landmark of sanity in his staggering universe.

"Nuts," Heimie said hollowly.

The Saint was not offended. He tucked the parcel under his arm.

"I'm afraid I must be going," he murmured. "But I'm sure we shall be getting together again soon. We seem to be destined . . ."

His voice dropped to nothing as he caught the sound of a footfall somewhere on his right. Staring into the bulging eyes of the man in front of him, he saw there a sudden flicker of hope; and his teeth showed very white in the moonlight.

"I think not," he advised softly.

His gun moved ever so slightly, so that a shaft of moonlight caught the barrel for a moment; and Heimie Felder was silent. The Saint shifted himself quietly in the darkness, so that his automatic half covered the visible target and yet was ready to turn instantly into the obscurity of the road at his side; and another voice spoke out of the gloom.

"You got it, Heimie?"

Heimie breathed hard, but did not speak; and the Saint answered for him. His voice floated airily through the night.

"No, brother," he said smoothly, "Heimie has not got it. I have it—and I also have Heimie. You will advance slowly with your hands well above your head, or else you may get it yourself."

For the third time that night the moon demonstrated its friendliness. On his right the Saint could make out a dark and shadowy figure, though he could not see the newcomer clearly on account of the trees at the roadside. But a vagrant beam of the moon danced glitteringly on something metallic in the intruder's hand, and the new voice spoke viciously.

"You rat!"

The gun banged in his hand, spitting a venomous squirt of orange flame into the blackness, and the bullet whisked through the leaves and thudded into the tree where the Saint stood. Simon's eyes narrowed over the sights, as coldly deliberate as if he had been firing on a range; his forefinger closed on the trigger, and the metallic object on which the moonbeam danced spun crazily from the man's hand and flew across the road. A roar of pain and an unprintable oath drowned the clatter of metal on the macadam, and the same voice yelled: "Get him, Heimie!"

In the next second the black bulk of the man was charging down on him. Simon pressed the trigger again coolly; but nothing happened—the hammer fell on a dud cartridge. He dropped the parcel under his arm and snatched at the sliding jacket, but the charging weight of the man caught him before the next shell was in the chamber.

Simon went back against the tree with a force that seemed to bruise his very lungs through the pads of muscle across his back. His breath came with a grunt and he rebounded out again, sluggishly, like a sandbag, and felt his fist smack into a chest like a barrel. Then the man's arms whipped round him and they went down together, rolling heavily over the uneven ground.

The sky was shot with daubs of vivid colour, while a blackness deeper than the blackness of night struggled to close over the Saint's brain. His chest was a dull mass of pain from that terrific crash against the tree, and the air had to be forced into it with a mighty effort at each agonizing breath, as if his face were smothered with a heavy cushion. Nothing but a titanic vitality of will kept him conscious and fighting. The man on top of him was thirty pounds heavier than he was; and he knew that if Heimie Felder recovered from the superstitious paralysis which had been gripping him, and located the centre of the fight soon enough, there would be nothing but a slab of carved marble to mark the spot where a presumptuous outlaw had bucked the odds once too often.

They crashed through a low bush and slithered down a slight gradient, punching and kicking and grappling like a pair of wildcats. The big man broke through Simon's arms and got hold of his head, gouging viciously. The Saint's head bumped twice against the hard turf, and the flashing daubs of colour whirled in giddy gyrations across his vision. Suddenly his body went limp, and the big man let out an exultant yell.

"I got him, Heimie! I got him! Where are ya?"

Simon saw the close-cropped bullet head for one instant clearly, lifted in black silhouette against the swimming stars. He swung up the useless automatic which he was still clutching and smashed it fiercely into the silhouette; and the grip on his head weakened. With a new surge of power the Saint heaved up and rolled them over again, straddling the cursing man with his legs and hammering the butt of his gun again and again into the dark sticky pulpiness from which the cursing came. . . .

A rough hand, which did not belong to the man underneath him, essayed to encircle his throat from the rear; and Simon gathered that the full complement of the opposition was finally gathered on the scene. The cursing had died away, and the heavy figure of his first opponent was soft and motionless under him and the Saint dropped his gun. His right hand reached over his shoulder and grasped the new assailant by the neck.

"Excuse me, Heimie," said the Saint, rather breathlessly—"I'm busy."

He got one knee up and lifted, pulling downwards with his right hand. Heimie Felder was dragged slowly from the ground: his torso came gradually over the Saint's shoulder: and then the Saint turned his wrist and straightened his legs with a quick jerk, and Heimie shot over and downwards and hit the ground with his head. Apart from that solid and soporific thump, he made no sound; and silence settled down once more upon the scene.

The Saint dusted his clothes and repossessed himself of his automatic. He wiped it carefully on Heimie's silk handkerchief, ejected the dud cartridge which had caused all the trouble, and replenished the magazine. Then he went in search of the parcel which had stimulated so much unfriendly argument, and carried it back to his car without a second glance at the two sleeping warriors by the roadside.

CHAPTER VI

HOW SIMON TEMPLAR INTERVIEWED MR. INSELHEIM, AND DUTCH KUHLMANN WEPT

It seems scarcely necessary to explain that Mr. Ezekiel Inselheim was a Jew. He was a stoutish man with black hair surrounding a shiny bald pate, pleasant brown eyes, and a rather attractive smile; but his nose would have driven Hitler into frenzies of belligerent Aryanism. Confronted by that shamelessly Semitic proboscis, no well-trained Nazi could ever have been induced to believe that he was a kindly and honest man, shrewd without duplicity, self-made without arrogance, wealthy without offensive ostentation. It has always been difficult for such wild possibilities to percolate into the atrophied brain cells of second-rate crusaders, and a thousand years of self-styled civilization have made no more improvements in the Nordic crank than they have in any other type of malignant half-wit.

He sat slumping wearily before the table in his library. The white light of his desk lamp made his sallow face appear even paler than it was naturally; his hands were resting on the blotter in front of him, clenched into impotent fists, and he was staring at them, with a dull, almost childish hurt creasing deep grooves into the flesh on either side of his mouth.

Upstairs, his daughter slept peacefully, resting again in her own bed with the careless confidence of childhood; and for that privilege he had been compelled to pay the price. In spite of the fact that that strange Robin Hood of the twentieth century who was called the Saint had brought her back to him without a fee, Inselheim knew that the future safety of the girl still depended solely on his own ability to meet the payments demanded of him. He knew that his daughter had been kidnapped as a warning rather than for actual ransom, knew that there were worse weapons than kidnapping which the Terror would not hesitate to employ at the next sign of rebellion; if he had ever had any doubts on that score, they had been swept away by the cold guttural voice which had spoken to him over the telephone that morning; and it was the knowledge of those things that clenched his unpractised fists at the same time as that dull bitter pain of helplessness darkened his eyes.

Ezekiel Inselheim was wondering, as others no less rich and famous had wondered before him, why it was that in the most materially civilized country in the world an honoured and peaceful citizen had still to pay toll to a clique of organized bandits, like medieval peasants meeting the extortions of a feudal barony. He was wondering, with a grim intensity of revolt, why the police, who were so impressively adept at handing out summonses for traffic violations, and delivering perjured testimony against unfortunate women, were so plaintively incapable of holding the racketeers in check. And he knew the answers only too well.

He knew, as all America knew, that with upright

legislators, with incorruptible police and judiciary, the gangster would long ago have vanished like the Western bad man. He knew that without the passive cooperation of a resigned and leaderless public, without the inbred cowardice of a terrorized population, the racketeers and the grafting political leaders who protected them could have been wiped off the face of the American landscape at a cost of one hundredth part of the tribute which they exacted annually. It was the latter part of that knowledge which carved the stunned, hurt lines deeper into his face and whitened the skin across his fleshy fists. It gave him back none of the money which had been bled out of him, returned him no jot of comfort or security, filled him with nothing but a cancerous ache of degradation which was curdling into a futile trembling agony of hopeless anger. If, at that moment, any of his extortioners had appeared before him, he would have tried to stand up and defy them, knowing that there could be only one outcome to his lonely, pitiful resistance. . . .

And it was at that instant that some sixth sense made him turn his head, with a gasp of fear wrenched from sheer overwrought nerves strangling in his throat.

A languid immaculate figure lolled gracefully on the windowsill, one leg flung carelessly into the room, the other remaining outside in the cool night. A pair of insolent blue eyes were inspecting him curiously, and a smile with a hint of mockery in it moved the gay lips of the stranger. It was a smile with humour in it which was not entirely humorous, blue eyes with an amused twinkle which did not belong to any conventional amusement. The voice, when it spoke, had a bantering lilt, but beneath the lilt was something harder and colder than Inselheim had ever heard before—something that reminded him of chilled steel glinting under a polar moon.

"Hullo, Zeke," said the Saint.

At the sound of that voice the pathetic mustering of anger drained out of Inselheim as if a stopcock had been opened, leaving nothing but a horrible blank void. Upstairs was his child—sleeping . . . . And suddenly he was only a frightened old man again, staring with fear-widened eyes at the revival of the menace which was tearing his self-respect into shreds.

"I've paid up!" he gasped hysterically. "What do you want? I've paid! Why don't you leave me alone——"

The Saint swung his other leg into the room and hitched himself nonchalantly off the sill.

"Oh, no, you haven't," he said gravely. "You haven't paid up at all, brother."

"But I have paid!" The broker's voice was wild, the words tumbling over each other in the ghastly incoherence of panic. "Something must have gone wrong. I paid—I paid tonight, just as you told me to. There must be some mistake. It isn't my fault. I paid——"

Simon's hands went to his pockets. From the breast pocket of his coat, the side pockets, the pockets of his trousers, he produced bundle after bundle of neatly stacked fifty-dollar bills, tossing them one by one onto the desk in an apparently inexhaustible succession, like a conjuror producing rabbits out of a hat.

"There's your money, Zeke," he remarked cheerfully. "Ninety thousand bucks, if you want to count it. I allotted myself a small reward of ten thousand, which I'm sure you'll agree is a very modest commission. So you see you haven't paid up at all."

Inselheim gaped at the heaps of money on the desk with a thrill of horror. He made no attempt to touch it. Instead, he stared at the Saint, and there was a numbness of stark terror in his eyes.

"Where—where did you get this?"

"You dropped it, I think," explained the Saint easily. "Fortunately I was behind you. I picked it up. You mustn't mind my blowing in by the fire escape—I'm just fond of a little variety now and again. Luckily for you," said the Saint virtuously, "I am an honest man, and money never tempts me—much. But I'm afraid you must have a lot more dough than is good for you, Zeke, if the only way you can think of to get rid of it is to go chucking scads of it around the scenery like that."

Inselheim swallowed hard. His face had gone chalk white.

"You mean you—you picked this up where I dropped it?"

Simon nodded.

"That was the impression I meant to convey. Perhaps I didn't make myself very clear. When I saw you heaving buckets of potatoes over the horizon in that absent-minded sort of way——"

"You fool!" Inselheim said, with quivering lips. "You've killed me—that's what you've done. You've killed my daughter!" His voice rose in a hoarse tightening of dread. "If they don't get this money—they'll kill!"

Simon raised his eyebrows. He sat on the arm of a chair.

"Really?" he asked, with faint interest.

"My God!" groaned the man. "Why did you have to interfere? What's this to you, anyway? Who are you?"

The Saint smiled.

"I'm the little dicky bird," he said, "who brought your daughter back last time."

Inselheim sat bolt upright.

"The Saint!"

Simon bowed his acknowledgment. He stretched out a long arm, pulled open the drawer of the desk in which long experience had taught him that cigars were most often to be found, and helped himself.

"You hit it, Zeke. The bell rings, and great strength returns the penny. This is quite an occasion, isn't it?" He

pierced the rounded end of the cigar with a deftly
wielded matchstick, reversed the match, and scraped fire
from it with his thumbnail, ignoring the reactions of his
astounded host. "In the circumstances, it may begin to
dawn on you presently why I have that eccentric
partiality to fire escapes." He blew smoke towards the
ceiling and smiled again. "I guess you owe me quite a
lot, Zeke; and if you've got a spot of good Bourbon to
go with this I wouldn't mind writing it off your
account."

Inselheim stared at him for a long moment in silence.
The cumulative shocks which had struck him seemed to
have deadened and irised down the entrances of his
mind, so that the thoughts that seethed in the anterooms
of consciousness could only pass through one by one.
But one idea came through more strongly and
persistently than any other.

"I know," he said, with a dull effort. "I'm sorry. I—
I guess I owe you—plenty. I won't forget it. But—you
don't understand. If you want to help me, you must get
out. I've got to think. You can't stay here. If they found
you were here—they'd kill us both."

"Not both," said the Saint mildly.

He looked at Inselheim steadily, with a faintly
humorous interest, like a hardened dramatic critic
watching with approval the presentation of a
melodrama, yet realizing with a trace of self-mockery
that he had seen it all before. But it was the candid
appraisement in his gaze which stabbed mercilessly into
some lacerated nerve that was throbbing painfully away
down in the depths of the Jew's crushed and battered
fibre—a swelling nerve of contempt for his own
weakness and inadequacy, the same nerve whose mute
and inarticulate reactions had been clenching his soft
hands into those pitifully helpless fists before the Saint
came. The clear blue light of those reckless bantering
eyes seemed to illumine the profundities of Inselheim's

very soul; but the light was too sudden and strong, and his own vision was still too blurred, for him to be able to see plainly what the light showed.

"What did you come here for?" Inselheim asked; and Simon blew one smoke ring and put another through the centre of it.

"To return your potatoes—as you see. To have a cigar, and that drink which you're so very inhospitably hesitating to provide. And to see if you might be able to help me."

"How could I help you? If it's money you want——"

"I could have helped myself." The Saint glanced at the stacks of money on the desk with one eyebrow cocked and a glimmer of pure enjoyment in his eye. "I seem to be getting a lot of chances like that these days. Thanks all the same, but I've got one millionaire grubstaking me already, and his bank hasn't failed yet. No—what I might be able to use from you, Zeke, is a few heart-to-heart confidences."

Inselheim shook his head slowly, a movement that seemed to be more of an automatic than a deliberate refusal.

"I can't tell you anything."

Simon glanced at his wrist watch.

"A rather hasty decision," he murmured. "Not to say flattering. For all you know, I may be ploughing through life in a state of abysmal ignorance. However, you've got plenty of time to change your mind. . . ."

The Saint rose lazily from his chair and stood looking downwards at his host, without a variation in the genial leisureliness of his movements or the cool suaveness of his voice; but it was a lazy leisureliness, a cool geniality, that was more impressive than any noisy dominance.

"You know, Zeke," he rambled on affably, "to change one's mind is the mark of a liberal man. It indicates that one has assimilated wisdom and experience. It indicates that one is free from stubbornness and pride and pimples and other deadly sins. Even scientists aren't dogmatic any more—they're always ready to admit they were wrong and start all over again. A splendid attitude, Zeke—splendid. . . ."

He was standing at his full height, carelessly dynamic like a cat stretching itself; but he had made no threatening movement, said nothing menacing . . . nothing.

"I'm sure you see the point, Zeke," he said; and for some reason that had no outward physical manifestation, Inselheim knew that the gangsters whom he feared and hated could never be more ruthless than this mild-mannered young man with the mocking blue eyes who had clambered through his window such a short while ago.

"What could I tell you?" Inselheim asked tremulously.

Simon sat on the edge of the desk. There was neither triumph nor self-satisfaction in his air—nothing to indicate that he had ever even contemplated any other ultimate response. His gentleness was almost that of a psycho-analyst extracting confessions from a nervous patient; and once again Inselheim felt that queer light illuminating hidden corners of himself which he had not asked to see.

"Tell me all, Zeke," said the Saint.

"What is there you don't know?" Inselheim protested weakly. "They kidnapped Viola because I refused to pay the protection money——"

"The protection money," Simon repeated idly. "Yes, I knew about that. But at least we've got started. Carry on, Uncle."

"We've all got to pay for protection. There's no way out. You brought Viola back, but that hasn't saved her. If I don't pay now—they'll kill. You know that. I told you. What else is there——"

"Who are *they?*" asked the Saint.

"I don't know."

Simon regarded him quizzically.

"Possibly not." Under the patient survey of those unillusioned eyes, the light in Inselheim's subconsciousness was very bright. "But you must have some ideas. At some time or another, there must have been some kind of contact. A voice didn't speak out of the ceiling and tell you to pay. And even a bloke with as many potatoes as you have doesn't go scattering a hundred grand across the countryside just because some maniac he's never heard of calls up on the phone and tells him to. That's only one of the things I'm trying to get at. I take it that you don't want to go on paying out hundreds of thousands of dollars to this unknown voice till the next new moon. I take it that you don't want to spend the rest of your life wondering from day to day what the next demand is going to be—and wondering what they'll do to your daughter to enforce it. I take it that you want a little peace and quiet—and that even beyond that you might like to see some things in this city changed. I take it that you have some manhood that goes deeper than merely wearing trousers, and I'm asking you to give it a chance."

Inselheim swallowed hard. The light within him was blinding, hurting his eyes. It terrified him. He rose as if in sheer nervousness and paced the room.

Simon watched him curiously. He knew the struggle that went on inside the man, and after a fashion he sympathized. . . . And then, as Inselheim reached the far wall, his hand shot out and pressed a button. He turned and faced the Saint defiantly.

"Now," he said, with a strange thickness in his voice, "get out! That bell calls one of my guards. I don't wish you any harm—I owe you everything—for a while. But I can't—I can't sign my own death warrant—or Viola's. . . ."

"No," said the Saint softly. "Of course not."

He hitched himself unhurriedly off the desk and walked to the window. There, he threw a long leg across the sill; and his unchanged azure eyes turned back to fix themselves on Inselheim.

"Perhaps," he said quietly, "you'll tell me the rest another day."

The broker shook his head violently.

"Never," he gabbled. "Never. I don't want to die. I won't tell anything. You can't make me. You can't!"

A heavy footstep sounded outside in the hall. Inselheim stood staring, his chest heaving breathlessly, his mouth half open as if aghast at the meaning of his own words, his hands twitching. The light in his mind had suddenly burst. He looked for contempt, braced himself for a retort that would shrivel the last of his pride, and instead saw nothing in the Saint's calm eyes but a sincere and infinite compassion that was worse than the bitterest derision. Inselheim gasped; and his stomach was suddenly empty as he realized that he had thrown everything away.

But the Saint looked at him and smiled.

"I'll see you again," he said; and then, as a knock came on the door and the guard's voice demanded an answer, he lowered himself briskly to the fire-escape landing and went on his way.

The profit from his visit had been precisely nil—in fact, a mercenary estimate might have assessed it as a dead loss of ninety thousand dollars—but that was his own fault. As he slid nimbly down the iron ladders he cursed himself gently for that moment's unwariness which had permitted Inselheim to put a finger on the bell. And yet, without the shock of seeing that last denial actually accomplished, without that final flurry of insensate panic, the broker's awakening might never have been completed. And Simon had a premonition that if Inselheim's chance came again the result would be a little different.

Oddly enough, in his preoccupation with that angle on the task in hand, the Saint had forgotten that there were other parties who would be likely to develop an interest in Sutton Place that night. He stepped off the last ladder into the inky blackness of the narrow alley where it let him down without a thought of immediate danger, and heard the slight movement behind him too late. He spun round with his right hand darting to his pocket, but before it had touched his gun a strong arm was flung round his neck from behind and the steel snout of an automatic jabbed into his back. A voice harsh with exultation snarled in his ear: "Come a little ways with us, will ya . . . pal?"

Not a shadow of uneasiness darkened the Saint's brow as he crossed the threshold of the back room of Charley's Place and stood for a moment regarding the faces before him. Behind him he heard the click of the latch as the door was closed; and the men who had risen from their seats in the front bar and followed him as his captors hustled him through ranged themselves along the walls. More than a dozen men were gathered in the room. More than two dozen eyes were riveted on him in the same calculating stares—eyes as hard and unwinking as coloured marbles, barren of all humanity.

He was unarmed. He had nothing larger than a pin which might have been used as an offensive weapon. His gun had been taken from him; and the knife which he carried in his sleeve, having left men alive the day before to tell the tale of its deadliness, had been removed almost as quickly. The new desperate suspicion of concealed weapons with which his earlier exploits had filled the minds of the mob had prompted a vastly less perfunctory search than the deceased Mr. Papulos had thought necessary—a search which had left no inch of his person untouched, and which had even seized on his penknife and cigarette case as possible sources of danger. The thoroughness of the examination had afforded the Saint some grim amusement at the time, but not for a moment had he lost sight of what it meant. Yet his poise had never been more easy and debonair, the steel masked down more deceptively in the mocking depths of his eyes, than it was as he stood there smiling and nodding to the assembled company like an actor taking a bow.

"How! my palefaced brothers," he murmured. "The council sits, though the pipe of peace is not in evidence. Well, well, well—every time we get together you think of new games, as the bishop said to the actress. And what do we play tonight?"

A weird light came into the eyes of Heimie Felder, who sat at the table with a fresh bandage round his head. He leaned across and whispered to Dutch Kuhlmann.

"Nuts," he said, almost pleadingly. "De guy is nuts. Dijja hear what he says?"

Kuhlmann's contracted pupils were fixed steadily on the Saint's face. He made no answer. And after that first general survey of the congregation in which he had been included, Simon had not looked at him. For all of the Saint's interest was taken up with the girl who also sat at the table.

It was strange what a deep impression she had made on him in the places where she had crossed his path. He realized that even now he knew nothing about her. He had heard, or assumed that he heard, her voice over the telephone; he had seen, or assumed that he saw, the owner of that disembodied voice in the house on Long Island where Viola Inselheim was held and Morrie Ualino died; and once he had felt her hand in the darkness and she had pressed a gun into his hand. But she had never identified herself to more than one of his senses at the same time; and he knew that his cardinal belief that this slim, fair-haired girl with the inscrutable

amber eyes was that mysterious Fay Edwards of whom
Fernack had spoken rested on nothing but intuition.
And yet, even while the active part of his brain had been
most wrapped up in the practical mechanics of his vendetta, her image had never been very far from his mind.

The sight of her in that room, the one glimpse of colour and beauty in the grim circle of silent men, brought
back to the Saint every question that he had asked himself about her. Every question had trailed off into the
same nebulous voids of guesswork in which the hope of
any absolute answer was more elusive than the end of a
rainbow; but to see her again at such a moment gave
him a throb of pleasure for which there was no logical
accounting. Once when he was in need she had helped
him; he might never know why. Now he was again in
need, and he wondered what she was thinking and what
she would do. Her face told him nothing—only a spark
of something to which he could give no name gleamed
for an instant in her eyes and was gone.

Dutch Kuhlmann turned to her.

"This is der Saint?" he asked.

She answered without shifting her gaze from Simon:
"Yes. That's the man who killed Morrie."

It was the first time he had ever seen her and heard her
speak at once, the first definite knowledge that his intuition had been right; and a queer thrill leapt through him
at the sound of her voice. It was as if he had been
fascinated by a picture, and it had suddenly come to life.

"Good-evening, Fay," he said.

She looked at him for a moment longer and then took
a cigarette from her bag and struck a match. The movement veiled her eyes, and the spark which he thought he
had seen there might have existed only in his imagination.

Kuhlmann nodded to a man who stood by the wall,
and another door was unlocked and opened. Through it,
after a brief pause, came two other men.

One of them was a big burly man with grey hair and a florid complexion on which the eyebrows stood out startlingly black and bushy, as if they had been gummed on by an absent-minded make-up artist. The other was a small bald-headed man with a heavy black moustache and gold-rimmed pince-nez, whose peering and fluttering manner reminded the Saint irresistibly of a weasel. Seen together, they looked rather like a vaudeville partnership which, either through mishap or design, had been obliged to share the props originally intended for one, and who had squabbled childishly over the division: between them they possessed the material for two normally sized men of normal hairiness, but on account of their disagreement they had both emerged with extravagant inequalities. Simon had an irreverent desire to remove the bushy eyebrows from the large man and glue them where it seemed they would be more appropriate, above the luxuriant moustache of the small one. Their bearing was subtly different from that of the others who were assembled in the room; and the Saint gave play to his flippant imaginings only for a passing second, for he had recognized them as soon as they came in and knew that the conference was almost complete. One of them was the district attorney, Marcus Yeald; the other was the political boss of New York City himself, Robert Orcread—known by his own wish as "Honest Bob."

They studied the Saint with open interest while chairs were vacated for them at the table. Yeald did his scrutinizing from a safe distance, peering through his spectacles nervously—Simon barely overcame the temptation to say "Boo!" to him and find out if he would jump as far as he seemed prepared to. Orcread, on the other hand, came round the table without sitting down.

"So you're the guy we've been looking for," he said; and the Saint smiled.

"I guess you know whom you were looking for,

Honest Bob," he said.

Orcread's face hardened.

"How did you know my name?"

"I recognized you from your caricature in the *New Yorker* last week, brother," Simon explained, and gathered at once that the drawing had not met with the Tammany dictator's approval.

Orcread chewed on the stump of dead cigar in his mouth and hooked a thumb into his waistcoat. He looked the Saint up and down again with flinty eyes.

"Better not get too fresh," he advised. "I been wanting a talk with you, but I'll do the wisecracking. You've given us plenty of trouble. I suppose you know you could go to the chair for what you've done."

"Probably," admitted the Saint. "But that was just ignorance. When I first came here, I didn't know that I had to get an official license to kill people."

"You should have thought of that sooner," Orcread said. His voice had the rich geniality of the professional orator, but underneath it the Saint's sensitive ears could detect a ragged edge of strain. "It's liable to be tough for a guy who comes here and thinks he can clean up the town by himself. You know what I ought to be doing now?"

The Saint's smile was very innocent.

"I can guess that one. You ought to be calling a cop and handing me over to him. But that would be a bit awkward for you—wouldn't it? I mean, people might want to know what you were doing here yourself."

"You know why I'm not calling a cop?"

"It must be the spring," Simon hazarded. "Or perhaps today was your old grandmother's birthday, and looking into her dear sweet face you felt the hard shell of worldliness that hides your better nature softening like an overripe banana."

Orcread took the cigar stub from between his teeth and rolled it in his fingers. The leaves crumpled and shredded under the roughness of his hand, but his voice did not rise.

"I'm trying to do something for you," he said. "You ain't so old, are you? You wouldn't want to get into a lot of trouble. It ain't right to go to the chair at your age. It ain't right to be taken for a ride. And why should you?"

"Don't ask me," said the Saint. "If I remember rightly, the suggestion was yours."

"I could do a lot for a guy like you. If you'd come and seen me first, none of this would have happened. But these things you've been doing don't make it easy for us. I don't say we got a grudge against you. Irboll was just a no-account hoodlum, and Ualino was getting too big for himself anyway—I guess he had it coming to him before long. But you're trying to go too fast, and you make too much noise about it. That sort of thing don't go with the public, and it's my job to stop it. It's Mr. Yeald's job to stop it—ain't it, Mark?"

"Certainly," said the lawyer's dry voice, like the voice of a parrot repeating a lesson. "These things have got to be stopped. They will be stopped."

Orcread tapped the Saint on the chest.

"That's it," he said impressively. "We have given our word to the electors that this sort of thing shall be stamped out, and we gotta keep our promises. But we don't want to be too hard on you. So I says to Mark: 'Look here, this Saint must be a sensible young guy. Let's make him an offer.'"

Simon nodded thoughtfully, but Orcread's words only touched the fringes of his attention. He had been trying to find a reason why Orcread and Yeald should ever have entered the conference at all; and in searching for that reason he had made a remarkable discovery. For about the first time in his career he had grossly underestimated himself. He knew that his spectacular advent upon the New York scene had caused no small stir in certain circles, as indeed it had been designed to do;

but he had not realized that his modest efforts could have raised so much dust as Orcread's presence appeared to indicate.

And then he began to understand what a small disturbance could throw a complicated machine out of gear, when the machine was balanced on an unstable foundation of bluff and apathy and chicane, and the disturbance was of that one peculiar kind. The newspaper headlines which he had enjoyed egotistically flashed across his mind's eye with a new meaning. He had not thought, until Orcread told him, that the coincidence of the right man and the right moment, coupled with the mercurial enthusiasms of the New World, could have flung the figure of the Saint almost overnight onto a pinnacle where the public imagination would see it as a rallying point and the banner of a reformation. He had not thought that his disinterested attempts to brighten the Manhattan and Long Island entertainments could have started a fresh wave of civic ambition whose advance ripples had already been felt under the sensitive thrones of the political rulers.

He listened to Orcread again with renewed interest.

"So you see, we're being pretty generous. Two hundred thousand bucks is worth something to any man. And we get you out of a tough spot. You get out of here without even feeling uncomfortable—you go to England or anywhere else you like. A young guy like you could have a good time with two hundred grand. And I'm here to tell you that it's on the up-and-up."

Simon Templar looked at him with a slow and deceptive smile. The glitter of amusement in the Saint's eyes was faint.

"You're making me feel almost sentimental, Bob," he said gravely. "And what is the trivial service I have to do to earn all these benefits?"

Orcread threw his mauled cigar away, and parked the thumb thus released in the other armhole of his waistcoat. He rocked back on his heels, with his prosperous paunch thrown out, and beamed heartily.

"Well . . . nothing," he said. "All we want to do is stop this sort of thing going on. Well, naturally it wouldn't be any good packing you off if things went on just the same. So all we'd ask you to do is tell us who it is that's backing you—tell us who the other guys in your mob are—so we can make them the same sort of proposition, and that'll be the end of it. What d'you say? Do we call it a deal?"

The Saint shook his head regretfully.

"You may call it a deal, if you like," he said gently, "but I'm afraid I call it bushwah. You see, I'm not that sort of a girl."

"He's nuts," said Heimie Felder doggedly, out of a deep silence; and Orcread swung round on him savagely.

"You shut your damn mouth!" he snarled.

He turned to the Saint again, the benevolent beam still hollowly half frozen on his face, as if he had started to wipe it off and had forgotten to finish the job, his jaw thrust out and his flinty eyes narrowed.

"See here," he growled, "I'm not kidding, and if you know what's good for you, you'll lay off that stuff. I'm giving you a chance to get out of this and save your skin. What's funny about it?"

"Nothing," said the Saint blandly, "except that you're sitting on the wrong flagpole. Nobody's backing me, and I haven't got a mob—so what can I do about it? I hate to see these tender impulses of yours running away with you, but——"

A vague anger began to darken Orcread's face.

"Will you talk English?" he grated. "You ain't been running this business by yourself just to pass the time. What are you getting out of it, and who's giving it to you?"

The Saint shrugged wearily.

"I've been trying to tell you," he said. "Nobody's

backing me, and I haven't got a mob. Ask any of this beauty chorus whether they've ever seen me with a mob. I, personally, am the whole works. I am the wheels, the chassis, and the gadget that squirts oil into the gudgeon pins. I am the one-man band. So all you've got to do is to hand me that two hundred grand and kiss me good-bye."

Orcread stared at him for a moment longer and then turned away abruptly. He walked across the room and plumped himself into a chair between Yeald and Kuhlmann. In the voiceless pause that followed, the lips of Heimie Felder could be seen framing tireless dogmas about nuts.

The Saint smiled to himself and bummed a cigarette from the nearest member of the audience. He was obliged dispassionately. Inhaling the smoke dreamily, he glanced around at the hard, emotionless faces under the lights and realized quite calmly that any amusement which he derived from the situation originated entirely in his own irresponsible sense of humour.

Not that he was averse to tight corners and dangerous games—his whole history, in fact, was composed of a long series of them. But it occurred to him that the profitable and amusing phase of the soiree, if there had ever been one, was now definitely over. He had established beyond question the fact that Orcread and the district attorney were in the racket up to their necks, but the importance of that confirmation was almost entirely academic. More important than that was the concrete revelation of their surprisingly urgent interest in his own activities. Judged solely on its merits, the hippopotamoid diplomacy of Honest Bob Orcread earned nothing but a sustained horselaugh—Simon had not once been under the delusion that any of the gentlemen present would have allowed him to be handed two hundred thousand dollars under their noses, or that after the ceremony they would have escorted him to the next out-

ward liner with mutual expressions of philanthropy and
good will—but the fact that the offer had been made at
all, and that Orcread had thought it worth while lending
his own rhetorical genius to it, wanted some thinking
over. And most certainly there were places in New York
more conducive to calm and philosophic thought than
the spot in which he was at present. In short, he saw no
good point in further dalliance at Charley's Place, and
the real difficulty was how he could best take his leave.

From the fragments of conversation that reached him
from the table, he gathered that altruistic efforts were
being made to solve his problem for him. The booming
voice of Honest Bob Orcread, even when lowered to
what its owner believed to be an airy whisper, was penetrating enough to carry the general theme of the discussion to the Saint's ears.

"How do we know it ain't a stall?" he could be heard
reiterating. "A guy couldn't do all that by himself."

The district attorney pursed his lips, and his answer
rustled dustily like dry leaves.

"Personally, I believe he is telling the truth. I was
watching him all the time. And nobody has seen anybody else with him."

"Dot's right," Kuhlmann agreed. "It's chust von man
mit a lot of luck, taking everybody by surprise. I can
look after him."

Orcread was worried, in a heavy and struggling way.

"I hope you're right. But that don't settle anything.
We gotta do something that'll satisfy the public. If you
make a martyr of him it'll only make things worse. Now,
if we could get him in court an' make a monkey out of
him, we could say: 'Well, we done our duty. We caught
the guy that was making all the trouble. And now look
at him.' We could fix things so he didn't get any sympathy."

"I doubt it," Yeald said. "Once he was in court it
would be difficult to stop him talking. I wouldn't dare to

hold the trial in camera; and all the reporters would be wanting interviews. You couldn't keep them away."

"Well, I think we oughta make an example. How would it be if . . ."

The rumbling and the rustling went on, and the Saint smoked his cigarette with no outward signs of concern. But not for a moment had he ceased to be aware that the old gentleman with the scythe, of whom he had undertaken to make an ally, was very close to him that night. Yet his smile was undimmed, and his eyes had the stillness of frozen sea water as he idly watched the whispering men who were debating how the processes of justice could best be turned to meet their own ends. And within him was a colder, deadlier contempt than anything he had felt since the beginning of that adventure.

In the room before him were more than a dozen men whose lives were dedicated to plunder and killing, mercenaries of the most amazing legion of crime that modern civilization had ever known; but it was not against them that he felt the deadliest chill of that cold anger. It was against the men who made their looting possible—the men who held positions of trust, whom a blind public had permitted to seize office, whose wages were paid over and over again out of the pockets of ordinary honest citizens, whose cooperation allowed robbery and murder to go unpunished and even commended. The law meant nothing; except when it was an expedient instrument to remove an obstacle to further pillage.

Outside, beyond that room, lay a great city, a monument in brick and granite to the ingenuity of man; and in that city seven million people paid tribute to a lawless handful. The Saint had never been given to glorifying himself into any kind of knightly hero; in the end he was a mercenary himself, hired by Valcross to do an outlaw's work; but if he had had any doubts of the justice of his cause, they would have been swept away that night.

Whether he acknowledged it or not, whether they knew it or not, he was the champion of seven million, facing sentence in that hushed room for a thing that perhaps none of the seven million could have put into words; and it had never seemed more vital that he should come out alive to carry the battle on. . . .

And then, as if in answer, Orcread's voice rammed itself into his consciousness again and brought him out of his reverie.

"You've heard all we've got to say, Saint. There's only two ways out for you—mine or yours. You can think again if you like."

"I've done all the thinking I can," said the Saint evenly.

"Okay. You've had your chance."

He got up heavily and stood staring at Simon with the same worried perplexity; he was not satisfied yet that he had heard the truth—it was beyond his comprehension that a menace which had attacked the roots of his domination could be so simple—but the consensus of opinion had gone against him. Marcus Yeald twiddled the locks of his briefcase, stood up, and fidgeted with his gloves. He glanced at the door speculatively, in his peering petulant way, and one of the men opened it.

Orcread hitched himself round reluctantly and nodded to Kuhlmann.

"Okay, Dutch," he said and went out, followed by Yeald. The door was closed and locked again, and a ripple of released suppression went over the room. The conference, as a conference, was over. . . .

"Come here, Saint," said Kuhlmann gutturally.

After that single scuffle of movement which followed Orcread's exit an electric tension had settled on the room—a tension that was subtly different from that which had just been broken. Kuhlmann's unemotional accents did not relieve it. Rather, they seemed to key up the tautness another notch; but the Saint did not appear to feel it. Cool, relaxed, serene as if he had been in a gathering of intimate friends, he sauntered forward a couple of steps and stood in front of the racketeer.

He knew that there was nothing he could do there. The odds were impossible. But he stood smiling quietly while Kuhlmann looked up into his face.

"You're a goot boy," Kuhlmann said. "You give us a liddle bit of trouble, und that is bad. But we cannot finish our talk here. So I think"—he swallowed a lump in his throat, and his voice broke—" I think you go outside und vait for us for a minute."

Quick hands grabbed the Saint's wrists and twisted him round, but he did not struggle. He was led to the door; and as he went out, Kuhlmann nodded, blinking, to two of the men who stood along the wall.

"You, Joe, und you, Maxie—give him der business. Und meet me here again aftervards."

Without a flicker of expression the two men detached themselves from the wall and followed the Saint out, their hands automatically feeling in their pockets. The door closed behind the cortege, and for a moment nobody moved.

And then Dutch Kuhlmann dragged out his large white handkerchief and dabbed with it at his eyes. A distinct sob sounded in the room; and the remaining gunmen glanced at each other with almost sheepish grins. Dutch Kuhlmann was crying.

The moon which had shed its light over the earlier hours of the evening, and which had germinated the romance of Mr. Bungstatter of Brooklyn, had disappeared. Clouds hung low between the earth and the stars, and the night nestled blackly over the city. A single booming note from the Metropolitan Tower announced the passing of an hour after midnight.

On the fringe of the town sleep claimed honest men. In the Bronx and the nearer portions of Long Island, in

Hoboken, Peekskill, and Poughkeepsie, families slept peacefully. In Brooklyn, Mr. Theodore Bungstatter slept in ecstatic bliss—and, it must be confessed, snored. And with the hard nozzle of Maxie's automatic grinding deep into his ribs Simon Templar was hurried across the pavement outside Charley's Place and into a waiting car.

Joe piled in on the other side, and a third man took the wheel. The muzzle of another gun stabbed into the Saint's other side, and there was a cold tenseness in the eyes of the escort which indicated that their fingers were taut on the triggers. On this ride they were taking no chances.

Simon looked out of the windows while the driver jammed his foot down on the starter. The few pedestrians who passed scarcely glanced aside. If they had glanced aside, they would have seen nothing extraordinary; and if they had seen anything extraordinary, the Saint reflected with a wry grin, they would have run for their lives. He had taken a hand in a game where he had to play alone, and there would be no help from anyone but himself. . . . But even as he looked back, he saw the slim figure of Fay Edwards framed in the dark doorway through which he had been brought; and the old questions leapt to his mind again.

The brim of her hat cast a shadow over her eyes, and he could not even tell whether she was looking in his direction. He had no reason to think that she would. Throughout his interview with Orcread she had sat like an inattentive spectator, smoking, and thinking her own thoughts. When Kuhlmann's sentence had been passed upon him she had been lighting another cigarette: she had not even looked up, and her hand had not shaken. When he was turned and hustled out of the room she had been raising her eyes to look at him again, with a calm impersonal regard that told him no more than her present pose.

"Better take a good look," advised Maxie.

There was no derision, no bitterness in his voice—it simply uttered a grim reminder of the fact that Simon Templar was doomed to have few more attractive things to look at.

The Saint smiled and saw the girl start off to cross the road behind the car, without looking round, before Joe reached forward and drew the curtains.

"She's worth a look," Simon murmured and slanted an eyebrow at the closed draperies which shut out his view on either side. "This wagon looks like a hearse already."

Joe grunted meaninglessly, and the car pulled away from the curb and circled the block. The blaze of Broadway showed ahead for a moment, like the reflection of a fire in the sky; then they were turned around and driving west, and the Saint settled down and made himself as comfortable as he could.

The situation had no natural facilities for comfort. There was something so businesslike, so final and confident, in the manner of his captors, that despite himself an icy finger of doubt traced its chill course down the Saint's spine. Except for the fact that no invisible but far-reaching hand of the Law sanctioned this strange execution, it had a disturbing similarity to the remorseless ritual of lawful punishment.

Before that he had been in tight corners from which the Law might have saved him if he had called for help; but he had never called. There was something about the dull, ponderous interventions of the Law which had never appealed to him, and in this particular case their potentialities appealed to him least of all. Intervention, even if it succeeded, meant arrest and trial; and his brief acquaintance with Orcread and Yeald had been sufficient to show him how much justice he could expect from that. Not that the matter of justice was very vital in his case. The most incorruptible court in the world, he had to admit, could do nothing else but sentence him to about forty years' imprisonment even if it didn't go so far as ordering execution, and on the whole he preferred his chances with the illicit sentence. It would not be the first time that he had sat in a game of life and death and played the cards out with a steady hand no matter how the luck ran; and now he would do it again, though at that precise moment he hadn't the faintest idea what method he would use. Yet for the first time in many years he wondered if he had not taken on too much.

But no hint of what passed in his mind showed on his face. He leaned back, calm-eyed and nonchalant, as if he were one of a party of friends on their way home; and even when they stopped at the driveway of a ferry he did not move. He cocked one quizzical blue eye at Maxie.

"So it's to be Jersey this time, is it?"

"Yeah," said the gunman, with a callous twist of humour. "We thought ya might like a change."

An efficient-looking blue-coated patrolman stood no more than four yards away; but no sixth sense, no clairvoyant flash of prescience, warned him to single out the gleaming black sedan from the line of other vehicles which were waiting their turn to go on board. He dreamed his dreams of an inspectorship in a division well populated with citizens who would be unselfishly eager to dissuade him with cash and credit from the obvious perils of overworking himself at his job; and the Saint made no attempt to interrupt him. The driver paid their fares, and they settled into their place on the ferry to wait until it chose to sail.

Simon gazed out at the inky waters of the Hudson and wondered idly why it should be that the departure of a ferry was always accompanied by twice as much fuss and anxiety as the sailing of an ocean liner; and he derived a rather morbid exhilaration even from that vivid detail of his experience. He had heard much, and speculated more, about that effective American method of removing an appointed victim; but in spite of his flippant remarks to Valcross he had not expected that he would have this unique opportunity of learning at first hand the sensations of the man who played the leading role in the drama. He felt that in this instance the country which had adopted the "ride" as a native sport for wet week-ends was rather overdoing itself in its eagerness to show him the works so quickly and comprehensively, but the tightness of his corner was not capable of damping a keen professional interest in the proceedings. And yet, all the time, he missed the reassuring pressure of the knife blade that should have been cuddling snugly along his forearm; and his eyes were very cold and bright as he flicked his cigarette end through the open front window and watched it spring like a red tracer bullet across the dark. . . .

Maxie rummaged in his pockets with his free hand, drew forth a crumpled pack of cigarettes, and extended it politely.

"Have another?"

"A last smoke for the condemned man, eh?"

Equally courteous and unruffled, the Saint thumbed a Chesterfield from the package and carefully straightened it out. Maxie passed him the cigar lighter from the arm rest and then lighted a smoke for himself; but in none of the motions of this studious observance of the rules of etiquette was there an opening for a surprise attack from the victim. Simon felt Joe's automatic harden against his side almost imperceptibly while the exchange of courtesies was going on, and knew that his companions had explored all the possibilities of such situations before they began to shave. He sighed and leaned back again, exhaling twin streams of smoke from his nostrils.

"What is that girl Fay?" he asked casually, taking up a natural train of thought from the gunman's penultimate remark.

Maxie tilted back his hat.

"Whaddaya mean, what is she? She's a doll."

Simon reviewed the difficulties of reaching Maxie's intellect with the argument that was occupying his own mind. He knew better than anyone else that the glamorous woman of mystery whose feminine charms rule hard-boiled desperadoes as with a rod of iron, and whose brilliant brain outwits criminals and detectives with equal ease, belonged only in the pages of highly spiced fictional romance, and that in the underworld of New York she was the most singular curiosity of all. To the American hoodlum and racketeer the female of the species has only one function, reserved for his hours of relaxation, and requiring neither intelligence nor outstanding personality. When he calls her a "doll," his vocabulary is an accurate psychological revelation. She is a toy for his diversion, on which he can squander his easily won dollars to the advertisement of his own wealth, to whom he can boast and in boasting expand his own ego and feel himself a great guy; but she has no place in the machinery of his profession except as a spy, a stringer of suckers, or a dumb instrument for putting a rival on the spot, and she has no place in his councils at all.

The Saint saw no easy approach to Maxie from that angle; but he said: "She's good to look at, all right, but I can't see anything else she's got that you could use. I wouldn't let any girls sit in on my business—you can never trust 'em."

Maxie regarded him pityingly.

"Say, why don't ya get wise? That dame has got it here." He tapped the area where his brain might be presumed to reside. "She's got more of it than you or anybody else like ya."

Simon shrugged dubiously.

"You ought to know. But I wouldn't do it. The cleverer a dame is, the more she's dangerous. You can't ever be sure of 'em. They ride along with you for a while, and then the first thing you know they've fallen for some other guy and they're working like hell to double-cross you."

"What, her?" Maxie's stare deepened with indignation as well as scorn. "I guess Heimie was right—you must be nuts. Who's she going to double-cross? She's the Big Fellow's mouthpiece."

The Saint's face was expressionless.

"Mouthpiece?" he repeated slowly.

"Yeah. She talks for him. If he's got something to say, she says it. If we got anything to say, she takes it back. She's the only one in the mob who knows everything that's going on."

Simon did not move. He sat perfectly still, watching the lights along the riverside begin to slide across the darkness as the ferry pulled out from the pier. The urgency of his predicament dropped out of his mind as if a trapdoor had fallen open, leaving a sensation of emptiness through which weaved an eerie squirm of excitement. Maxie's frank expansiveness fairly took his breath away.

It was about the last thing he had expected to develop from that ride. And then, in another moment, he realized how it came about. The callous confidence of his executioners was an attitude which worked two ways; the utter, irrevocable finality of it was sufficient to make conversations possible which could never have happened otherwise. In a different setting, threats and torture and even the menace of certain death would have received no response but a stony, iron-jawed silence, according to that stoical gangland code of which the late Mr. Papulos had been such a faithless exponent; but to a condemned prisoner on the road to execution a gunman could legitimately talk, and might even derive some pleasure from the dilation of his ego and the proof of his own omniscience and importance in so doing—death loomed so inevitably ahead, and dead men told no tales. It gave the Saint a queer feeling of fatality to realize that he had to come to the end of his usefulness before he could make any headway in his quest, but even if dissolution had been a bare yard away he could never have separated himself from the instinct to learn all that he could while knowledge was being offered. And even at that stage he had not lost hope.

"I'm sorry I didn't meet this Big Fellow," he remarked, without a variation in his even tone of casual conversation. "He must be worth knowing."

"You got too near as it was," Joe said matter-of-factly. "You shouldn't of tried it, pal."

"He sounds an exclusive sort of bird," Simon admitted; and Maxie took the cigarette out of his mouth to grin widely.

"You ain't said nuth'n yet. Exclusive ain't the word for it. Say, you don't know how good we're bein' to ya. You're lucky to of got away from Morrie Ualino—Morrie 'd 've had ya in the hot box for sure."

As if he felt a glow of conscious pride at this discovery of his own share in such an uncustomary humaneness, he pulled out his crumpled pack of Chesterfields and offered them again. Simon took one and accepted a light, the procedure being governed by exactly the same courtesy and caution as before.

"Yes," he said thoughtfully, "your Big Fellow must be the wrong kind of bloke to buck."

"You're learning late," Maxie agreed laconically.

"All the same," pursued the Saint, with an air of vague puzzlement, "I can't quite see what makes you and the rest of the mob take your orders from a fellow who isn't in the racket—a bird you haven't ever even seen. I mean, what have you got to gain by it?"

Maxie hitched himself round and tapped a nicotine-stained forefinger on his brain pan again, in that occult gesture which appeared to be his synonym for a salute to intelligence.

"Say, that guy has got what it takes. An' if a guy has

got what it takes, an' shoots square an' can find the dough, I'll take orders from him. And that goes for Joe an' Heimie an' Dutch and the rest of the mob, too. The dough ain't been so easy since they made liquor legal, see?"

The Saint frowned with inviting perplexity; and Maxie, not at all reluctant, endeavoured to clarify his point.

"When we had prohibition, a bootlegger an' his mob were all right, see? They were breaking the law, but it wasn't a law that anybody cared about. Everybody, even respectable citizens, guys on Park Avenue an' everything, useta know bootleggers and ring 'em up and talk to 'em an' be proud to know them. Why, guys would boast about their bootleggers like they would about their doctors or their lawyers, and get into arguments and fights with other guys about whose bootlegger was the best. They paid us our dough an' didn't grumble, because they knew we had to take risks to get the stuff they wanted; and the cops was sort of enemies of the public because they tried to stop us getting the stuff— sometimes. Ya couldn't get a guy to testify against a guy that was getting him his liquor, in favour of another guy who was trying to stop the liquor comin' through, see?"

"Mmm," conceded the Saint doubtfully, more for punctuation than anything else.

"Well, when prohibition went out, that changed everything, see? A bootlegger wasn't any guy's friend any more. He was just a racketeer that was trying to stick something on the prices of stuff that any guy could go and buy legitimate, an' the cop was a guy that was trying to put the racketeer out of business an' keep the prices down; and everybody suddenly forgot everything we'd done for 'em in the dry years, an' turned right round on us." Maxie scowled mournfully at the flimsiness of human gratitude. "Well, we hadda do something, hadn't we? A guy's gotta live."

"I suppose so," said the Saint. "Which guy is this?"

Maxie wrinkled his nose.

"A lotta guys got in trouble about that time," he said reminiscently. "We had a sort of reform drive, an' got hunted about a lot. It got worse all the time. A lotta guys couldn't get it into their coconuts that it wasn't going to be easy money any more, an' it was too bad about them. You had to have it here." He thumbed his forehead again mysteriously. "Business wasn't good, so we hadn't got the money to pay the cops; an' the cops not getting money started going after us again an' makin' things worse." Maxie sighed reminiscently. "But then the Big Fellow came along," he said, cheering up, "an' everything was jake again."

"Why?" Simon asked, with the same ingenuously puzzled air.

"Well, he put us in the big dough again, see?"

"With the same old rackets?"

"Yeah. But he's got brains. An' information. He's got everything taped out. When he says: 'The layout is like this and that, we gotta fix it this way and that way,' we know it's going to be just like he says. So we don't make no mistakes."

The lights of the waterside had ceased to move, and there was a general stir of voyagers gathering themselves to continue on their way. The driver climbed back into the car and settled himself, waiting for their turn to pull out in the line of disembarking traffic.

Keeping their place decorously in the procession, they climbed the winding road that leads upwards from the Jersey shore, and in a short time they were speeding across the Jersey meadows. The drive became a monotonous race through unfamiliar country—straight lines of highway which might have been laid across the face of the moon for all the landmarks that Simon could pick out, straggling lights of unidentifiable small towns, blazing headlights of other cars which leapt up out of the blackness and roared by in an instant of noise, to be swallowed up in the gulf of dark behind. The powerful sedan, guided by the expert hands of the silent driver, flashed at a reckless pace through the countryside, slowed smoothly down from time to time to keep well within the prescribed speed limits of a village, then leapt ahead down another long stretch of open road. Despite the speed at which they were travelling, the journey seemed interminable: the sense of utter isolation, of being shut away from the whole world in that mass-produced projectile whirling through the uncharted night, would have had an overwhelmingly soporific effect if it had not been for the doom to which they were driving.

The Saint had no means of knowing how far ahead that destination lay, and a cold fatalism would not let him ask. He knew that it could not be very far away— knew that his time must be getting short and his need more desperately urgent—but still he had had no opportunity to save himself. The vigilance of his companions had never relaxed, and if he made the slightest threatening move it would hardly inconvenience them at all to shoot him where he sat and fling his body out of the car without slackening speed.

They could have done that anyhow, might even be preparing to do it. He did not know why he had assumed that he was being taken to a definite place of execution, to be slain there according to a crude gangland ritual; but it was on that expectation that he had based his only hopes of escape.

He stole a glance at Maxie. The gunman was lounging nonchalantly in his corner, the backward tilt of his hat serving to emphasize the squat impassivity of his features, twirling an unlighted cigar in one side of his thick mouth. To say that he was totally unimpressed by the enormity of the thing he was there to do would convey only the surface of his attitude. He was, if anything, rather bored.

Simon fought to maintain his outward calm. The

length of the journey, the forced inaction under the strain of such a deadly suspense, was slowly wearing down his nerves; but at all costs he had to remain master of himself. His chance would be thin enough even if it ever came, he knew; and the faintest twitch of panic, the very slightest disordering of the swift, cold precision and coordination of brain and arm, would eliminate that chance to vanishing point. And all the time another aloof and wholly dissociated thread in his mind, akin to the phlegmatic detachment of a scientist who notes his own symptoms on his deathbed, was weaving the fact that Maxie might still go on talking to a man whom he believed to be helpless. . . .

The Saint cleared his throat and tried to resume the conversation in the same tone of innocent puzzlement as before—as if it had never been broken off. He had to go on trying to learn those things which he might never be able to turn to advantage, had to do something to occupy his mind and ease the strain on his aching self-control.

"How do you mean, the Big Fellow came along?" he said. "If he wasn't even in the racket, if you'd never heard of him before and haven't even seen him yet— how did you know he'd be any use to you?"

"How did we know he'd be any use to us? Say, he showed us. Ya can't get around facts. He had it all worked out."

"Yes, I know; but he must have started somewhere. How did he get in touch with you? What was the first you heard of him?"

Maxie grunted and peered ahead through the windshield.

"I guess you'll have to figure that out yourself—you'll have plenty of time," he said; and Simon looked out and saw that the car was slowing down.

CHAPTER VII

HOW DUTCH KUHLMANN SAW
A GHOST, AND SIMON
TEMPLAR RETURNED HOME

At first the Saint could see nothing but a stretch of deserted highway that seemed to reach for endless miles into the distance; and then the driver spun the wheel sharply to the right, and the car bounced off the road into a narrow lane.

Simon was not surprised that he had failed to spot it. The sweeping branches of trees almost met over the bumpy disused bypath: their foliage scraped the top of the sedan and brushed with a slithering sound against the sides as they went down the side road at a considerably reduced speed. Before they had gone five yards they were effectively screened from the view of any car that might be travelling along the main thoroughfare.

With both hands clinging to the wheel, which leapt and shuddered in his grasp like a live thing, the driver headed deeper and deeper along the narrow track. If the combined bulks of Joe and Maxie had not formed a system of human wedges pinning him tightly to the cushions, the Saint would have been bumped clear of the seat each time the tires caromed off the boulders that studded the roadbed.

Simon Templar was aware of the quickened beating of his heart. There was a dryness in his throat and a vague feeling of constriction about his chest that made him breathe a little deeper than normally; but the breathing was slow, steady, and deliberate, not the quick, shallow gasps of fear. The tension of his nerves had passed the vibrating point—they were strung down to a terrific immobility that was as impermanent as the stillness of a compressed spring. The waiting and suspense was over; now there was nothing but the end of the ride to see, and a chance for life to be taken if fate offered it. And if the chance did not offer, that was the end of adventures.

The lane was growing even narrower as they went on; the trees and bushes that lined its sides closed in upon them. Plainly it had been derelict for years: the march of macadamized arteries had swept by and left it for no other service but for such journeys as they were on, and its destination, if it had ever had one, had long since found other and faster communications with the outside world. At last, when the streamlined body of the sedan could make no further headway, the driver jammed on the brakes and brought the car to a lurching halt. Then he snapped off the headlights, leaving only the bright glow of the parking lights to illuminate the scene.

A good enough spot for a murder, the Saint was forced to admit; and he wondered how many other men had dared the vengeance of Dutch Kuhlmann and the Big Fellow, only to pay for their temerity in that lonely place. With the switching off of the purring engine all sound seemed to have been blotted out of the night, as if the world had been folded under a dense pack of wool; even the distant hum of other cars away back on the highway they had left, if there were any, was inaudible.

As far as the Saint could see, there was nothing around them but a wilderness of trees and shrubbery scattered over an undulating stony common; a man could die there with no sound that the world would ever hear, and his body might lie there for weeks before some chance passer-by stumbled on it and sent a new blare of headlines screaming across the front pages. Suddenly the Saint guessed why he had been taken so far, with such precautions, instead of simply being pushed out on any New York street and riddled with bullets as the car drove away. It had been sufficient often enough for other victims; but this case was different. The handling of it linked up with certain things that Orcread and Yeald had discussed. The Saint was not to become a martyr or even a sensation: he was to disappear, as swiftly and unaccountably as he had come, like a comet —all questions could go unanswered perhaps for ever, and the fickle public would soon forget . . . .

Something creaked at the back of the car, breaking the stillness; and Maxie roused himself. He climbed out unhurriedly and turned round again as soon as he was outside, his automatic glinting dully in the subdued light. He jerked it at the Saint expressively.

"Out, buddy."

Behind the Saint, Joe's gun added its subtle pressure to the command.

Simon pulled himself up slowly. Now that the climax of the ride was reached, he had ceased speculating upon the reactions of a doomed man. Every cell in his keen brain, every nerve and fibre of his body, was dynamically alive and watchful. His mind had never worked more clearly and smoothly, his body had never been keyed to a more perfect pitch of physical fitness, than they were at that moment in the deepening shadow of death. It was impossible to think that in a few brief moments, with one inconceivably numbing, crashing shock, that vibrant, pulsing life could be stilled, the brilliant mind dulled for ever, the play and delight of sensual experience and the sweet awareness of life swallowed up in a black nothingness from which there was no return.

He stepped down gradually to the running board. A yard from him, Maxie's automatic was levelled steadily at his chest; behind him, Joe's gun pushed no less steadily into his back. The wild thought crossed his mind that he might launch himself onto Maxie from the running board in a desperate smothering leap, trusting to the surprise to bowl him over before he could shoot, and to the beneficent darkness to take care of the rest. But in the next instant he knew that there was no hope there. In spite of his outward stolidity, Maxie was watching him like a cat; and he had measured his distance perfectly. To have jumped then would have been to jump squarely into a bullet, and Joe would probably have got him from behind at the same time.

With a face of iron the Saint lowered himself to the ground and straightened up, but his eyes met Maxie's calmly enough.

"Is this as far as we go?" he inquired.

"You said it," Maxie assented curtly.

Behind him, Simon could hear the crunch of Joe's brogans on the soil as the other gunman followed him out, and the brusque click of the door closing again. The weight of the gun muzzle touched his back again. He was gripped between two potential fires as securely as if he had been held in a pair of tangible forceps; and for the second time that icy qualm of doubt squirmed clammily in the pit of his stomach. In every movement that was made there was a practised confidence, an unblinking vigilance, such as he had never encountered before. No other two men he had ever met could have held him in the car so long, talking to him and lighting his cigarettes, without giving him a moment's chance to take them off their guard. No other two men that he could think of could have manoeuvred him in and out of it without offering at least one even toss-up on a break for freedom. He had always known, at the back of his mind, that one day he must meet his match—that sometime, somewhere, the luck which had followed him so faithfully throughout his career must turn against him, as it does in the life of every gambler and adventurer who refuses to acknowledge any limits. But he had not thought that it would happen there—just as no man ever believes that he will die tomorrow, although he knows that there must come a tomorrow when he will die . . . . A thin shadow of the old Saintly smile touched his lips and did not reach his eyes.

"I hope you're going to do this with all the regular formalities," he said gently. "You know, I've often wondered just how the thing was done. I'd be awfully disappointed if you didn't bump me off in the most approved style."

At the back of him, Joe choked on an oath; but Maxie was unimpressed.

"Sure," he agreed affably. "We'll give you a show. But there ain't much to it. Just in the line of business, see?"

"I see," said the Saint quietly.

The complete unconcern, the blandly brutal callousness of Maxie's reply, seemed to have frozen something deep in his heart. He had faced death before —death that flamed out at him in violent, seething hate, death that dispassionately proposed his annihilation as a matter of cold expediency. He had dealt out death himself, in various ways. But never had he known a man to attempt to snuff out another's life so casually, with such an indescribable absence of all personal feeling, as this ruthless killer who was preparing to send a bullet through his vitals—"just in the line of business. . . ."

The Saint had had his own rules of the game; but at that moment they were forgotten. If he ever broke loose from the trap in which he was held, if Destiny offered him that one lone ghost of a break to get away and join in the game again, for the rest of that adventure he would play it as his opponents played it—giving no quarter. He would be the same as they were—utterly without mercy or compunction. He would have only one remedy for all mistakes—the same as theirs.

In the dim light his eyes had lost all expression. Their gaze was narrowed down to a mere frosty gleam of jagged ice.

"Over by that tree," directed Maxie conversationally. "That's the best spot."

His phrasing of the words held a sinister implication that many other spots in that locality had been tried, and that his choice was based on the findings of long experience; but the suggestion was absolutely unconscious. He seemed even more indifferent than if he had been posing the Saint for a photograph.

Simon looked at him for a moment and then turned away. There was nothing else he could do. Sometimes he had wondered why even on the way to certain death a man should still submit to the dictation of a gun; now, with a terrible clarity of reason, he knew the answer. Until death had actually struck him, until the ultimate unanswerable instant of annihilation, he would cling to the hope that some miracle must bring reprieve; obedient to some illogical blind instinct of self-preservation, he would do nothing to precipitate the end.

Under the turning muzzle of Maxie's gun, the Saint took up his position against the trunk of a towering elm and turned round again. Joe nodded approvingly and at a sign from Maxie stepped closer to prepare the victim for execution according to the gangland code.

Methodically he unbuttoned the Saint's coat and opened it; then began a similar task upon his shirt.

"Some guys started wearin' bullet-proof vests,"

Maxie explained cheerfully.

Simon's nerves were tensed to the last unbearable ounce; his body was rigid like a steel bar. Now there was only Maxie covering him: Joe was fully taken up with his gruesome ritual, and the voiceless driver had raised the hood of the car and was seemingly engrossed in some minor ailment that he had detected in its mechanism. If he was to have a chance at all, it could only be now.

He moved slightly, as if to help Joe with his unbuttoning. Then, with a lightning movement, his left hand shot up. Lean fingers closed on Joe's left wrist as he fumbled with the Saint's shirt, and a sudden whipping contraction of steel sinews jerked the man aside, throwing him off balance and turning him half round on the leverage of his extended arm. The gun in his right hand was flung out of aim: Simon heard the crack of the explosion and saw the vicious splash of flame from the barrel, but the shot went off at right angles to the line it should have taken.

Simon's fist snapped over and thudded into the back of the gunman's neck, accurately at the base of his skull, smacking into the hard flesh and bone in a savage punch that must have almost jarred the bones loose from their sockets. The man grunted stupidly and lurched forward; but the Saint's left arm lashed round his upper body and held him up as a human shield, while his right hand grabbed at the man's gun wrist and held it to prevent Joe twisting it up behind his back and firing at point-blank range. He had had no time to wonder what Maxie might be doing during that flurry of hectic action; when the Saint had last observed him he had been three yards away and a trifle to his left; but the first jerk which had hurled Joe across the line of fire had made that position useless. Simon looked for him over Joe's shoulder and did not see him. He hauled his living shield round in a frantic spin; and then he heard the deafening peal of an automatic exploding somewhere close behind him on his right, and something hit him in the right side of his back below the shoulder with terrific force.

The Saint stumbled and caught his breath as a redhot anguish stabbed through him from the point of impact of that fearful blow; and at the same moment Joe's body kicked convulsively in his grasp and became a dead weight. Simon's right arm was numb to his fingertips from the shock. He turned further, dragging Joe with him, and heard a dull bump as the dead man's automatic slipped from his nerveless fingers and fell to the ground, but he could not reach it. To have tried to do so, with one arm useless, would have meant letting go his only protection; and he knew he would never have had time to cover the distance and locate the fallen weapon in the dark. He looked up and saw Maxie's pitiless face, a white blotch in the faint light.

"You got two minutes to say your prayers, Saint," Maxie grated, with the first trace of vindictiveness that he had shown. He tilted his head and spoke louder.

"Hi, Hunk, you damn fool! Where are ya?"

Then Simon remembered the driver of the car and knew that the chance which he thought he had seen was only a chimera, a last sadistic jest on the part of the fortune which had deserted him. Between them, the two men would get him easily. He couldn't watch both at once, or protect himself from the two of them together. One of them would outflank him, as simply as walking round a table, without risk and without effort; and that would be the finish.

The Saint did not pray. He had no deities to call on, except the primitive pagan gods of battle and sudden death who had carried him on a flood tide of favour into that blind alley and left him there to pay the last account alone. But he looked up at the dark sky and saw that the clouds had broken, and a star twinkled millions of miles aloft in the blue rift. A light breeze passed across the common, stirring the fresh scents of the night; and he knew that, whatever the reckoning might be, he would have asked for no other life.

"Hunk!" Maxie called again, raspingly.

He dared not turn his head for fear of taking his eyes off the Saint; but the Saint looked beyond him and saw a strange thing.

The driver was not probing into the vitals of the car, as he had been. He was not even approaching at a lumbering trot to throw his taciturn weight into the unequal scale. It took the Saint a second or two to discover where he was—a second or two longer to realize that the blurred form extended at full length beside the car was the driver, lying as if in sleep.

And then he saw something else—a slender graceful figure that was coming up behind Maxie on soundless feet. And as he saw it, she spoke.

"The Big Fellow says wait a minute, Maxie."

Maxie's eyes went wide in hurt surprise, and his jaw sagged foolishly. Only the aim of his automatic did not waver. It clung to its mark as if his brain stubbornly refused to accept the evidence of his ears; and his astounded gaze did not shift away from the Saint.

"Wha—whass that?" he got out.

"This is Fay," said the girl.

Simon Templar opened his nostrils to a vast lung-easing breath. The cool sweet air of the unwalled fields went down into his lungs like ethereal nectar and sent the blood racing again along his stagnant veins. He lifted his head and looked up at the lone twinkling star in that slim gap in the black canopy of cloud, and over the abyss of a thousand million light-years the star seemed to wink at him. He was alive.

There are no words to describe what he felt at that moment. When a man has been down into the uttermost depths, when the shadow of the dark angel's wings has blotted out the last light and their cold breath has touched his brow, not in sudden accident or the anaesthetic heat of passion, but with a remorseless deliberation that wrings the last dram of self-control from every second of hopeless knowledge, his return to life is beyond the reach of words. To say that the weight of all mortality is swept from his shoulders, that the snapping of the strain leaves every heroically disciplined nerve loose and inert like a broken thread, that the precious response of every living sense takes away his breath with its intolerably brilliant beauty, is to say nothing. He is like a man who has been blind from birth, to whom the gift of sight has been given in the middle of his life; but he is far more than that. He has been dumb and deaf, without taste or smell or hearing, without mind or movement; and all those things have been given to him at the same time.

As in a dream, the Saint heard Maxie's blank bewildered voice again.

"How did you get here?"

"I walked," said the girl coldly. "Did you hear what I told you? The Big Fellow says to lay off him."

"But—but——" Maxie was floundering in a bottomless morass of incredulity that had taken the feet from under him. "But he killed Joe," he managed, in a sudden gasp.

The girl had advanced coolly until she was at his side. She gazed across at the limp form gripped in the Saint's left arm.

"Well?"

The monosyllable dropped from her lips with a pellucid serenity that was void of the faintest tinge of interest. She did not care what had happened to Joe. She was at a loss to find any connection whatsoever between his death and the object of her arrival. Maxie struggled for speech.

And the Saint realized that Joe's automatic was still on the ground close by, where it had fallen.

His arm was beginning to ache with the dead weight on it, and he heaved the body up and got a fresh grip while his keen eyes probed the darkness. There was a throbbing pain growing up in his wound that turned to a sharp twinge in his chest every time he breathed, but he scarcely noticed the discomfort. Presently he found a dull gleam of metal in the grass somewhere to his left front.

He edged himself towards it, inch by inch, with infinite patience. Every instinct urged him to drop his encumbering load and make a swift, desperate dive for it, but he knew that the gamble would have been hopelessly against him. With every muscle held relentlessly in check, he worked himself across the intervening space with movements so smooth and minute that they could never have been noticed. There was only about a yard and a half to go, but it might have been seven miles. And at last Maxie recovered his voice.

"What does the Big Fellow want us to do?" he demanded harshly. "Kiss him?"

"The Big Fellow says to let him go."

The dull gleam of metal was only six inches away then. Simon extended a cautious toe, touched it here and there, drew it gently towards him. It was the gun he was looking for. His right arm was still useless; but if he could drop Joe and dive for it with his left—the instant Maxie's attention was distracted, as it must be soon . . . .

"Let him go?" Maxie's eyes were wild, his mouth twisted. "Like hell I'll let him go! You must be nuts. He killed Joe." Maxie's forearm stiffened, and the gun in his hand moved slightly. "You're too late, Fay—we'd done the job before you got here. This is how we let him go, the dirty double-crossing——"

"Don't be a fool!"

In a flash the girl's hands were on his wrist, dragging his arm down; and in that moment the Saint had his chance. With a swift jerk of his sound shoulder he flung the body of his shield away, well away to one side, and his hand plunged downwards to the automatic that he was still marking with his toe. His fingers closed on the butt, and he straightened up again with it in his hand.

"I think that's pretty good advice, Maxie," he said gently.

There was a trace of the old Saintly lilt in his voice, a lilt of triumphant mockery that was born in the surge of new power and confidence which went through him at the feel of gun metal in his hands again. Maxie stared at him frozenly, with his right arm still stretched downwards in the girl's grasp, and the muzzle of his automatic pointed uselessly into the ground. Simon's finger itched on the trigger. He had sworn to be without mercy. The indifference of his executioners had hardened the last dregs of pity out of his heart.

"Wasn't it two minutes that we had to say our prayers, Maxie?" he whispered.

The gunman glared at him with dilated eyes. All at once, in a physical quiver of comprehension, he seemed to take in the situation—that the Saint was alive and free and the tables were turned. With a foul oath, heedless of the menace of the Saint's automatic, he broke loose from the girl with a savage fling of his arm and brought up his gun.

Simon's forefinger tightened on the trigger—once. Maxie's gun was never fired. His arms flew wide, and his head snapped back. For one swaying moment he stared at the Saint with all the furies of hell concentrated in his flaming eyes; and then a dull glaze crept over his eyeballs and the fires died out. His head sagged forward as if he were tired; his knees buckled, and he pitched headlong to the ground.

Simon gazed down at the two sprawled figures for a second or two in silence, while the jagged ice melted out of his eyes without softening their expression. A faint gesture of repugnance crinkled a thin line into one corner of his mouth; but whether the repugnance was for the two departed killers, or for the manner in which they had been exterminated, he did not know himself. He dismissed the proposition with a shrug, and the careless movement sent a sharp twinge of pain through his injured shoulder to bring him finally back to reality. With an inaudible sigh, he put the gun away in his pocket and turned his eyes back to the girl.

She had not moved from where he had last seen her. The dead body of Maxie lay at her feet; but she was not looking at it, and she had made no attempt to possess herself of the automatic that was still clutched in his hand. The light was too dim for the Saint to be able to see the expression on her face; but the poise of her body reminded him irresistibly of the night when she had watched him kill Morrie Ualino, and more recently of the time, only an hour or two ago, when he himself had been sent out from the back room of Charley's Place on the ride which had only just ended. There was the same impregnable aloofness, the same inscrutable carelessness of death, as though in some impossible way she had detached herself from every human emotion and dominated even the last mystery of dissolution. He walked up closer to her, slowly, because it hurt him a little when he breathed, until he could see the brightness of her tawny eyes; but they told him nothing.

She did not speak, and he hardly knew what to do. The situation was rather beyond him. He saluted her vaguely, with the ghost of a bow, and let his arm fall to his side.

"Thank you," he said.

Her eyes were pools of amber, still and unreadable.

"Is that all?" she asked in a low voice.

Again he felt that queer leap of expectation at the husky music which she made of words. He moved his hands in a slight helpless gesture.

"I suppose so. It's the second time you've helped me —I don't know why. I haven't asked. What else is there?"

"What about this?"

Suddenly, before he knew what she was doing, her arms were around his neck, her soft slenderness pressed close to him, the satin of her cheek against his. For a moment he was too amazed to move. Hazily, he wondered if the terrible strain he had been through had unhinged some weak link in his imagination. The tenuous perfume of her skin and hair stole in upon his senses, sending a creeping trickle of fire along his veins; her lips found his mouth, and for one mad second he was shaken by the awareness of her passion. He winced imperceptibly, and she drew back.

"I'm sorry," he said. "You see, you didn't get here quite soon enough. I stopped one."

Instantly she forgot everything else. She drew him over to the car, switched on the headlights, and made him take off his coat. With quick, gentle hands she slipped his shirt down over his shoulder; he could feel the warm stickiness of blood on his back. On the ground close by, the chauffeur still lay as if asleep.

"Better make sure he doesn't wake up while you're doing the first aid," said the Saint, with a rather weary gesture towards the unconscious man.

"He won't wake up," she answered calmly. "I killed him."

Then Simon saw that the shadow between the driver's shoulder blades was the hilt of a small knife, and a phantom chill went through him. He understood now why Maxie's call had gone unanswered. The girl's hands were perfectly steady on his back; he couldn't see her face because she was behind him, but he knew what he would have found there. It would have been masked with the same cold beauty, the same unearthly contempt of life and death and all their associations, which he had only once seen broken—so strangely, only a few moments before.

She fastened his handkerchief and her own over the wound, replaced his shirt, and drew his coat loosely over the shoulder. Her hand rested there lightly.

"You'll have to see a doctor," she said. "I know a man in Passaic that we can go to."

He nodded and moved round to the side of the car. Competently, she lowered the hood over the engine and forestalled him at the wheel. He didn't protest.

It was impossible to turn the car about in the confined space, and she had to back up the lane until they reached the highway. She did it as confidently as he would have expected her to, although he had never met a woman before who had really achieved a complete mastery of the art of backing. Inanimate stones seemed to have become alive, judging by the way they thrust malicious obstacles into the path of the tires and threatened to pitch the car into the shrubbery, but her small right hand on the wheel performed impossible feats. In a remarkably short time they had broken through the trees and swung around in the main road; and the powerful sedan, responding instantly to the pressure of her foot on the accelerator, whirled away like the wind towards Passaic. The Saint saw no other car near the side road and was compelled to repeat Maxie's question.

"How did you get here?"

"I was in the trunk behind," she explained. "Hunk was hanging around so long that I thought I'd never be able to get out. That's why I was late."

The strident horn blared a continuous warning to slower cars as the speedometer needle flickered along the dial. She drove fast, flat out, defiantly, yet with a cold machine-tooled precision of hand and eye that took the recklessness out of her contempt for every other driver's rights to the road. Perhaps, as they scrambled blasphemously out of her path, they caught a glimpse of her fair hair and pale careless face as she flashed by, like a valkyrie riding past on the gales of death.

Simon lay back in his corner and lighted a cigarette. His shoulder was throbbing more painfully, and he was glad to rest. But the puzzle in his mind went on. It was the second time she had intervened, this time to save his life; and he was still without a reason. Except—the obvious one. There seemed to be no doubt about that; although until that moment she had never spoken a word to him. The Saint had lived his life. He had philandered and roistered with the best, and done it as he did most other things, better than any of them; but in that mad moment when she had kissed him he had felt something which was unlike anything else in his experience, something of which he could almost be afraid. . . .

He was too tired to go deeper into it then. Consciously, he tried to postpone the accounting which would be forced on him soon enough; and he was relieved when the lights of Passaic sprang up around them, even though he realized that that only lessened the time in which he must make up his mind.

The girl stopped the car before a small house on the outskirts of the town and climbed out. Simon hesitated.

"Hadn't you better wait here?" he suggested. "If this bird is connected with your mob——"

"He isn't. Come on."

She was ringing the bell when he reached the door. After a lengthy interval the doctor opened it, sleepy-eyed and dishevelled, in his shirt and trousers. He was a swarthy stocky man with a loose lower lip and rather prominent eyes which shifted salaciously behind thick pebble glasses—Simon would not have cared to take his wife there, but nevertheless the doctor's handling of the present circumstances was commendable in every way. After one glance at the Saint's stained shirt and empty sleeve he led the way to his surgery and lighted the gas under a sterilizing tray.

He gave the Saint a long shot of brandy and proceeded to wash his hands methodically in a cracked
basin.

"How've you been keeping, Fay?" he asked.

"Pretty well," she replied casually. "How about
you?"

He grunted, drying his hands.

"I've been fairly busy. I haven't taken a vacation since
I went to the Chicago exhibition."

The bullet had entered the Saint's back at an angle,
pierced cleanly through the latissimus dorsi, ricochetted
off a rib, and lodged a few inches lower down in the
chest wall. Simon knew that the lung had not been
touched—otherwise he would probably have been dead
before that—but he was grateful for knowing the exact
extent of the injury. The doctor worked with impersonal
efficiency; and the girl took a cigarette and watched,
passing him things when he asked for them. Simon
looked at her face—it was impassive, untouched by her
thoughts.

"Have another drink?" asked the doctor, when he had
dressed the wound.

Simon nodded. His face was a trifle pale under his
tan.

Fay Edwards poured it out, and the doctor went back
to his cracked basin and washed his hands again.

"It was worth going to, that exhibition," he said. "I
was too hot to enjoy it, but it was worth seeing. I don't
know how they managed to put on some of those shows
in the Streets of Paris."

He came back and peered at the Saint through his
thick lenses, which made his eyes seem smaller than they
were.

"That will cost you a thousand dollars," he said
blandly.

The Saint felt in his pockets and remembered that he
hadn't a nickel. Fortunately, he had deposited his ten-

thousand-dollar bonus in a safe place before he went to interview Inselheim, but all his small change had been taken when he was searched after his capture. That was a broad departure from the underworld tradition which demands that a man who is taken for a ride shall be left with whatever money he has on him, but it was a tribute to the fear he had inspired which could transform even a couple of five-dollar bills and some silver into potential lethal weapons in his hands. He smiled crookedly.

"Is my credit good?"

"Certainly," said the surgeon without hesitation. "Send it to me tomorrow. In small bills, please. Leave the dressing on for a couple of days, and try to take things easy. You may have a touch of fever tomorrow. Take an aspirin."

He ushered them briskly down the hall, fondling the girl's hand unnecessarily.

"Come and see me any time you want anything, Fay. Good-night."

Throughout their visit he had not raised an eyebrow or asked a pertinent question: one gathered that a wounded man waking him up for attention in the small hours of the morning was nothing epoch-making in his practice, and that he had long since found it wise and profitable to mind his own business.

They sat in the car, and Simon lighted a cigarette. The doctor's brandy had taken off some of the deathly lassitude which had drained his vitality before; but he knew that the stimulation was only temporary, and he had work to do. Also there was still the enigma of Fay Edwards, which he would have to face before long. If only she would be merciful and leave the time to him, he would be easier in his mind: he had his normal share of the instinct to put off unpleasant problems. He didn't know what answer he could give her; he wanted time to think about it, although he knew that time and thought would bring him no nearer to an answer. But he knew she would not be merciful. The quality of mercy was rare enough in women, and in anyone like her it would be rarest of all. She would face his answer in the same way that she faced the fact of death, with the same aloof, impregnable detachment; he could only sense, in an indefinable intuitive way, what would lie behind that cold detachment; and the sensation was vaguely frightening.

"Where would you like to go?" she asked.

He smoked steadily, avoiding her eyes.

"Back to New York, I suppose. I haven't finished my job tonight. But you can drop me off anywhere it suits you."

"You're not fit to do any more today."

"I haven't finished," he said grimly.

She regarded him inscrutably; her mind was a thousand miles beyond his horizon, but the fresh sweetness of her body was too close for comfort.

"What did you come here to do?"

"I had a commission," he said.

He put his hand in his breast pocket, took out his wallet, and opened it on his knee. She leaned towards him, looking over his shoulder at the scrap of paper that was exposed. His forefinger slid down the list of names written on it.

"I came here to kill six men. I've killed three—Jack Irboll, Morrie Ualino, and Eddie Voelsang. Leaving three."

"Hunk is dead," she said, touching the list. "That was Jenson—the man who drove this car tonight."

"Leaving two," he amended quietly.

She nodded.

"I wouldn't know where to find Curly Ippolino. The last I heard of him, he was in Pittsburgh." Her golden-yellow eyes turned towards him impassively. "But Dutch Kuhlmann is next."

The Saint forced himself to look at her. There was nothing else to be done. It had to be faced; and he was spellbound by a tremendous curiosity.

"What will you do? He's one of your friends, isn't he?"

"I have no . . . friends," she said; and again he was disturbed by that queer haunting music in her voice. "I'll take you there. He'll just about be tired of waiting for Joe and Maxie by the time we arrive. You'll see him as he comes out."

Simon looked at the lighted panel of instruments on the dash. He didn't see them, but they were something to which he could turn his eyes. If they went back to find Dutch Kuhlmann, her challenge to himself would be in abeyance for a while longer. He might still escape. And his work remained: he had made a promise, and he had never yet failed to keep his word. He was certain that she was not leading him into a trap—it would have been fantastic to imagine any such complicated plan, when nothing could have been simpler than to allow Maxie to complete the job he had begun so well. On the other hand, she had offered the Saint no explanation of why she should help him, had asked him to give no reasons for his own grim mission. He felt that she would have had no interest in reasons. Hate, jealousy, revenge, a wager, even justice—any reasons that logic or ingenuity might devise would be only words to her. She was waiting, with her hand on the starting switch, for anything he cared to say.

The Saint bowed his head slowly.

"I meant to go back to Charley's Place," he said.

A little more than one hour later Dutch Kuhlmann gulped down the dregs of his last drink, up-ended his glass, pulled out his large old-fashioned gold watch, yawned with Teutonic thoroughness, and shoved his high stool back from the bar.

"I'm goin' home," he said. "Hey, Toni—when Joe an' Maxie get here, you tell them to come and see me at my apartment."

The barman nodded, mechanically wiping invisible stains from the spotless mahogany.

"Very good, Mr. Kuhlmann."

Kuhlmann stood up and glanced towards the two sleek sphinx-faced young men who sat patiently at a strategic table. They finished their drinks hurriedly and rose to follow him like well-trained dogs as he waddled towards the door, exchanging gruff good-nights with friends and acquaintances as he went. In the foyer he wanted for them to catch up with him. They passed him and stood between him and the door while it was opened. Also they went out first and inspected the street carefully before they nodded to him to follow. Kuhlmann came out and stood between them on the sidewalk—he was as thorough and methodical in his personal precautions as he was in everything else, which was one reason why his czardom had survived so long. He relighted his cigar and flicked the match sportively at one of his equerries.

"Go und start der car, Fritzie," he said.

One of the sphinx-faced young men detached himself from the little group and went and climbed into the driving seat of Kuhlmann's Packard, which was parked a little distance up the road. He was paid handsomely for his special duty, but the post was no sinecure. His predecessor in office, as a matter of fact, had lasted only three weeks—until a bomb planted under the scuttle by some malicious citizen had exploded when the turning of the ignition key had completed the necessary electrical circuit.

Kuhlmann's benign but restless eyes roved over the scene while the engine was being warmed up for him, and so he was the first to recognize the black sedan which swept down the street from the west. He nudged the escort who had remained with him.

"Chust in time, here is Joe and Maxie comin' back."

He went forward towards the approaching car as it

drew closer to the curb. He was less than two yards from it when he saw the ghost—too late for him to turn back or even cry out. He saw the face of the man whom he had sent away to execution, a pale ghost with stony lips and blue eyes cold and hard like burnished sapphires, and knew in that instant that the sands had run out at last. The sharp crack of a single shot crashed down the echoing channel of the street, and the black sedan was roaring away to the east before his body touched the pavement.

The police sirens were still moaning around like forlorn banshees in the distances of the surrounding night when Fay Edwards stopped the car again in Central Park. Simon had a sudden vivid memory of the night when he had sat in exactly the same spot, in another car, with Inspector Fernack; it was considerably less than thirty-six hours ago, and yet so much had happened that it might as well have been thirty-six years. He wondered what had happened to Fernack, and what that grim-visaged, massive-boned detective was thinking about the volcano of panic and killing which had flamed out in the underworld since they had had that strange, irregular conversation. Probably Fernack was scouring the city for him at that moment, harried to superhuman efforts by the savage anxiety of commissioners and politicians and their satellites; their next conversation, if they ever had one, would probably be much less friendly and tolerant. But that also seemed as far away as if it belonged in another century. Fay Edwards was waiting.

She had switched off the engine, and she was lighting a cigarette. He saw the calm, almost waxen beauty of her face in the flicker of the match she was holding, the untroubled quiet of her eyes, and had to make an effort to remember that she had killed one man that night and helped him to kill another.

"Was that all right?" she asked.

"It was all right," he said.

"I saw your list," she said reflectively. "You had my name on it. What have I done? I suppose you want something with me. I'm here—now."

He shook his head.

"There should have been a question mark after it. I put you down for a mystery. I was listening in when you spoke to Nather—that was the first time I heard your voice. I was watching you with Morrie Ualino. You gave me the gun that got me out of there. I wanted to know who you were—what you had been—why you were in the racket. Just curiosity."

She shrugged.

"Now you know the answer."

"Do I?" The response was automatic, and at once he wished he had checked it. He felt her eyes turning to looked at him, and added quickly: "When you came and told Maxie tonight that the Big Fellow said he was to let me go—that wasn't the truth."

"What makes you think so?"

"I'm guessing. But I'll bet on it."

She drew on her cigarette placidly. The smoke drifted out and floated down the beam of the lights.

"Of course it wasn't true. The Big Fellow was on your list as well, wasn't he?" she said inconsequently. "Do you want him, too?"

"Most of all."

"I see. You're very determined—very single-minded, aren't you?"

"I have to be," said the Saint. "And I want to finish this job. I want to write 'The End' to it and start something else. I'm a bit tired."

She was smoking thoughtfully, a very faint frown of concentration cutting one tiny etched line between her brows—the only wrinkle in the soft perfection of her skin. She might have been alone in her room, preparing to go out, choosing between one dress and another. It meant nothing to her emotions that the only thing they shared in their acquaintance were killings, that the Saint's mission was set down in an unalterable groove of battle and sudden death, that all the paths they had taken together were laid to the same grim goal. He had an eerie feeling that death and killings were the things she understood best—that perhaps there was nothing else she really understood.

"I think I could find the Big Fellow," she said; and he tried to appear as casual and unconcerned as she was.

"You know him, don't you?"

"I'm the only one who knows him."

It was indescribably weird to be sitting there with her, wounded and tired, and to be discussing with her the greatest mystery that the annals of New York crime had ever known, waiting on the threshold of unthinkable revelations, where otherwise he would have been faced with the same illimitable blank wall as had confronted him from the beginning. In his wildest day-dreams he had never imagined that the climax of his quest would be reached like that, and the thought made him feel unwontedly humble.

"He's a great mystery, isn't he?" said the Saint meditatively. "How long have you known him?"

"I met him nearly three years ago, before he was the Big Fellow at all—before anyone had ever heard of him. He picked me up when I was down and out." She was as casual about it as if she had been discussing an ephemeral scandal of nine days' importance, as if nothing of great interest to anyone hung on what she said. "He told me about his idea. It was a good one. I was able to help him because I knew how to contact the sort of people he had to get hold of. I've been his mouthpiece ever since—until tonight."

"D'you mean you—parted company?"

"Oh, no. I just changed my mind."

"He must be a remarkable fellow," said the Saint.

"He is. When I started, I didn't think he'd last a week, even though his ideas were good. It takes something more than good ideas to hold your own in the racket. And he couldn't use personality—direct contact—of any kind. He was determined to be absolutely unknown to anyone from beginning to end. As a matter of fact, he hasn't got much personality—certainly not of that kind. Perhaps he knows it. That may be why he did everything through me—he wouldn't even speak to any of the mob over the telephone. Probably he's one of those men who are Napoleons in their dreams, but who never do anything because directly they meet anyone face to face it all goes out of them. The Big Fellow found a way to beat that. He never met anyone face to face—except me, and somehow I didn't scare him. He just kept on dreaming, all by himself."

A light was starting to glimmer in the depths of Simon Templar's understanding. It wasn't much of a light, little more than a faint nimbus of luminance in the caverns of an illimitable obscurity; but it seemed to be brightening, growing infinitesimally larger with the crawling of time, as if a man walked with a candle in the infinities of a tremendous cave. He had an uncanny illogical premonition that perhaps after all the threads were not so widely scattered—that perhaps the wall might not be so blank as he had thought. Some unreasonable standard of the rightness of things demanded it; anything else would have been out of tune with the rest of his life, a sharp discord in a smooth flow of harmony; but he did not know why he should have that faith in such a fantastic law of coincidence.

"Were his ideas very clever?" he asked.

"He had ways for us to communicate that nobody ever found out," she replied simply. "Morrie Ualino tried to find out who he was—so did Kuhlmann. They tried every trick and trap they could think of, but there was never any risk. I call that clever. He had a way of handling ransom money, between the man who picked it up and the time when he eventually got his share himself, which took the dicks into a blind alley every time. You know the trouble with ransom money—it's nearly always fixed so that it can be traced. The Big Fellow never ran the slightest risk there, either, at any time. That was only the beginning. Yes, he's clever.''

Simon nodded. All of that he could follow clearly. It was grotesque, impossible, one of the things that do not and cannot happen; but he had known that from the start. And yet the impossible things had to happen sometimes, or else the whole living universe would long since have sunk into a stagnant morass of immutable laws, and the smug pedants whose sole ambition is to bind down all surprise and endeavour into their smugly catalogued little pigeonholes would long since have inherited their empty earth. That much he could understand. To handle thugs and killers, the brutal, dehumanized cannon fodder of the underworld, men whose scruples and loyalties and dissensions are as volatile and unpredictable as the flight of a flushed snipe, calls for a peculiar type of dominance. A man who would be a brilliant success in other fields, even a' man who might organize and control a gigantic industry, whose thunder might shake the iron satraps of finance on their golden thrones, might be an ignoble failure there. The Big Fellow had slipped round the difficulty in the simplest possible way—had possibly even gained in prestige by the mystery with which he shielded his own weakness. But the question which Maxie had not had time to answer still remained.

"How did the Big Fellow start?" asked the Saint.

"With a hundred thousand dollars." She smiled at his quick blend of puzzlement and attention. "That was his capital. I went to Morrie Ualino with the story that this man, whose name I couldn't give, wanted another man kidnapped and perhaps killed. I had the contact, so we could talk straight. You can find some heels who'll bump off a guy for fifty bucks. Most of the regulars would charge you a couple of hundred up, according to how big a noise the job would make. This man was a big shot. It could probably have been done for ten thousand. The Big Fellow offered fifty thousand, cash. He knew everything—he had the inside information, knew everything the man was doing, and had the plans laid out with a footrule. All that Morrie and his mob had to do was exactly what the Big Fellow told them, and ask no questions. They thought it was just some private quarrel. They put the snatch on this man, and then I went behind their backs and put in the ransom demand, just as the Big Fellow told me. It had to be paid in thirty-six hours, and it wasn't. The Big Fellow passed the word for him to be rubbed out, and on the deadline he was thrown out of a car on his own doorstep. That was Flo Youssine."

"The theatrical producer? . . . I remember. But the ransom story came out as soon as he was killed——"

"Of course. Morrie sent back to the Big Fellow and said he could do that sort of thing himself, without anybody telling him. The Big Fellow's answer was, 'Why didn't you?' At the same time he ordered another man to be snatched off, at the same price. Morrie did it. There was just as much information as before, the plan was just as perfect, there wasn't a hitch anywhere. Youssine having been killed was a warning, and this time the ransom was paid."

"I see." Simon was fascinated. "And then he worked on Kuhlmann with the same line——"

"More or less. Then he linked him up with Ualino. Naturally it wasn't all done at once, but it was moving all the time. The Big Fellow never made a mistake. After Youssine was killed, nobody else refused until Inselheim hung out the other day. The mobs began to think that the Big Fellow must be a god—a devil—their mascot—

anything. But he brought in the money, and that was good enough. He was smarter than any of them had ever been, and they weren't too dumb to see it."

It was so simple that the Saint could have gasped. It had the perfection of all simple things. It was utterly and comprehensively satisfactory, given the initial genius and the capable mouthpiece; it was so obvious that he could have kicked himself for ever allowing the problem to swell to such proportions in his mind, although he knew that nothing is so mysterious and elusive as the simple and obvious. It was like the thimble in the old parlour game—one came on it after an intensive search with a shock of surprise, to find that it had been staring everyone in the face from the beginning.

The development of which Papulos had spoken followed easily. Once a sufficient terrorism had been established, the crude mechanics of kidnapping could be dispensed with. The threat of it alone was enough, with the threat of sudden death to follow if the first warning were ignored. He felt a little less contemptuous of Zeke Inselheim than he had been: the broker had at least made his lone feeble effort to resist, to challenge the terror which enslaved a thousand others of his kind.

"And it's been like that ever since?" Simon suggested.

"Not quite," said the girl. "That was only the beginning. As soon as the racket was established, the Big Fellow organized it properly. There was nothing new about it—it's been done for years, here and there—but it had never been done so thoroughly or so well. The Big Fellow made an industry of it. He couldn't go on hiring Ualino and Kuhlmann to do isolated jobs at so much a time. Their demands would have gone up automatically —they might have tried to do other jobs on their own, and one or two failures would have spoiled the market. All the Big Fellow's victims were handpicked—he was clever there, too. None of them were big public figures, none of them would make terrific newspaper stories, like Lindbergh, none of them would get a lot of public sympathy, none of them had a political hook-up which might have made the cops take special interest, none of them would be likely to turn into fighters; but they were all rich. The Big Fellow wanted things to go on exactly as he had started them. He organized the industry, and the other big shots came in on a profit-sharing basis."

"How was that worked?"

"All the profits were paid into one bank, and all the big shots had a drawing account on it limited to so much per week. The Big Fellow had exactly the same as the rest of them—I handled it all for him. The rest of the profits were to accumulate. It was agreed that the racket should run for three years exactly, and at the end of that time they should divide the surplus equally and organize again if they wanted to. Since you've been here," she added dispassionately, "there aren't many of them left to divide the pool. That means a lot of money for somebody, because last month there were seventeen million dollars in the account."

Her cool announcement of the sum took Simon Templar's breath away. Even though he vaguely remembered having heard astronomical statistics of the billions of dollars which make up America's annual account of crime, it staggered him. He wondered how many men were still waiting to split up that immense fortune, now that Dutch Kuhlmann and Morrie Ualino were gone. There could not be many; but the girl's eyes were turned on him again with quiet amusement.

"Is there anything else you want to know?"

"Several things," he said and looked at her. "You can tell me—who is the Big Fellow?"

She shook her head.

"I can't."

"But you said you could find him for me."

"I think I can. But when we began, I promised him I would never tell his name to anyone, or tell anyone how to get in touch with him."

The Saint took a cigarette. His hand was steady, but the steadiness was achieved consciously.

"You mean that if you found him, and I met you in such a way that I accidentally saw him and jumped to the conclusion that he was the men I wanted—your conscience would be clear."

"Why not?" she asked naively. "If that's what you want, I'll do it."

A slight shiver went through the Saint—he did not know whether the night had turned colder, or whether it was a sudden, terrible understanding of what lay behind that flash of almost childish innocence.

"You're very kind," he said.

She did not reply at once.

"After that," she said at length, "will you have finished?"

"That will be about the end."

She threw her cigarette away and sat still for a moment, contemplating the darkness beyond the range of their lights. Her profile had the aloof, impossible perfection of an artist's ideal.

"I heard about you as soon as you arrived," she said. "I was hoping to see you. When I had seen you, nothing else mattered. Nothing else ever will. When you've waited all your life for something, you recognize it when it comes."

It was the nearest thing to a testament of herself that he ever heard, and for the rest of his days it was as clear in his mind as it was a moment after she said it. The mere words were unimpassioned, almost commonplace; but in the light of what little he knew of her, and the time and place at which they were said, they remained as an eternal question. He never knew the answer.

He could not tell her that he was not free for her, that

even in the lawless workings of his own mind she was for ever apart and unapproachable although to every sense infinitely desirable. She would not have understood. She was not even waiting for a response.

She had started the car again; and as they ran southwards through the park she was talking as if nothing personal had ever arisen between them, as if only the ruthless details of his mission had ever brought them together, without a change in the calm detachment of her voice.

"The Big Fellow would have liked to keep you. He admired the way you did things. The last time I saw him, he told me he wished he could have got you to join him. But the others would never have stood for it. He told me to try and make things easy for you if they caught you —he sort of hoped that he might have a chance to get you in with him some day."

She stopped the car again on Lexington Avenue, at the corner of 50th Street.

"Where do we meet?" she asked.

He thought for a moment. The Waldorf Astoria was still his secret stronghold, and he had a lurking unwillingness to give it away. He had no other base.

"How long will you be?" he temporized.

"I ought to have some news for you in an hour and a half or two hours."

An idea struck him from a fleeting, inconsequential gleam of memory that went back to the last meal he had enjoyed in peace, when he had walked down Lexington Avenue with a gay defiance in the tilt of his hat and the whole adventure before him.

"Call Chris Cellini, on East 45th Street," he said. "I probably shan't be there, but I can leave a message or pick one up. Anything you say will be safe with him."

"Okay." She put a hand on his shoulder, turning a little towards him. "Presently we shall have more time— Simon."

Her face was lifted towards him, and again the fragrant perfume of her was in his nostrils; the amazing amber eyes were darkened, the red lips parted, without coquetry, in acquiescence and acknowledgment. He kissed her, and there was a fire in his blood and a delicious languor in his limbs. It was impossible to remember anything else about her, to think of anything else. He did not want to remember, to strive or plot or aspire; in the surrender to her physical bewitchment there was an ultimate rest, an infinity of sensuous peace, beyond anything he had ever dreamed of.

"Au revoir," she said softly; and somehow he was outside the car, standing on the pavement, watching the car slide silently away into the dark, and wondering at himself, with the freshness of her lips still on his mouth and a ghost of fear in his heart.

Presently he awoke again to the throbbing of his shoulder and the maddening tiredness of his body. He turned and walked slowly across to the private entrance of the Waldorf apartments. "Well," he thought to himself, "before morning I shall have met the Big Fellow, and that'll be the end of it." But he knew it would only be the beginning.

He went up in the private elevator, lighting another cigarette. Some of the numbness had loosened up from his right hand: he moved his fingers, gingerly, to assure himself that they worked, but there was little strength left in them. It hurt him a good deal to move his arm. On the whole, he supposed that he could consider himself lucky to be alive at all, but he felt the void in himself which should have been filled by the vitality that he had lost, and was vaguely angry. He had always so vigorously despised weariness and lassitude in all their forms that it was infuriating to him to be disabled—most of all at such a time. He was hurt as a sick child is hurt, not knowing why; until that chance shot of Maxie's had found its mark, the Saint had never seriously imagined that anything could attack him which his resilient health would not be able to throw off as lightly as he would have thrown off the hangover of a heavy party. He told himself that if everything else about him had been normal, if he had been overflowing with his normal surplus of buoyant energy and confidence, not even the strange sorcery of Fay Edwards could have troubled him. But he knew that it was not true.

The lights were all on in the apartment when he let himself in, and suddenly he realized that he had been away for a long time. Valcross must have despaired of seeing him again alive, he thought, with a faint grim smile touching his lips; and then, when no familiar kindly voice was raised in welcome, he decided that the old man must have grown tired in waiting and dozed off over his book. He strolled cheerfully through and pushed open the door of the living room. The lights were on there as well, and he had crossed the threshold before he grasped the fact that neither of the two men who rose to greet him was Valcross.

He stopped dead; and then his hand leapt instinctively towards the electric-light switch. It was not until then that he realized fully how tired he was and how much vitality he had lost. The response of his muscles was slow and clumsy, and a twinging stab of pain in his shoulder checked the movement halfway and put the seal on its failure.

"Better not try that again, son," warned the larger of the two men harshly; and Simon Templar looked down the barrel of a businesslike Colt and knew that he was never likely to hear a word of advice which had a more soberly overwhelming claim to be obeyed.

CHAPTER VIII

HOW FAY EDWARDS KEPT HER WORD, AND SIMON TEMPLAR SURRENDERED HIS GUN

"Well, well, well!" said the Saint and was surprised at the huskiness of his own voice. "This is a pleasant surprise." He frowned at one of the vacant chairs. "But what have you done with Marx?"

"Who do you mean—Marx?" demanded the large man alertly.

The Saint smiled.

"I'm sorry," he said genially. "For a moment I thought you were Hart & Schaffner. Never mind. What's in a name?—as the actress said to the bishop when he told her that she reminded him of Aspasia. Is there anything I can do for you, or has the hotel gone bankrupt and are you just the bailiffs?"

The two men looked at each other for a moment and found that they had but a single thought. The smaller man voiced it, little knowing that a certain Heimie Felder had beaten him to it by a good number of hours.

"It's a nut," he affirmed decisively. "That's what it is. Let's give it the works."

192

Simon Templar leaned back against the door and regarded them tolerantly. He was stirred to no great animosity by the opinion which the smaller man had expressed with such an admirable economy of words— he had been hearing it so often recently that he was getting used to it. And at the back of his mind he was beginning to wonder if it might contain a germ of truth. His entrance into that room had been one of the most ridiculously careless manoeuvres he had ever executed, and his futile attempt to reach the light switch still made him squirm slightly to think of. Senile decay, it appeared, was rapidly overtaking him. . . .

He studied the two men with grim intentness. They have been classified, for immediate convenience, as the larger and the smaller man; but in point of fact there was little to choose between them—the effect was much the same as establishing the comparative dimensions of a rhinoceros and a hippopotamus. The "smaller" man stood about six feet three in his shoes and must have weighed approximately three hundred pounds; the other, it should be sufficient to say, was a great deal larger. Taken as a team, they summed up to one of the most undesirable deputations of welcome which the Saint could imagine at that moment.

The larger man bulked ponderously round the intervening table and advanced towards him. With the businesslike Colt jabbing into the Saint's middle, he made a quick and efficient search of Simon's pockets and found the gun which had belonged to the late lamented Joe. He tossed it back to his companion and put his own weapon away.

"Now, you," he rasped, "what's your name?"

"They call me Daffodil," said the Saint exquisitely. "And what's yours?"

The big man's eyebrows drew together, and his eyes hardened malevolently.

"Listen, sucker," he snarled, "you know who we are."

"I don't," said the Saint calmly. "We haven't been introduced. I tried a guess, but apparently I was wrong. You might like to tell me."

"My name's Kestry," said the big man grudgingly, "and that's Detective Bonacci. We're from headquarters. Satisfied?"

Simon nodded. He was more than satisfied. He had been thinking along those lines ever since he had looked down the barrel of the big man's gun and it had failed to belch death at him instantly and unceremoniously, as it would probably have done if any of the Kuhlmann or Ualino mobs had been behind it. The established size of the men, the weight of their shoes, and the dominant way they carried themselves had helped him to the conclusion; but he liked to be sure.

"It's nice of you to drop in," he said slowly. "I suppose you got my message."

"What message?"

"The message I sent asking you to drop in."

Kestry's eyes narrowed.

"*You* sent that message?"

"Surely. I was rather busy at the time myself, but I got a bloke to do it for me."

The detective expanded his huge chest.

"That's interesting, ain't it? And what did you want to see me about?"

The Saint had been thinking fast. So a message had actually been received—his play for time had revealed that much. He wondered who could have given him away. Fay Edwards? She knew nothing. The taxi driver who had been so interested in him on the day when Papulos died? He didn't see how he could have been followed——

"What did you want to see me about?" Kestry was repeating.

"I thought you might like to hear some news about the Big Fellow."

"Did you?" said the detective, almost benignly; and then his expression changed as if a hand had smudged over a clay model. "Then, you lousy liar," he roared suddenly, "why did the guy that was phoning for you say: 'This is the Big Fellow—you'll find the Saint in the tower suite of the Waldorf Astoria belonging to a Mr. Valcross—he's been treading on my toes a damn sight too long'?"

Simon Templar breathed in and out in a long sigh.

"I can't imagine," he said. "Maybe he'd had too much to drink. Now I come to think of it, he was a bit cockeyed——"

"You're damn right you can't imagine it," Kestry bit out with pugnacious satisfaction. He had been studying the Saint's face closely, and Simon saw suspicion and confirmation pass in procession through his mind. "I know who you are," Kestry said. "You *are* the Saint!"

Simon bowed. If he had had a chance to inspect himself in a mirror and discover the ravages which the night's ordeal had worked on his appearance, he might have been less surprised that the detective had taken so long to identify him.

"Congratulations, brother," he murmured. "A very pretty job of work. I suppose you're just practising tracking people down. Let's see—is there anything else I can give you to play with? . . . We used to have a couple of fairly well-preserved clues in the bathroom, but they slipped down the waste pipe last Saturday night——"

"Listen again, sucker," the detective cut in grittily. "You've had your gag, and the rest of the jokes are with me. If you play dumb, I'll soon slap it out of you. The best thing you can do is to come clean before I get rough. Understand?"

The Saint indicated that he understood. His eyes were still bright, his demeanour was as cool and debonair as it had always been; but a sense of ultimate defeat hung over him like a pall. Was this, then, the end of the adventure and the finish of the Saint? Was he destined after all to be ignominiously carted off to a cell at last, and left there like a caged tiger while on four continents the men who had feared his outlawry read of his downfall and gloated over their own salvation? He could not believe that it would end like that; but he realized that for the last few hours he had been playing a losing game. Yet there was not a hint of despair or weakness in his voice when he spoke again.

"You don't want much, do you?" he remarked gently.

"I want plenty with you," Kestry shot back. "Where's this guy Valcross?"

"I haven't the faintest idea," said the Saint honestly.

Before he realized what was happening, Kestry's great fist had knotted, drawn back, and lashed out at his face. The blow slammed him back against the door and left his brain rocking.

"Where do I find Valcross?"

"I don't know," said the Saint, with splinters of steel glittering in his eyes. "The last time I saw him, he was occupying a private cage in the monkey house at the Bronx Zoo, disguised as a retired detective."

Kestry's fist smacked out again with malignant force, and the Saint staggered and gripped the edge of the door for support.

"Where's Valcross?"

Simon shook his head mutely. There was no strength in his knees, and he felt dazed and giddy. He had never dreamed of being hit with such power.

Kestry's flinty eyes were fixed on him mercilessly.

"So you think you won't talk, eh?"

"I'm rather particular about whom I talk to, you big baboon," said the Saint unsteadily. "If this is your idea of playing at detectives, I don't wonder that you're a flop."

Kestry's stare reddened.

"I've got you, anyhow," he grated, and his fist swung

round again and sent the Saint reeling against a bookcase.

He caught the Saint by his coat lapels with one vast hand and dragged him up again. As he did so, he seemed to notice for the first time that one of Simon's sleeves was hanging empty. He flung the coat off his right shoulder and saw the dull red of drying stains on his shirt.

"Where did you get that?" he barked.

"A louse bit me," said the Saint. "Now I come to think of it, he must have been a relation of yours."

Kestry grabbed his wrist and twisted the arm up adroitly behind his back. The strength of the detective's hands was terrific. A white-hot blaze of pure agony went through the Saint's injured shoulder, and a kind of mist swam across his eyes. He knew that he could not hold up much longer, even though he had nothing to tell. But the medieval methods of the third degree would batter and torture him into unconsciousness before they were satisfied with the consolidation of their status as the spiritual heirs of Sherlock Holmes.

And then, through the hammering of many waters that seemed to be deadening his ears, he heard the single sharp ring of a bell, and the racking of his arm eased.

"See who it is, Dan," ordered Kestry.

Bonacci nodded and went out. Kestry kept his grip on the Saint's arm, ready to renew his private entertainment as soon as the intrusion was disposed of, but his eyes were watching the door.

It was Inspector Fernack who came in.

He stood just inside the room, pushing back his hat, and took in the scene with hard and alert grey eyes. His craglike face showed neither elation nor surprise; the set of his massive shoulders was as solid and immutable as a mountain.

"What's this?" he asked.

"We got the Saint," Kestry proclaimed exultantly.

"The other guy—Valcross—ain't been here, but this punk'll soon tell me where to look for him. I was just puttin' him on the grill——"

"You're telling me?" Fernack roared in on him abruptly, in a voice that dwarfed even the bull-throated harshness of his subordinate's. "You bloody fool! Who told you to do it here? Where d'you get that stuff, anyway?"

Kestry gulped as if he could not believe his ears.

"But say, Chief, where's the harm? This mug wouldn't come through—he was wisecrackin' as if this was some game we were playin' at—and I didn't want to waste any time gettin' Valcross as well——"

"So that's what they taught you at the Police Academy, huh?" Fernack ripped in searingly. "I always wondered what that place was for. That's a swell idea, Kestry. You go ahead. Tear the place to pieces. Wake all the other guests in the hotel up an' get a crowd outside. Bonacci can be ringing up the tabloids an' gettin' some reporters in to watch while you're doing it. The commissioner'll be tickled to death. He'll probably resign and hand you his job!"

Kestry let go the Saint's wrist and edged away. Simon had never seen anything like it. The great blustering bully of a few moments ago was transformed into the almost ludicrous semblance of a schoolboy who has been caught stealing apples. Kestry practically wriggled.

"I was only tryin' to save time, Chief," he pleaded.

"Get outside, and have a taxi waiting," Fernack commanded tersely. "I'll bring the Saint down myself. After that you can go home. Bonacci, you stay here an' wait for Valcross if he comes in. . . ."

Simon had admired Fernack before, but he had never appreciated the dominance of the man's character so much. Fernack literally towered over the scene like a god, booming out curt, precise directions that had the effect of cannon balls. In less than a minute after he had

entered the room he had cleaned it up as effectively as if
he had gone through it with a giant's flail. Kestry almost
slunk away, vacating the apartment as if he never wished
to see it again. Bonacci, who had been edging away into
an inconspicuous corner, sank into a chair as if he hoped
it would swallow him up completely until the thunder
had gone. Fernack was left looming over the situation
like a volcano, and there was a gleam in his frosted gaze
which hinted that he would not have cared if there had
been another half-dozen pygmies for him to destroy.

He eyed the Saint steadily, taking in the marks of
battle which were on him. The detective's keen stare
missed nothing, but no reaction appeared on the granite
squareness of his face. From the beginning he had given
no sign of recognition; and Simon, accepting the cue,
was equally impassive.

"Come on," Fernack grunted.

He took the Saint's sound arm and led him out to the
elevator. They rode down in silence and found Kestry
waiting sheepishly with a taxi. Fernack pushed the Saint
in and turned to his lieutenant.

"You can go with us," he said.

They journeyed downtown in the same atmosphere of
silent tension. Kestry's muteness was aggrieved and
plaintive, yet wisely self-effacing; Fernack refrained
from talking because he chose to refrain—he was
majestically unconcerned with what reasons might be
attributed to his taciturnity. Simon wondered what was
passing in the iron detective's mind. Fernack had given
him his chance once, had even confessed himself
theoretically in sympathy; but things had passed beyond
a point where personal prejudices could dictate their
course. The Saint thought that he had discerned a trace
of private enthusiasm in the temperature of the bawling
out which Fernack had given Kestry, but even that
meant little. The Saint had given the city of New York a
lot of trouble since that night when he had talked to

Fernack in Central Park, and he respected Fernack's rugged honesty too much to think of any personal appeal. As the cards fell, so they lay.

The Saint was getting beyond caring. The vast weariness which had enveloped him had dragged him down to the point where he could do little more than wait with outward stubbornness for whatever Fate had in store. If he must go down, he would go down as he had lived, with a jest and a smile; but the fight was sapped out of him. His whole being had settled down to the acceptance of an infinity of pain and fatigue. He only wanted to rest. He scarcely noticed the brief order from Fernack which switched the cab across towards Washington Square; and when it stopped and the door was opened he climbed out apathetically, and was surprised to find that he was not in Centre Street.

Fernack followed him out and turned to Kestry.

"This is my apartment," he said. "I'm going to have a talk to the Saint here. You can go on. Report to me in the morning. Good-night."

He took the Saint's arm again and led him into the house, leaving the bewildered Kestry to find his own explanations. Fernack's apartment was on the street level, at the back—Simon was a trifle perplexed to find that it had a bright, comfortable living room, with a few good etchings on the walls and bookcases filled with books which looked as if they had been read.

"You're never too old to learn," said Fernack, who missed nothing. "I been tryin' to get some dope about these Greeks. Did you ever hear of Euripides?" He pronounced it Eury-pieds. "I asked a Greek who keeps a chop house on Mott Street, an' he hadn't; but the clerk in the bookstore told me he was a big shot." He threw his hat down in a chair and picked up a bottle. "Would you like a drink?"

"I could use it," said the Saint with a wry grin.

Fernack poured it out and handed him the glass. It

was a liberal measure. He gave the Saint time to swallow some of it and light a cigarette, and then spat at the cuspidor which stood out incongruously by the hearth.

"Saint, you're a damn fool," he said abruptly.

"Aren't we all?" said the Saint helplessly.

"I mean you more than most. I've talked to you once. You know what it's all about. You know what I'm supposed to do now."

"Fetch out the old baseball bat and rubber hose, I take it," said the Saint savagely. "Well, I know all about it. I've met your Mr. Kestry. As a substitute for intelligence and a reasonable amount of routine work, it must be the slickest thing that was ever invented."

"We use it here," Fernack said trenchantly. "We've found that it works as well as anything. The only thing is, some fools don't know when you've gotta use it and when you're wastin' your time. That ain't the point. I got you here for something else. You've been out and around for some time since we had our talk. How close have you got to the Big Fellow?"

The question slammed out like a shot, without pause or artifice, and something in the way it was put told Simon that the time for evasions and badinage was over.

"I was pretty damn near it when I walked into Kestry's loving arms," he said. "In fact, I could have picked up a message in about an hour that ought to have taken me straight to him."

Fernack nodded. His keen grey eyes were fixed steadily on the Saint's face.

"I'm not askin' you how you did it or who's sending you the message. You move fast. You're clever. It's queer that one little bullet can break up a guy like you."

He put a hand in his hip pocket, as if his last sentence had suggested a thought which required concrete expression, and pulled out a pearl-handled gun. He tossed it in the palm of his hand.

"Guns mean a lot in this racket," he said. "If a bullet

out of a gun hadn't hit you, you might have got away from Kestry and Bonacci. I wouldn't put it beyond you. If you had this gun now, you'd be able to get away from me." He dropped the revolver carelessly on the table and stared at it. "That would be pretty tough for me," he said.

Simon looked at the weapon, a couple of yards away, and sank back further into his chair. He took another drink from his glass.

"Don't play cat-and-mouse, Fernack," he said. "It isn't worthy of you."

"It would be pretty tough," Fernack persisted, as if he had not heard the interruption. "Particularly after I brought Kestry as far as the door an' then sent him home. There wouldn't be anything much I could put up for an alibi. I didn't have to see you alone in my own apartment, without even a guy waitin' in the hall in case you gave any trouble, when I could've taken you to any station house in the city or right down to Centre Street. If anything went wrong, I'd have a hell of a lot of questions to answer; an' Kestry wouldn't help me. He must be feelin' pretty sore at the way I bawled him out at the Waldorf. It'd give him a big kick if I slipped up an' gave him the laugh back at me. Yeah, it'd be pretty tough for me if you got away, Saint."

He scratched his chin ruminatively for a moment and then turned and walked heavily over to the far end of the room, where there was a side table with a box of cheap cigars. Simon's eyes were riveted, in weird fascination, on the pearl-handled revolver which the detective had left behind. It lay in solitary magnificence in the exact centre of the bare table—the Saint could have stood up and reached it in one step—but Fernack was not even looking at him. His back was still turned, and he was absorbed in rummaging through the cigar box.

"On the other hand," the deep voice boomed on abstractedly, "nobody would know before morning. An' a lot of things can happen in a few hours. Take the Big Fellow, for instance. There's a guy that this city is wantin' even worse than you. It'd be a great day for the copper that brought him in. I'm not sure that even the politicians could get him out again—because he's the man that runs them, an' if he was inside they'd be like a snake with its head cut off. We've got a new municipal election comin' along, and this old American public has a way of waking up sometimes, when the right thing starts 'em off. Yeah—if I lost you but I got the Big Fellow instead, Kestry'd have to think twice about where he laughed."

Fernack had found the cigar which he had been hunting down. He turned half round, bit off the end, and spat it through his teeth. Then he searched vaguely for matches.

"Yeah," he said thoughtfully, "there's a lot of responsibility wrapped up in a guy like you."

Simon cleared his throat. It was oddly difficult to speak distinctly.

"Suppose any of those things happened—if you did get the Big Fellow," he said jerkily. "Nobody's ever seen him. Nobody could prove anything. How would that help you so much?"

"I don't want proof," Fernack replied, with a flat arrogance of certitude that was more deadly than anything the Saint had ever heard. "If a guy like you, for instance, handed a guy to me and said he was the Big Fellow—I'd get my proof. That's what you don't understand about the third degree. When you know you're right, a full confession is more use than any amount of evidence that lawyers can twist around backwards. Don't worry. I'd get my proof."

Simon emptied his glass. His cigarette had gone out and he had not noticed it—he threw it away and lighted another. A new warmth was spreading over him, driving away the intolerable fatigue that gripped his limbs, crushing down pain; it might have been the quality of

Fernack's brandy, or the dawn of a hope that had been dead for a long time. The unwonted hoarseness still clogged his throat.

But the fight was back in him. The hope and courage, the power and the glory, were creeping back through his veins in a mighty tide that washed defeat and despondency away. The sound of trumpets echoed in his ears, faint and far away—how faint and far, perhaps no one but himself would ever know. But the sound was there. And if it was a deeper note, a little less brazen and flamboyant than it had ever been before, only the Saint knew how much that also meant.

He stood up and reached for the gun. Even then, he could scarcely believe that it was in his power to touch it—that it wouldn't vanish into thin air as soon as his fingers came within an inch of it, a derisive will-o'-the-wisp created by weariness and despair out of the fumes of unnatural stimulation. At least, there must be a string tied to it—it would be jerked suddenly out of his reach, while the detective jeered at him ghoulishly. . . . But Fernack wasn't even looking at him. He had turned away again and was fumbling with a box of matches as if he had forgotten what he had picked them up for.

Simon touched the gun. The steel was still warm from Fernack's pocket. His fingers closed round the butt, tightened round its solid contours; it fitted beautifully into his hand. He held it a moment, feeling the supremely balanced weight of it along the muscles of his arm; and then he put it away in his pocket.

"Take care of it," Fernack said, striking his match. "I'm rather fond of that gun."

"Thanks, Fernack," said the Saint quietly. "I'll report to you by half-past nine—with or without the Big Fellow."

"You'd better wash and clean up a bit and get your coat on properly before you go," said Fernack casually.

"The way you look now, any dumb cop would take you in on sight."

Ten minutes later Simon Templar left the house. Fernack did not even watch him go.

Chris Cellini himself appeared behind the bars of his basement door a few moments after Simon rang the bell. He recognized the Saint almost at once and let him in. In spite of the hour, his rich voice had not lost a fraction of its welcoming cordiality.

"Come in, Simon! I hope you don't want a steak now, but you can have a drink."

He was leading the way back towards the kitchen, but Simon hesitated in the corridor.

"Is anyone else here?"

Chris shook his head.

"Nobody but ourselves. The boys have only just gone —we had a late night tonight, or else you'd of found me in bed."

He sat the Saint down at the big centre table, stained with the relics of an evening's conviviality, and brought up a bottle and a couple of clean glasses. His alert brown eyes took in the pallor of Simon's face, the marks on his shirt which showed beyond the edge of his coat, and the stiffness of his right arm.

"You've been in the wars, Simon. Have you seen a doctor? Are you all right?"

"Yes, I'm all right," said the Saint laconically.

Chris regarded him anxiously for a moment longer; and then his rich habitual laugh pealed out again—a big, meaningless, infectious laugh that was the ultimate expression of his sunny personality. If there was a trace of artificiality about it then, Simon understood the spirit of it.

"Say, one of these days you'll get into some serious trouble, and I shall have to go to your funeral. The last time I went to a funeral, it was a man who drank himself to death. I remember a couple of years ago . . ."

He talked with genial inconsequence for nearly an hour, and Simon was unspeakably glad to have all effort taken out of his hands. Towards the end of that time Simon was watching the slow crawling of the hands of the clock on the wall till his vision blurred; the sudden jangle of the bell in the passage outside made him start. He downed the rest of his drink quickly.

"I think that's for me," he said.

Chris nodded, and the Saint went outside and picked up the receiver.

"Hullo," said a thick masculine voice. "Is dat Mabel?"

"No, this is not Mabel," said the Saint viciously. "And I hope she sticks a knife in you when you do find her."

Over in Brooklyn, a disconsolate Mr. Bungstatter jiggered the hook querulously and then squinted blearily at the dancing figures on his telephone dial and stabbed at them doggedly again.

The Saint went back to the kitchen and shrugged heavily in answer to Chris's unspoken question. Chris was silent for a short while and then went on talking again as if nothing had happened. In ten minutes the telephone rang again.

Simon lighted a fresh cigarette to steady his nerves—he was surprised to find how much they had been shaken. He went out and listened again.

"Simon? This is Fay."

The Saint's heart leaped, and his hand tightened on the receiver; he was pressing it hard against his ear as if he were afraid of missing a word. She had no need to tell him who it was—the cadences of her voice would ring in his memory for the rest of his life.

"Yes," he said. "What's the news?"

"I haven't been able to get him yet. I've tried all the

usual channels. I'm still trying. He doesn't seem to be around. He may get one of my messages at any time, or try to get through to me on his own. I don't know. I'll keep on all night if I have to. Where will you be?"

"I'll stay here," said the Saint.

"Can't you get some rest?" she asked—and he knew that he would never, never again hear such soft magic in a voice.

"If we don't find him before morning," he said gently, "I shall have all the time in the world to rest."

He went back slowly into the kitchen. Chris took one look at his face and stood up.

"There's a bed upstairs for you, Simon. Why don't you lie down for a bit?"

Simon spread out his hands.

"Who'll answer the telephone?"

"I'll hear it," Chris assured him convincingly. "The least little thing wakes me up. Don't worry. Directly that telephone rings, I'll call you."

The Saint hesitated. He was terribly tired, and there was no point in squandering his waning reserve of strength. There was nothing that he himself could do until the vital message came through from Fay Edwards. His helplessness, the futile inaction of it, maddened him; but there was no answer to the fact. The rest might clear his mind, restore part of his body, freshen his brain and nerves so that he would not bungle his last chance as he had bungled so much of late. Everything, in the end, would hang on his own quickness and judgment; he knew that if he failed he would have to go back to Fernack, squaring the account by the same code which had given him this one fighting break. . . .

Before he had mustered the unwilling instinct to protest, he had been shepherded upstairs, his coat taken from him, his tie loosened. Once on the bed, sleep came astoundingly. His weariness had reached the point where even the dizzy whirligig of his mind could not stave off the healing fogs of unconsciousness any longer.

When he woke up there was a brilliant New York morning in the translucent sky, and Chris was standing beside his bed.

"Your call's just come, Simon."

The Saint nodded and looked at his watch. It was just before eight o'clock. He rolled out of bed and pushed back his disordered hair, and as he did so felt the burning temperature of his forehead. His shoulder was stiffened and aching. Yet he felt better and stronger than he had been before his sleep.

"There'll be some coffee and breakfast for you as soon as you're ready," Chris told him.

Simon smiled and stumbled downstairs to the telephone.

"I'm glad you've had a rest," said the girl's voice.

The Saint's heart was beating in a rhythmic palpitation which he could feel against his ribs. His mouth was dry and hot, and the emptiness was trying to struggle back into his stomach.

"It's done me good," he said. "Give me anything to fight, and I'll lick it. What do you know, Fay?"

"Can you be at the Vandrick National Bank on Fifth Avenue at nine? I think you'll find what you want."

His heart seemed to stand still for a second.

"I'll be there," he said.

"I had to park the car," she went on. "There were too many cops looking for it after last night. Can you fix something else?"

"I'll see what I can do."

"*Au revoir,* Simon," she whispered; and he hung up the receiver and went through into the kitchen to a new day.

There was the good rich smell of breakfast in the air. A pot of coffee bubbled on the table, and Chris was frying eggs and bacon at the big range. The door to the backyard stood open, and through it floated the crisp invigorating tang of the Atlantic, sweeping away the last mustiness of stale smoke and wine. Simon felt magnificently hungry.

He shaved with Chris's razor, clumsily left-handed, and washed at the sink. The impact of cold water freshened him, swept away the trailing cobwebs of fatigue and heaviness. He wasn't dead yet. Inevitably, yet gradually because of the frightful hammering it had sustained, his system was working towards recovery; the resilience of his superb physique and dynamic health was turning the slow balance against misfortune. The slight feeling of hollowness in his head, the consequence of over-tiredness and fever, was no more than a minor discomfort. He ate hugely, thinking over the problem of securing the car which Fay Edwards had asked for; and suddenly a name and number flashed up from the dim hinterlands of reminiscence—the name and number of the garrulous taxi driver who had driven him away from the scene of Mr. Papulos's Waterloo. He got up and went to the telephone, and admitted himself lucky to find the man at breakfast.

"This is the Saint, Sebastian," he said. "Didn't you say I could call you if I had any use for you?"

He heard the driver's gasp of amazement, and then the eager response.

"Sure! Anyt'ing ya like, pal. What's it woit?"

"Twice as much as you're asking," replied the Saint succinctly. "Meet me on the corner of Lexington and 44th in fifteen minutes."

He hung up and returned to his coffee and a cigarette. He knew that he was taking a risk—the possibility of the chauffeur having had a share in the betrayal of his hideout at the Waldorf Astoria was not completely disposed of, and the prospect of a substantial reward might be a temptation to treachery in any case—but it was the only solution Simon could think of.

Nevertheless the Saint's mouth was set in a grim line

when he said good-bye to Chris and walked along 45th
Street to Lexington Avenue. He walked slowly and kept
his left hand in his pocket with the fingers fastened
round the comforting butt of Fernack's revolver. There
was nothing out of the ordinary about his appearance,
no reason for anybody to notice him—he was still bet-
ting on the inadequacy of newspaper photographs and
the blindness of the average unobservant man, the only
two advantages which had been faultlessly loyal to him
from the beginning. And if there was a hint of fever in
the brightness of the steel-blue eyes that raked the sidewalks watchfully as he sauntered down the block to the
rendezvous at 44th Street, it subtracted nothing from
their unswerving vigilance.

But he saw nothing that he should not have seen—no
signs of a collection of large men lounging against lamp-
posts or kicking their heels in shop doorways, no suspi-
ciously crawling cars. The morning life of Lexington Avenue flowed normally on and was not concerned with
him. Thus far the breaks were with him. Then a familiar
voice hailed him, and he stopped in his tracks.

"Hi-yah, pal!"

The Saint looked round and saw the cab he had ordered parked at the corner. And in the broad grin of the
driver were no grounds for a solid belief that he was a
police stool pigeon or a scout of the Big Fellow's.

"Better get inside quick, before anyone sees ya, pal,"
he advised hoarsely; and the Saint nodded and stepped
in. The chauffeur twisted round to continue the conversation through the communicating window. "Where
ja wanna go dis time?"

"The Vandrick National Bank on Fifth Avenue," said
the Saint.

The driver started up his engine and hauled the cab
out into the stream of traffic.

"Chees!" he said in some awe, at the first crosstown

traffic light. "Ya don't t'ink we can take dat joint wit' only two guns?"

"I hadn't thought about it," Simon confessed mildly.

The driver seemed disappointed in spite of his initial skepticism.

"I figgered dat might be okay for a guy like you, wit' me helpin' ya," he said. "Still, maybe ya ain't feelin' quite yourself yet. I hoid ja got taken for a ride last night —I was t'inkin' I shouldn't be seein' ya for a long while."

"A lot of other people are still thinking that," murmured the Saint sardonically.

They slowed up along Fifth Avenue as they came within a block of the Vandrick Bank Building.

"Whadda we do here, pal?" asked the driver.

"Park as close to the entrance as you can get," Simon told him. "I'll wait in the cab for a bit. If I get out, stay here and keep your engine running. Be ready for a getaway. We may have a passenger—and then I'll tell you more."

"Okay," said the chauffeur phlegmatically; and then an idea struck him. He slapped his thigh. "Chees!" he said. "I t'ought ya was kiddin'. Dat's better 'n hoistin' de bank!"

"What is?" inquired the Saint, with slight puzzlement.

"Aw, nuts," said the driver. "Ya can't catch me twice. Why, puttin' de arm on Lowell Vandrick himself, of course. Chees! I can see de headlines. 'Sebastian Lipski an' de Saint Snatches off de President of de Vandrick National Bank.' Chees, pal, ya had me guessin' at foist!"

Simon grinned silently and resigned himself to letting Mr. Lipski enjoy himself with his dreams. To have disillusioned the man before it was necessary, he felt, would have been as heartless as robbing an orphan of a new toy.

He sat back, mechanically lighting another cigarette in the chain that stretched far back into the incalculable past, and watched the imposing neo-Assyrian portals of the bank. A few belated clerks arrived and scuttled inside, admitted by a liveried doorkeeper who closed the doors again after each one. An early depositor arrived, saw the closed doors, scowled indignantly at the doorkeeper, and drifted aimlessly round the sidewalk in small circles, chewing the end of a pencil. The doorkeeper consulted his watch with monotonous regularity every half-minute. Simon became infected with the habit and began counting the seconds until the bank would open, finding himself tense with an indefinable restlessness of expectation.

And then, with an effect that gripped the Saint into almost breathless immobility, the first notes of nine o'clock chimed out from somewhere nearby.

Stoically the doorkeeper dragged out his watch again, corroborated the announcement of the clock to his own satisfaction, opened the doors, and left them open, taking up his impressive stance outside. The early investor broke off in the middle of a circle and scurried in to do his business. The bank was open.

Otherwise Fifth Avenue was unchanged. A few other depositors arrived, entered the bank, and departed, with the preoccupied air of men who were carrying the weight of the nation's commerce. A patrolman strolled by, with the preoccupied air of a philosopher wondering what to philosophize about, if anything. Pedestrians passed up and down on their own mysterious errands. And yet Simon Templar felt himself still clutched in the grip of that uncanny suspense. He could give no account for it. He could not even have said why he should have been so fascinated by the processes of opening the bank. For all he knew, it might merely have been a convenient landmark for a meeting place, and even if the building itself was concerned there were hundreds of other offices on the upper floors which might have an equal claim on his attention; nine o'clock was the hour, simply an hour for him to be there, without any evidence that something would explode at that instant with the precision of a timed bomb; but he could not free himself from the almost melodramatic sense of expectation that made his left hand close tightly on the pearl grips of Fernack's gun.

And then, while his eyes were searching the street restlessly, he suddenly saw Valcross sauntering by, and for the moment forgot everything else.

In a flash he was out of the cab, crossing the pavement —he did not wish to make himself conspicuous by yelling from the window of the taxi. He clapped Valcross on the shoulder, and the older man turned quickly. His eyes widened when he saw the Saint.

"Why, hullo, Simon. I didn't know you were ever up at this hour."

"I'm not," said the Saint. "Where on earth have you been?"

"Didn't you find my note? It was on the mantelpiece."

Simon shook his head.

"There are reasons why I haven't had a chance to look for notes," he said. "Come into my taxi and talk— I don't want to stand around here."

He seized Valcross by the arm and led him back to the cab. Mr. Lipski's homely features lighted up in applause mingled with delirious amazement—if that was kidnapping, it was the slickest and simplest job that he had ever dreamed of. Regretfully, Simon told him to wait where he was, and slammed the communicating window on him.

"Where have you been, Bill?" he repeated.

"I had to go to Pittsburgh and see a man on business. I heard about it just after you'd gone out, and I didn't know how to get in touch with you. I had supper with him and came back this morning—flying both ways. I've only just got in."

"You haven't been to the Waldorf?"

"No.. I was short of cash, and I was going into the bank first."

Simon drew a deep breath.

"It's the luckiest thing that ever happened to you that you had business in Pittsburgh," he said. "And the next luckiest is that you ran short of cash this morning. Somebody's snitched on us, Bill. When I got into the Waldorf in the small hours of this morning it was full of policemen, and one detachment of 'em is still waiting there for you unless it's starved to death!"

Valcross was staring at him blankly.

"Policemen?" he echoed. "But how——"

"I don't know, and it isn't much use asking. The Big Fellow did it—apparently he said I was treading on his toes. Since his own mobs hadn't succeeded in getting rid of me, I suppose he thought the police might have a try. He's paying their wages, anyway. That needn't bother us. What it means is that you've got to get out of this state like a bat out of hell."

"But what about you?"

The Saint smiled a little.

"I'm afraid I shall have to wait for my million dollars," he said. "I've got five of your men out of six, but I don't know whether I shall be able to get the sixth."

He told Valcross what had been happening, in terse crackling sentences pared down to the uttermost parched economy of words. The other's eyes were opening wider from the intervention of Fay Edwards at the last moment of the ride—on through the slaying of Dutch Kuhlmann to the pleasantness of Mr. Kestry and the amazing reprieve that Fernack had offered. The whole staggering course of those last few hectic hours was sketched out in clipped impressionistic phrases that punched their effect through like a rattle of bullets. And all the while the Saint's eyes were scanning the road and sidewalks, his fingers were curled round the butt of Fernack's gun, his nerves were keyed to the last milligram of vigilance.

"So you see it's been a big night," he wound up. "And there isn't much of it left. Fernack's probably wondering already whether I haven't skipped into Canada and left him to hold the baby."

"And Fay Edwards told you the Big Fellow would be here at nine?" said Valcross.

"Not exactly. She asked me to be here at nine—and she was looking for the Big Fellow. I'm hoping it means she knows something. I'm still hoping."

"It's an amazing story," said Valcross thoughtfully. "Do you know what to make of that girl?"

Simon shrugged.

"I don't think I ever shall."

"I shall never understand women," Valcross said. "I wonder what the Big Fellow will think. That marvellous brain—an organization that's tied up the greatest city in the world into the greatest criminal combine that's ever been known—and a harlot who falls in love with an adventurer can tear it all to pieces."

"She hasn't done it yet," said the Saint.

Valcross was silent for a few moments; and then he said: "You've done your share. You've got five men out of the six names I gave you. In the short time you've been working, that's almost a miracle. The Big Fellow's your own idea—you put him on the list. If you fail—if you feel bound to keep your word and go back to Fernack—I can't stop you. But I feel that you've earned the reward I promised you. I've had a million dollars in a drawing account, waiting for you, ever since you came over. I'd like to give it to you, anyhow. It might be some use to you."

Simon hesitated. Valcross's eyes were fixed on him eagerly.

"You can't refuse," he insisted. "It's my money, and

I think it's due to you. No one could have earned it better."

"All right," said the Saint. "But you can pay me in proportion. I haven't succeeded—why try to make out that I have?"

"I think I'm the best judge of that," said Valcross and let himself out of the cab with a quick smile.

Simon watched him go with a troubled frown. There was an unpleasant taste in his mouth which he had not noticed before. So the accounts of death would be paid according to their strict percentages, the blood money handed over, and the ledger closed. Six men to be killed for a million dollars. One hundred and sixty-six thousand, six hundred and sixty-six dollars and sixty-six cents per man. He had not thought of it that way before —he had taken the offer in his stride, for the adventure, without seriously reckoning the gain. Well, he reflected bitterly, there was no reason why a man who in a few short weeks would be a convicted felon should try to flatter his self-esteem. He would go down as a hired killer, like any of the other rats he had killed. . . .

Valcross was closing the door, turning away towards the bank; and at that moment another taxi flashed past the one in which Simon sat, and swung in to the curb in front of them. The door opened, and a woman got out. It was Fay Edwards.

Simon grabbed at the door handle and flung himself out onto the sidewalk. And then he saw that the girl was not looking at him, but at Valcross.

The Saint had never known anything to compare with that moment. There was the same curious constricted feeling at the back of his knees as if he had been standing with his toes over the edge of a sheer precipice, looking down through space into an unimaginable gulf; seconds passed before he realized that for a time he had even stopped breathing. When he opened his lungs again, the blood sang in his ears like the hissing of distant surf.

There was no need for anything to be said—no need for a single question to be asked and answered. The girl had not even seen him yet. But without seeing her face, without catching a glimpse of the expression in her eyes —he knew. Facts, names, words, events, roared through his mind like a turmoil of machinery gone mad, and fell one by one into places where they fitted and joined. Kestry's harsh voice stating: "Why did the guy that was phoning for you say 'This is the Big Fellow'?" He had never been able to think who could have given him away —except the one man whom he had never thought of. Fay Edwards saying: "The last I heard of Curly Ippolino, he was in Pittsburgh." Valcross had just returned from Pittsburgh. Fay Edwards saying: "All the profits were paid into one bank. It was agreed that the racket should run for three years . . . divide the surplus equally . . . Since you've been here, there aren't many of them left to divide . . . That means a lot of money for somebody." Valcross on his way to the bank—Valcross on his way back from Pittsburgh, where the last surviving member of the partnership had been. Fay Edwards saying: "He told me to try and make things easy for you." Naturally—until the job was finished. Valcross meeting him in Madrid. The list of men for justice—all of them dead now. The story of his kidnapped and murdered son, which it had never occurred to the Saint to verify. "I'll pay you a million dollars." With seventeen million at stake, the fee was very modest. "You might clean up this rotten mess of crooks and grafters." Oh, God, what a blind fool he'd been!

In that reeling instant of time he saw it all. Jack Irboll dead. Morrie Ualino and Eddie Voelsang dead. The news flashed over the underworld grapevine, long before the newspapers caught up with it, that Hunk Jenson and Dutch Kuhlmann had also died. The knowledge that the Saint's sphere of usefulness was rapidly drawing to a close, and the bill would remain for payment. The trip to

Pittsburgh and the telephone message to police head-quarters. The last Machiavellian gesture of that devilish warped genius which had gone out and picked up the scourge of all secret crime, the greatest fighting outlaw in the world, bought him with a story and the promise of a million dollars, used him for a few days of terror, and cast him off before his curiosity became too dangerous. The final shock when Valcross saw the Saint that morning, alive and free. And the simple, puerile, obvious excuse to continue into the bank—and, once there, to slip out by another exit, and perhaps send a second message to the police at the same time. Simon Templar saw every detail. And then, as Fay Edwards turned at last and saw him for the first time, he read it all again, without the utterance of a single word, in that voiceless interchange of glances which was the most astounding solution to a mystery that he would ever know.

Aeons of time and understanding seemed to have rocketed past his head while he stood there motionless, taking down into his soul the last biting, shattering dregs of comprehension; and yet in the chronology of the world it was no time at all. Valcross had not even reached the doors of the bank. And then, as Fay Edwards saw the Saint and took two quick steps towards him, some supernatural premonition seemed to strike Valcross as if a shout had been loosed after him, and he turned round.

He saw Fay Edwards, and he saw the Saint.

Across the narrow space Simon Templar stared at Valcross and saw the whole mask of genial kindliness destroyed by the blaze of horrible malignity that flamed out of the old man's eyes. The change was so incredible that even though he understood the facts in his mind, even though he had assimilated them into the immutable truths of his existence, for that weird interval of time he was paralyzed, as if he had been watching a spaniel turn into a snake. And then Valcross's hand streaked down towards his hip pocket.

Simon's right hand started the hundredth part of a second later, moving with the speed of light—and the stiffness of his wounded shoulder caught it in midflight like a cruel brake. A stiletto of pain stabbed through his back like a hot iron. In the hypnotic grasp of that uncanny moment his disability had been driven out of his mind: he had used his right hand by instinct which moved faster than thought. In an instant he had corrected himself, and his left hand was snatching at Fernack's revolver in his coat pocket; but by that time Valcross was also holding a gun.

A shot smacked past his ear, stunning the drum like the blast of an express train concentrated twenty thousand times. His revolver was stuck in his pocket. Of the next shot he heard only the report. The bullet went nowhere near him. Then he twisted his gun up desperately and fired through the cloth; and Valcross dropped his automatic and clutched at his side, swaying where he stood.

Simon hurled himself forward. The street had turned into pandemonium. White-faced pedestrians blocked the sidewalk on either side of the bank, crushing back out of the danger zone. The air was raucous with the screams of women and the screech of skidding tires. He caught Valcross round the waist with his sound arm, swung him mightily off his feet, and started back with him towards the cab. He saw Mr. Lipski, his features convulsed with intolerable excitement, scrambling down from his box to assist. And he saw Fay Edwards.

She was leaning against the side of the taxi, holding onto it, with one small hand pressed to the front of her dress; and Simon knew, with a terrible finality, where Valcross's second shot had gone.

Something that was more than a pang came into his

throat; and his heart stopped beating. And then he went on.

He jerked open the door and flung Valcross in like a sack. And then he took Fay Edwards in his arms and carried her in with him. She was as light in his arms as a child; he could not even feel the pain in his shoulder; and yet he carried the weight of the whole world. He put her down on the seat as tenderly as if she had been made of fragile crystal, and closed the door. The cab was jolting forward even as he did so.

"Where to, pal?" bellowed the driver over his shoulder.

Simon gave him Fernack's address.

There was a wail of police sirens starting up behind them—far behind. Weaving through the traffic, cornering on two wheels, whisking over crossroads in defiance of red lights, supremely contemptuous of the signs on one-way streets, performing hair-raising miracles of navigation with one hand, Mr. Sebastian Lipski found opportunities to scratch the back of his head with the other. Mr. Lipski was worried.

"Chees!" he said bashfully, as if conscious that he was guilty of unpardonable sacrilege, and yet unable to overcome the doubts that were seething in his breast. "What is dis racket, anyway? Foist ya puts de arm on a guy wit' out any trouble. Den ya lets him go. Den ya shoots up Fift' Avenue an' brings him back again. Howja play dis snatch game, what I wanna know?"

"Don't think about it," said the Saint through his teeth. "Just drive!"

He felt a touch on his arm and looked down at the girl. She had pulled off her hat, and her hair was falling about her cheeks in a flood of soft gold. There were shadows in her amazing amber eyes, but the rest of her face was untroubled, unlined, like unearthly satin, with the bloom of youth and life undimmed on it. The parting of her lips might have been the wraith of a smile.

"Don't worry," she said. "I'm not going with you—very far."

"That's nonsense," he said roughly. "It's nothing serious. You're going to be all right."

But he knew that he lied.

She knew, too. She shook her head, so that the golden curls danced.

"It doesn't hurt," she said. "I'm comfortable here."

She was nestling in the crook of his arm, like a tired child. The towers and canyons of New York whirled round the windows, but she did not see them. She went her way as she had lived, without fear or pity or remorse, out of the unknown past into the unknown future. Perhaps even then she had never looked back, or looked ahead. All of her was in the present. She belonged neither to times nor seasons. In some strange freak of creation all times and seasons had been mingled in her, were fused in the confines of that flawless incarnation; the eternal coordinates of the ageless earth, death and desire. She sighed once.

"I'm so sorry," she said. "I suppose it wasn't meant to happen—this time."

He could not speak.

"Kiss me again, Simon," she said quietly.

He kissed her. Why had she seemed unapproachable? She was himself. It was his own lawless scorn of life and death which had conquered her, which had brought her twice to save his life and taken her own life in the end. If the whole world had condemned her, he could not have cast a stone. He did not care. They moved in the same places, the wide sierras of outlawry where there were no laws.

She slipped back, gazing into his face as if she were trying to remember every line of it for a hundred years. She was smiling, and there was a light in her darkening amber eyes which he would never understand. He could see her take breath to speak.

"*Au revoir*, Simon," she said; and as she had lived with death, so she died.

He let her go gently and turned away. Strange tears were stinging his eyes so that he could not see. The taxi lurched round a corner with its engine growling. The noises of the city ebbed and swelled like the beat of a tidal sea.

He became aware that Valcross was tugging at his arm, whining in a horrible mouthy incoherence of terror. The yammering words came dully through into his brain:

"Can't you do something? I don't want to die. I've been good to you. I didn't mean to cheat you out of your million dollars. I'll do anything you say. I don't want to die. You shot me. You've got to take me to a doctor. I've got money. You can have anything you like. I've got millions. You can have all of them. I don't want them. Take what you want——"

"Be quiet," said the Saint in a dreadful voice.

"Millions of dollars—in the bank—they're all yours ——"

Simon struck him on the mouth.

"You fool," he said. "All the money in the world couldn't pay for what you've done."

The man shrank away from him, and his babbling rose to a scream.

"What is it you want with me, then? I can give you anything. If it isn't money, what do you want? Damn you, what is your racket?"

Then the Saint turned towards him, and even Valcross was silent when he saw the look on the Saint's face. His mouth worked mutely, but the words would not leave his throat. His trembling hands went up as if to shield himself from the stare of those devilish blue eyes.

"Death," said the Saint, in a voice of terrible softness. "Death is my racket."

They turned into Washington Square from the south.

Simon had never noticed what route they took to shake off pursuit, but the wail of sirens had ceased. The muttering thunder of the city had swallowed it up. The taxi was slowing down to a more normal pace. Buses rumbled ponderously by; the endless stream of cars and vans and taxis flowed along, as it would flow day and night while the city stood, one of a myriad impersonal rivers on which human activities took their brief bustling voyages, coming and going without trace. A newsboy ran down the sidewalk, bawling his ephemeral sensation. In a microscopic corner of one infinitesimal speck of dust floating through the black abysses of infinity, inconsiderable atoms of human life hurried and fumed and fretted and were broken and triumphant in the trivial affairs of their brief instant in eternity. Lives began and lives ended, but the primordial accident of life went on.

The cab stopped, and the driver looked round.

"Dis is it," he announced. "What next?"

"Wait here a minute," said the Saint; and then he saw Fernack standing on the steps of his house.

He got out and walked slowly towards the detective, and Fernack stood and watched him come. The strong, square-jawed face did not relax; only the flinty grey eyes under the shaggy brows had any expression.

Simon drew out the pearl-handled gun, reversed it, and held it out as if he were surrendering a sword.

"I've kept my word," he said. "That's the end of my parole."

Fernack took the revolver and slid it into his hip pocket.

"Didn't you find the Big Fellow?"

"He's in the taxi."

A glimmer of immeasurable content passed across Fernack's eyes, and he looked over the Saint's shoulder, down towards the waiting cab. Then, without a word, he went past the Saint, across the pavement, and opened the door. Valcross half fell towards him. Fernack caught him with one hand and hauled the slobbering man out and upright. Then he saw something else in the taxi, and stood very still.

"Who's this?" he said.

There was no answer. Fernack turned round and looked up and down the street. Simon Templar was gone.

EPILOGUE

Mr. Theodore Bungstatter, of Brooklyn, espoused his cook on the eleventh day of June in that year of grace, having finally convinced her that his inability to repeat his devotion coherently on a certain night was due to nothing more unregenerate than a touch of influenza. They spent their honeymoon at Niagara Falls, and on the third day of it she induced him to sign the pledge; but in spite of this concession to her prejudices she never cooked for him again, and the rest of their wedded bliss was backgrounded by a procession of disgruntled substitutes who brought Mr. Bungstatter to the direst agonies of dyspepsia.

Mr. Ezekiel Inselheim paced his library and said to a deputation of reporters: "It is the duty of all public-spirited citizens to resist racketeering and extortion even at the risk of their own lives or the lives of those who are nearest and dearest to them. The welfare of the state must override all considerations of personal safety. We are fighting a war to the death with crime, and the same code of self-sacrifice must guide every one of us as if we were at war with a foreign power. It is the only way in which this vile cancer in our midst can be rooted out." And while he spoke he remembered the cold appraising eyes of the outlaw who had faced him in that same room, and behind the pompous phrasing of his words was the pride of a belief that if he himself were tried again he would not be found wanting.

Mr. Heimie Felder, wrestling in argument with a circle of boon companions in Charley's Place, said: "Whaddya mean, de guy was nuts? Coujja say a guy dat bumped off Morrie Ualino an' Dutch Kuhlmann was nuts? Say, listen, I'm tellin' ya. . . ."

Mr. Chris Cellini laid a magnificent juicy steak, two inches thick, tenderly on the bars of his grill. His sleeves were rolled up to the elbows, his strong hands moved with the deft sureness and delight of an artist. The smell of food and wine and tobacco was perfume in his nostrils, the babel of human fellowship was music in his ears. His rich laugh rang jovially through his beloved kitchen. "No, I ain't seen the Saint a long while. Say, he was a wild fellow, that boy. I'll tell you a story about him one day."

Mr. Sebastian Lipski said to an enraptured audience in his favourite restaurant at Columbus Circle: "Say, dijja never hear about de time when me an' de Saint snatched off de Big Fellow? De time when we took de Vandrick National Bank wit' two guns? Chees, youse guys ain't hoid nut'n' yet!"

Mr. Toni Ollinetti wiped invisible stains from the shining mahogany of his bar, mechanically, with a spotless white napkin. His smooth face was expressionless, his brown eyes carried their own thoughts. Whenever anything was ordered, he served it promptly, unobtrusively, and well; his flashing smile acknowledged every word that was addressed to him with the most perfect allotment of politeness, but the smile went no further than the gleam of his white teeth. It was impossible to tell whether he was tired—he might have just come on duty, or he might have had no sleep for a week. The life of Broadway and the bright lights passed before him, new faces appearing, old faces dropping out, the

whole endlessly shifting pageant of the half-world. He
saw everything, heard everything, and said nothing.

Inspector John Fernack caught a train down from Ossining twenty minutes after the Big Fellow went to the
chair. He was a busy man, and he could not afford to
linger over ancient cases. In his spare time he was still
trying to catch up with Euripides; but he had very little
spare time. There had been a change of regime at the last
municipal election. Tammany Hall was in the background, organizing its forces for the next move to the
polls; Orcread was taking a world cruise for his health,
Marcus Yeald was no longer district attorney; but
Quistrom was still police commissioner, and a lot of old
accounts were being settled. There was the routine copy
of a letter on his desk:

METROPOLITAN POLICE,
SPECIAL BRANCH,
SCOTLAND HOUSE, LONDON, S.W.I.

Police Commissioner, New York City.
Dear Sir:
      Re: SIMON TEMPLAR *("The Saint")*
   Referring to our previous letter to you on the subject, we
have to inform you that this man, to our knowledge, has
returned to England, and therefore that we shall not need
to request further assistance from you for the time being.

Faithfully yours,
C. E. Teal, Chief Inspector.

Fernack looked at the calendar on the wall, where he
had made marks against certain dates. Teal's letter
brought no surprising news to him. In three days, to his
knowledge, the Saint had come and gone, having done
his work; and the last word on that case which entered
Fernack's official horizon had just been said at Ossin-

ing. But his hand went round to his hip, where the butt of his pearl-handled revolver lay, and the touch of it brought back memories.

Perhaps that was one reason why, at the close of his talk to the senior students of the Police Academy that night, when the dry, stern, ruthless facts had been dealt with in their textbook order, the stalwart young men who listened to him saw him put away his notes and straighten up to look them over empty-handed—a towering giant whose straight shoulders would have matched those of any man thirty years younger, whose face and hair were marked with the iron and granite of his grim work, whose flinty grey eyes went over them with a strange softening of pride and affection.

"You boys have taken up the finest job in the world," were his last words to them; and the harshness of thirty years dropped out of his great voice for that short time. "I've given my whole life to it, an' I'd do it ten times over again. It ain't an easy job. It ain't easy to stand up an' take a slug in the guts. It ain't easy to see your best friends go out that way—plugged by some lousy rat that happened to be quick with a gun. It ain't easy to remember the oath you take when you go out of here, when you see guys higher up takin' easy money, an' that same money is offered to you just for shuttin' your eyes at the right moment. It's a tough job. You gotta be rough. You're dealin' with rats and killers, guys that would shoot their own mother in the back for five bucks, the whole scum of the earth—an' they don't understand any other language. We here, you an' me, are carryin' on the toughest police job in the world. But"—and at that point they saw John Fernack, Iron John Fernack, square his tremendous shoulders like a man settling an easy load, while a light that was almost beautiful came into his eyes—"don't let it make you too tough. Because some day, out of all the scum, you're gonna meet a guy who's as good a man as you, an' if you don't know when to give him a break you're gonna miss the greatest thing in the world, which is seein' your faith in a guy made good."

And in the garden of an inn beside the Thames, in the cool of the darkness after a summer day, with a new moon turning the stream to a river of silver, Miss Patricia Holm, who had long ago surrendered all her days to the Saint, said: "You've never told me everything that happened to you in New York."

His cigarette glowed steadily, a red spark in the darkness, and his quiet voice answered her gently out of the shadows.

"Maybe I shall never know everything that happened to me there," he said; but his memories were three thousand miles away from the moon on the river and the black sentinels of the trees, and there was the thunder of a city in his ears, and the whisper of a voice that was all music, which said: *"Au revoir. . . ."*

WATCH FOR THE SIGN OF
THE SAINT

HE WILL BE BACK!

THE LIBRARY OF CRIME CLASSICS®

GEORGE BAXT TITLES
The Affair at Royalties
0-930330-77-3 $4.95
The Alfred Hitchcock Murder Case
0-930330-55-2 $5.95
The Dorothy Parker Murder Case
0-930330-36-6 $4.95
"I!" Said the Demon
0-930330-57-9 $4.95
A Parade of Cockeyed Creatures
0-930330-47-1 $4.95
A Queer Kind of Death
0-930330-46-3 $4.95
Satan Is a Woman
0-930330-65-X $5.95
Swing Low Sweet Harriet
0-930330-56-0 $4.95
The Talullah Bankhead Murder Case
0-930330-89-7 $5.95
Topsy and Evil
0-930330-66-8 $4.95
Who's Next?
0-930330-99-4 $17.95

JOHN DICKSON CARR TITLES
Below Suspicion
0-930330-50-1 $4.95
The Burning Court
0-930330-27-7 $4.95
Death Turns the Tables
0-930330-22-6 $4.95
Hag's Nook
0-930330-28-5 $4.95
He Who Whispers
0-930330-38-2 $4.95
The House at Satan's Elbow
0-930330-61-7 $4.95

The Problem of the Green Capsule
0-930330-51-X $4.95
The Sleeping Sphinx
0-930330-24-2 $4.95
The Three Coffins
0-930330-39-0 $4.95
Till Death Do Us Part
0-930330-21-8 $4.95

WRITING AS CARTER DICKSON
The Gilded Man
0-930330-88-9 $4.95
He Wouldn't Kill Patience
0-930330-86-2 $4.95
The Judas Window
0-930330-62-5 $4.95
Nine—and Death Makes Ten
0-930330-69-2 $4.95
The Peacock Feather Murders
0-930330-68-4 $4.95
The Punch and Judy Murders
0-930330-85-4 $4.95
The Red Widow Murders
0-930330-87-0 $4.95

MARGARET MILLAR TITLES
An Air That Kills
0-930330-23-4 $4.95
Ask for Me Tomorrow
0-930330-15-3 $4.95
Banshee
0-930330-14-5 $4.95
Beast in View
0-930330-07-2 $4.95
Beyond This Point Are Monsters
0-930330-31-5 $4.95
The Cannibal Heart
0-930330-32-3 $4.95
The Fiend
0-930330-10-2 $5.95

Fire Will Freeze
0-930330-59-5　$4.95
How Like An Angel
0-930330-04-8　$4.95
The Iron Gates
0-930330-67-6　$4.95
The Listening Walls
0-930330-52-8　$4.95
The Murder of Miranda
0-930330-95-1　$4.95
Rose's Last Summer
0-930330-26-9　$4.95
Spider Webs
0-930330-76-5　$5.95
A Stranger in My Grave
0-930330-06-4　$4.95
Wall of Eyes
0-930330-42-0　$4.95

BACKLIST

CHARLOTTE ARMSTRONG
A Dram of Poison
0-930330-98-6　$4.95
Mischief
0-930330-72-2　$4.95
The Unsuspected
0-930330-84-6　$4.95
JACQUELINE BABBIN
Bloody Special
0-930330-83-8　$4.95
ANTHONY BOUCHER
Nine Times Nine
0-930330-37-4　$4.95
Rocket to the Morgue
0-930330-82-X　$4.95
CARYL BRAHMS & S.J. SIMON
A Bullet in the Ballet
0-930330-12-9　$5.95

Murder a la Stroganoff
0-930330-33-1 $4.95
Six Curtains for Stroganova
0-930330-49-8 $4.95

CHRISTIANNA BRAND
Cat and Mouse
0-930330-18-8 $4.95

MAX BRAND
The Night Flower
0-930330-48-X $4.95

HERBERT BREAN
The Traces of Brillhart
0-930330-81-1 $4.95
Wilders Walk Away
0-930330-73-0 $4.95

LESLIE CHARTERIS
The Last Hero
0-930330-96-X $4.95
The Saint in New York
0-930330-97-8 $4.95

CARROLL JOHN DALY
Murder from the East
0-930330-01-3 $4.95

LILLIAN DE LA TORRE
Dr. Sam: Johnson, Detector
0-930330-08-0 $6.95
The Detections of Dr. Sam: Johnson
0-930330-09-9 $4.95
The Return of Dr. Sam: Johnson, Detector
0-930330-34-X $4.95
The Exploits of Dr. Sam: Johnson, Detector
0-930330-63-3 $5.95

PAUL GALLICO
The Abandoned
0-930330-64-1 $5.95
Too Many Ghosts
0-930330-80-3 $5.95
Thomasina
0-930330-93-5 $5.95

JAMES GOLLIN
Eliza's Galliardo
0-930330-54-4 $4.95
The Philomel Foundation
0-930330-40-4 $4.95
DOUGLAS GREENE with ROBERT ADEY
Death Locked In
0-930330-75-7 $12.95
DASHIELL HAMMETT & ALEX RAYMOND
Secret Agent X-9
0-930330-05-6 $9.95
RICHARD HULL
The Murder of My Aunt
0-930330-02-1 $4.95
E. RICHARD JOHNSON
Mongo's Back in Town
0-930330-90-0 $4.95
Silver Street
0-930330-78-1 $4.95
JONATHAN LATIMER
The Lady in the Morgue
0-930330-79-X $4.95
Solomon's Vineyard
0-930330-91-9 $4.95
VICTORIA LINCOLN
A Private Disgrace
Lizzie Borden by Daylight
0-930330-35-8 $5.95
BARRY MALZBERG
Underlay
0-930330-41-2 $4.95
WILLIAM F. NOLAN
Look Out for Space
0-930330-20-X $4.95
Space for Hire
0-930330-19-6 $4.95
WILLIAM O'FARRELL
Repeat Performance
0-930330-71-4 $4.95

ELLERY QUEEN
Cat of Many Tails
0-930330-94-3 $4.95
Drury Lane's Last Case
0-930330-70-6 $4.95
The Ellery Queen Omnibus
1-55882-001-9 $9.95
The Tragedy of X
0-930330-43-9 $4.95
The Tragedy of Y
0-930330-53-6 $4.95
The Tragedy of Z
0-930330-58-7 $4.95

S.S. RAFFERTY
Cork of the Colonies
0-930330-11-0 $4.95
Die Laughing
0-930330-16-1 $4.95

CLAYTON RAWSON
Death from a Top Hat
0-930330-44-7 $4.95
Footprints on the Ceiling
0-930330-45-5 $4.95
The Headless Lady
0-930330-60-9 $4.95
No Coffin for the Corpse
0-930330-74-9 $4.95

JOHN SHERWOOD
A Shot in the Arm
0-930330-25-0 $4.95

HAKE TALBOT
Rim of the Pit
0-930330-30-7 $4.95

DARWIN L. TEILHET
The Talking Sparrow Murders
0-930330-29-3 $4.95

P.G. WODEHOUSE
Service with a Smile
0-930330-92-7 $4.95

Write For Our Free Catalog:
International Polygonics, Ltd.
Madison Square, P.O. Box 1563
New York, NY 10159

3840